PRAISE FOR *SAINT SEBAS*

T0273609

"Haber's comic novel tracks the friendship, falling-out and sort-of reconciliation of two critics who have devoted their careers to a 16th-century painting of St. Sebastian that both find sublime—though for different reasons. What is it about art that can move us to extremes? This absurdist take on very serious people hazards a guess."

—*The New York Times,* "Editor's Choice"

"A meditation on art that meticulously builds a fictional painter's world and critical legacy, only to playfully yet ruthlessly tear it all down. This tale of two art historical frenemies traces an apocalyptic obsession that circumscribes every waking moment of their lives."

—**New York Public Library**

"[A] sparkling comic novel. . . . Every few pages Haber, the author of one other novel and a story collection, throws in a gem. . . . Schmidt is one of Haber's keenest inventions."

—**Jackson Arn,** *The New York Times*

"In sinuous, recursive sentences infused with equal parts reverence and venom, Haber constructs a darkly parodic portrait of aesthetic devotion and intellectual friendship, in which the redemptive practice of collaborative interpretation becomes a cage that two egos relentlessly rattle."

—**Nathan Goldman,** *Jewish Currents*

"*Saint Sebastian's Abyss* feels exactly like the description of the painting—deceitfully small in scale, containing a cosmic abyss at its center. The mimetic impulse between the book and its themes pervades the whole reading experience."

—**Hernan Diaz, author of** *In the Distance*

PRAISE FOR *REINHARDT'S GARDEN*

Longlisted for the 2020 PEN/Hemingway Award
The Millions, **"Most Anticipated of 2019"**
Texas Observer, **"Best Texas Books of the Decade"**

"Outstanding . . . the descent into the heart of darkness at the very core of modernity."

—*BOMB Magazine*

"Haber, who has been called 'one of the most influential yet low-key of tastemakers in the book world,' is about to raise it up a level with the debut of his novel."

—*The Millions*

"An adventurous journey into the country of melancholy. A fascinating dissection of human vulnerability."

—**Guadalupe Nettel, author of** *After the Winter*

LESSER RUINS

**ALSO BY MARK HABER,
FROM COFFEE HOUSE PRESS**

Reinhardt's Garden

Saint Sebastian's Abyss

Ada (forthcoming, 2026)

LESSER RUINS

MARK HABER

COFFEE HOUSE PRESS

MINNEAPOLIS

2024

Coffee House Press books are available to the trade through our primary distribu-
tor, Consortium Book Sales & Distribution, cbsd.com or (800) 283-3572. For personal orders, catalogs, or other information, write to info@coffeehousepress.org.

Coffee House Press is a nonprofit literary publishing house. Support from private
foundations, corporate giving programs, government programs, and generous individuals helps make the publication of our books possible. We gratefully acknowledge their support in detail in the back of this book.

LIBRARY OF CONGRESS CATALOGING-IN-PUBLICATION DATA

Names: Haber, Mark, 1972- author.
Title: Lesser ruins / Mark Haber.
Description: Minneapolis : Coffee House Press, 2024.
Identifiers: LCCN 2023057447 (print) | LCCN 2023057448 (ebook) | ISBN
  9781566897198 (paperback) | ISBN 9781566897204 (e-pub)
Subjects: LCGFT: Novels.
Classification: LCC PS3608.A23835 L47 2024 (print) | LCC PS3608.A23835
  (ebook) | DDC 813/.6—dc23/eng/20231218
LC record available at https://lccn.loc.gov/2023057447
LC ebook record available at https://lccn.loc.gov/2023057448

PRINTED IN THE UNITED STATES OF AMERICA

31 30 29 28 27 26 25 24   2 3 4 5 6 7 8 9

To Ülrika

They had not been privileged to experience the dizzy descent he had surrendered to ... only an all-consuming, all-encompassing idea could liberate a man, make him free and place him above everything else.

—LEONID TSYPKIN,
SUMMER IN BADEN-BADEN

He had sunk into the morgue of time, he had become a cadaver wrapped in senselessness, in idiocies, in the grotesquely devised absurdity of soldiering with an aura of the dramatic.

—DAŠA DRNDIĆ,
BELLADONNA

"Do you want to join us?" I was recently asked by an acquaintance when he ran across me alone after midnight in a coffee-house that was already almost deserted. "No, I don't," I said.

—FRANZ KAFKA,
DIARIES, 1914

LESSER RUINS

I

Anyway, I think, she's dead, and though I loved her, I now have both the time and freedom to write my essay on Montaigne, an essay requiring not only extraordinary focus and intellect but also time and freedom, time and freedom being necessary for the composition of my essay on Montaigne, since freedom, specifically financial freedom, will provide the means to set my plans in motion, meaning the time required to visit the libraries, universities, and archives vital to finish the book-length essay I vowed more than twenty years ago to complete. Both of these, meaning time and financial freedom, rely on each other; one is as essential as the other because having one but not both is meaningless. A person may possess time but lack financial freedom, thus that person can do absolutely nothing, or worse, *less* than nothing, except contemplate how they have half of what's needed, nothing but brood and sulk about having the time but not the means, which is to say financial freedom, and people like this, I'm certain, make up most of the world's population, and, conversely, the rest may possess financial freedom but *not* the time which, in a similar sense, is also meaningless because the money is there, asking to be spent, but the time necessary to *spend* the money isn't and, in point of fact, this often happened during our tumultuous though very happy marriage, a marriage I might add, that was affectionate and warm and though not blessed by many children, indeed only one, was teeming with love. Anyway, the money was there, time wasn't. *Time, time, time,* I said to myself for years, driving back and forth from the community college, teaching humanities and philosophy at the community college, wanting nothing more than to be alone, to contemplate and meditate, to escape mediocrity by working on my Montaigne essay, meaning researching and ruminating on Montaigne, a writer and a philosopher who demands vast swathes of fathomless time, not just intellectual time but the time *leading up* to intellectual time, the *prerequisite* to time, the period during which one prepares to advance into the deep balmy waters of an intellectual campaign; I yearned for the time to ponder and deliberate and do the *slow thinking* banished from our contemporary world, *slow thinking* absolutely required yet absolutely ravaged by our contemporary climate and culture, a climate and culture that would laugh at a man, myself for example, a man who would like nothing more than to sit alone in a dark room at dusk, staring at the wall, listening to Stravinsky at a low, delicate volume, tapping his foot, biting his bottom lip, in short, *slow thinking,* the lost art of ignoring, expunging, even annihilating the outside world for the sake of enjoying prolonged and undisturbed thoughts, thoughts like an endless desert, a *mental Sahara,* profound and illuminating thoughts, the kind of thoughts that lead inevitably to ideas, ideas impervious to the distractions offered by the world at large, our world's onslaught of half-baked howls and shrieks, rants and inanities, in short, our world's *incoherence,* and for years I'd come home, kiss my wife, ask about her day, and then retreat into the bedroom to punch and kick the air in silent rage, indignant at the scarcity of the two things I needed most: time and financial freedom. Now I have both and I recognize that I should be happy and yet I'm clearly quite lost because my wife's illness was drawn out, years I'm talking, an interminable span during which work on my Montaigne essay effectively ceased; it became neglected, gathered dust, lost the power to speak. Anyone familiar with intellectual endeavors understands, knows a dialogue must be established, a conversation between the writer and their work, because the work must be tended to, must be cultivated and caressed, spoken *and* listened to because the work speaks (if you know how to listen) and this I'd failed to do, having put my work, my Montaigne essay, away in the rolltop desk to better endure the litany of demands issuing from my wife, or rather coming from my wife's physical ailments via my wife, the immeasurable, almost dizzying burden of nursing and bathing, feeding and placating, measuring out her medicines and making sure she wasn't a threat to herself, in short, three years of hardship and horror, and when I again thought of my work I was frightened of what I'd find because part of me believed I'd find only bad ideas badly stated, in short mediocrity and incoherence, and this is *exactly* what I found after years of tending to my wife, burying my wife, sitting shiva or *attempting* to sit shiva in mourning for my wife, mediocrity and incoherence, not to mention bad writing and bad ideas, half-formed, unfinished ideas, ideas that took me *away* from Montaigne rather than toward Montaigne. And soon the slow orbit of grieving friends quit coming around, including Marcel, our son, who returned to his apartment once the weeping and mourning waned, though his grief wasn't so easily extinguished because it was his mother after all and, moreover, Marcel sought the sympathy of others, had understood since earliest youth the benefits gained from pity. He had no qualms making a show of his emotional state in front of friends and strangers alike because to him it made no difference, what difference does it make, he asked, she's gone, she was my mother and I loved her, and think of the sacrifices I made, he said, think about the *remixes* and DJ *sets* I've given up, the shows I wanted to play but didn't, pinching his face, feigning dejection, the way he'd done since infancy, and on he would go about his music, what he called *house music,* speaking what might as well have been another language, peppered with words I'd picked up begrudgingly over the years and was now forced to admit I recognized, because the boy had no sense of restraint, no notion of how to judge his audience, endlessly sermonizing about his passion for *electronic dance music,* what he called *deep house* or *microhouse* or *minimal techno.* Anyway, Marcel returned to his life with his countless roommates and his dance music, *house music,* he constantly corrects me, and though we live in the same city we're no more than strangers, because Marcel was always closer to his mother, always felt more attached and connected to his mother, and she, his mother, always claimed they *understood* one another better than he and I. Now she's gone, the house empty; me, widowed and alone, a mountain of half-formed ideas taunting me from the rolltop desk. Decades gone and the work resembles a stranger, or worse, an *intruder,* hostile and malicious, hundreds of typed pages haunted and harassed by the ghost of Michel de Montaigne, a subtle mixture of history, biography, and literary criticism, an expanded version of my master's thesis, *Montaigne and the Lugubrious Cherubs,* written decades before, when the world was a verdant meadow, opulent and rich, when the world, to quote Paz, was *a gallery of sound,* before I met my now-dead wife, before Marcel was born and those subsequent years of vexation and fatigue: fatherhood, husbandhood, driving back and forth from the community college, attempting to escape mediocrity while simultaneously contemplating my book-length essay, a work intended to *liberate* me from mediocrity, to reinvent and reimagine the work of Montaigne, a work intended to expand upon the humanism Montaigne introduced to an unprepared world. I always envisioned my book as an exploration of the inner-life, therefore a work *rebuking* the contemporary world, a world that aims to *annihilate* the inner-life, a world that refutes any serious intellectual enterprise. I'd had the reviews in my head for years, as I parked my car at the community college, as I taught Humanities 101 and Philosophy 103 at the community college, as I left for home from the community college. I sought the acclaim before the work, the adulation and adoration my work would elicit, but the work remained elusive and *still* remains elusive because only yesterday, last mourner gone, front door locked, I went straight to the study, picked up a sample page, read a few lines, and dropped it in disgust because there's nothing worse than catching oneself trying to be intelligent or original when one lacks intelligence or originality; no different than seeing a photograph of yourself taken from a curious angle, glimpsing the crooked nose, the too-large paunch, wanting desperately to believe you're looking at a stranger. Now however the time I've sought for decades trembles at my feet, and I find myself daunted and unnerved because my wife, who embraced and encouraged and supported me, is dead, and, it seems to me, the completion of my Montaigne essay, its success or failure, will be my ruin or my salvation. I retired, or was fired, depending on who you ask, I nursed my now-dead wife, and, not unlike Montaigne who—bereaved due to the death of his father, retired to his estate outside Bordeaux to devote his life to reading, writing, and reflection, a *holy* or *saintly* calling, which today would doubtless be seen as a sickness, a form of lunacy, and in any case quite impossible due to the incursion of public idiocy into our private spaces of thought—had quite happily invented the essay. Montaigne withdrew to his estate to banish the *outer world* and invite the *inner world,* to spend his days in *learned leisure* devoted to *rational thought.* Under a more critical eye the similarities between myself and Montaigne pale, yet I yearn to live a life not unlike Montaigne's, a life of reading, writing, and reflection, but due to the intrusions on my *mental Saharas,* I find only tiny islets of *coherence* amid vast continents of *incoherence.* I blame the modern world. There's too much stimulus, I think, an *overabundance* of stimulus, when all one needs are the depths of the deepest ocean or a dry desert's worth of time or the luminous notes of a Chopin sonata and surely none of these lesser, petulant stimuli that are as aggressive as they are infinite but do nothing to improve *slow thinking,* but instead hamper *slow thinking* and attack *slow thinking* and diminish *slow thinking,* meaning encourage fast and dull thinking, non-thinking, or the *impression* and the *facade* of thinking but not thinking at all, not the *mental Saharas* required to lift one's thoughts from earthly concerns, the sort of thinking essential for producing a Chopin concerto or the Acropolis or the works of, for example, Montaigne. A world that won't let a person think, I think, a world that distracts and creates *obstacles* for thinking, that compels a person to resist the natural instinct to engage in deep reflection and to jump instead from frivolous thought to frivolous thought. Anyway, I continue to think, I don't have the large estate nor the time to devote myself *wholly* to reflection, but time enough, and just now the phone chirps because today even the interruptions have interruptions. It's Marcel asking how I'm holding up, which is Marcel's way of nudging me to ask how *he* is holding up. Marcel says he's making an album dedicated to his mother, a *concept album,* he says, minimal and refined, balmy but bone dry too. Sounds good, I mumble, eyeing the tower of papers, the stacks of legal pads, thousands of words *reaching* for Montaigne but taking me *further* from Montaigne, countless insights, tenuous revelations, concepts both rare and implausible, all yearning for something symbolic, transgressive, oneiric, pages upon pages confirming the certainty of my own failure. Marcel sounds distant, submerged, as if he's trying to convince himself of his own idea beneath a large body of water, not a pool but a vast lake or an ocean. He's talked of making a dance album for years, blaming the setbacks and delays on his mother's illness, says he couldn't record an album intended for the listener to, in his words, *lose themselves in ecstatic oblivion,* songs steeped in *reckless euphoria* and *divine exaltation,* when his own mother lay dying mere miles away. Marcel continues to speak and I drift. When I return, he's describing *Norwegian Space Disco* and I drift again. When I return, he's discussing gospel samples in early *Chicago house* and once more I drift. When I return, he's remembering his first lessons on the piano, how his mother, my late wife, was radiant, practically celestial, her walnut-brown hair, her easy mirth, how she clapped when he'd played his first piece, he can't remember exactly what, something decidedly easy and for beginners, but it had stayed with him, that memory, and it was the seed, he says, the seed she'd planted and which had grown inside of him for all of these years and Marcel begins lamenting about the album he's planning to write, record, and produce, dedicated to his mother and *about* his mother, the woman who'd planted the seed, but an album that will never be heard, hence never appreciated, by the *subject* of his album, meaning his mother. We're all plagued by nostalgia, I think, we all want to go back and live in different times; my son would like to live in Chicago or Detroit or some other city in the 1970s when disco and cocaine were everywhere, passed around without consequence, and some DJ in his holy omnipotence was *playing* records or *spinning* records or whichever verb he prefers and do you know where the best *house music* is currently coming from, Marcel asks, and before I can plead ignorance he goes on to explain that the *best house music* is currently being made in Berlin, and Marcel begins a sermon on Berlin, how the best clubs are in Berlin, how the best *underground dance music* is getting played, produced, and recorded in Berlin, a *haven* for electronic artists, he says, a *shrine,* he declares, and these artists aren't all German, he insists, no, they're just as likely *expats,* DJs hailing from New York and Perth and Seoul, artists like Helen Adwande, one of my personal favorites, he says, Adwande, raised in the slums of Cape Town but nestled now in Berlin like she's always been there, Adwande, who uses handclaps in her twelve-minute downtempo tracks like secret weapons, handclaps like machetes or guillotines, with an elastic *four-on-the-floor* thump that's unmistakable, with a cadence and a rhythm that's insatiable, and when someone with even the tiniest modicum of taste hears it they know immediately that it's Adwande, it couldn't be anyone *but* Adwande, and Berlin, he says ardently, is filled with German electronic artists too, Dana Ruh and DJ Koze, both natives, all meshing to create an *electronic music utopia,* much of it underground and much of it spread across the city like one enormous kiss and not only *house* he says, but *breakbeat* and *dubstep* and *Dutch techno,* the kind of techno that trades in build-and-release, techno that gains momentum like you're driving off the edge of a cliff, Kasper Marott for instance, the most exciting techno artist working today, at least in my opinion, and his songs, meaning Kasper Marott's, are considered *fast techno,* but he can slow it down too, his best songs in fact take their time, the pulse and the rhythm gaining intensity over the course of nine, ten, twelve minutes, throwing in Latin tempos, analog basslines, stabs of piano, slivers of *acid house,* until the song is *unrecognizable* from where it began, from what it was ten minutes earlier, and Marcel continues to evangelize about techno while I stare at the rolltop desk with longing and trepidation because the rolltop desk has always been the one furnishing necessary, I feel, for me to begin my work, the one item absolutely indispensable for the production of my book-length essay on Montaigne, my work utterly inconceivable without the rolltop desk and its myriad contents, its repositories organized for both contemplation and industry, a fixture whose very existence confirms its owner as a person of the utmost seriousness, which is to say a person who sits down and gets started, meaning, in my case, revising, improving, and ultimately finishing my book-length essay on Montaigne. Heedless, Marcel continues, exhorting the elegance of a good drum machine as well as classic synthesizers and let's not forget the samples of vocals, Marcel says, Marcel suddenly ecstatic about the samples of vocals he plans to use for his album, gospel and disco and soul, he says, and I pace the house in my pale-yellow slippers listening to Marcel proselytize the majesty of *electronic dance music,* especially *underground dance music* and its dozen other iterations, Marcel pontificating about the *pulsing beeps* and *handcrafted breakbeats,* the *silky pads of downy strings,* the *glossy loops* and *shifting tempos,* before he suddenly stops and his stopping makes me pause, waiting for Marcel to continue and it's silent and inside the silence it's just the two of us, I think, no one left, I also think, the last remnants of a family and what a strange word, I think, *family,* wondering if it's even a family when only two remain. *Widower,* I also think, such a tragic word, a word suffused with pathos, conjuring the image of some lone survivor, the last vestige of a cataclysmic event. Life is incurable, wrote the Berber poet Ahmed Hamidi, a long, sluggish process of destruction; tediously predictable, all unavoidable, complicated no doubt by love, death, and the disease of despair, all the natural villains, and still we go on, still we persist. Why? Why not turn on the gas or jump from the bridge, I think, when there are no surprises in store and never have been? It seems Marcel is finished because he says he's tired. Promising to talk soon we hang up and I leave the study, pace the house, enter the kitchen to just as quickly leave the kitchen. I'm tempted to return to the study, sit at my desk, search out the best ideas from my Montaigne essay, extract the small scraps of wisdom and begin anew, but once again my phone chirps, that shrill chirp that births a goddamn knot in my chest each time it chirps, every chirp another attack against sanity and solitude and *fucking Christ,* I think, growing frustrated, growing antsy and aggrieved, pacing the house in my pale-yellow slippers, the modern world has destroyed the ability to have a single unfettered thought, humankind has demolished discernment and irony, the parsing of ideas with the slightest nuance because all of these require sustained, undisturbed time,

time that is now plagued either by interruption or by the *antici-pation* of interruption. What's left, I think, but to grunt at one another like baboons? Have I, along with the rest of the world, been trained to sabotage myself at every turn, to interject, de-flect, change subjects, and consider folly instead? The moment I have a thought it lifts into the ether and dissipates. I ignore the phone, consider writing down this sentiment instead, because, if handled deftly, I can insert this into my Montaigne essay, intro-duce the idea that what Montaigne was able to create (an enor-mous body of philosophical work; the birth of the essay) would be all but impossible today; there's too much distraction and not only the distraction one *seeks* but the distraction *foisted* upon a person against their will, a person who only wants to crawl in-side a cave and be left alone and imagine wanting to be left alone, I think, to live in solitude with one's thoughts, consider the bar-riers constructed at every turn, the way society plants one's feet in quickly drying concrete so you, along with the rest of the world, are paralyzed by the noise and the clamor and, instead of vast swathes of endless time, instead of *mental Saharas,* one is forced to live in mental swamps and mental quagmires and men-tal quicksand and suddenly the title *The Intrusion of Distraction* drifts into my mind like a fine, airy cloud and I see the essay opening like a verdant flower with deep observations and argu-ments because what one needs, I've always thought, is a title and then one writes *toward* that title; a title like a destination, a flaw-less end point, the title a summary that encapsulates everything it aims to represent and I run to the study and before it evaporates jot down *The Intrusion of Distraction* and I nod; I put quotations around *The Intrusion of Distraction* and nod again; I underline *The Intrusion of Distraction* and a third time I nod because it looks and sounds important, relevant and sagacious too. I often lectured on this very subject in Ethics 101 and Philosophy 103, the barriers to sustained thinking, the myriad ways in which the fractured modern world had invited itself into our rapidly eroding imaginations; I was passionate, devoted, but my students (dullards delivered like clockwork each semester) were frightened of my passion, since my passion was strange and unfamiliar, not just *my* passion but passion in general because my students were unaccustomed to fierce and fervent feelings, acquainted instead with lives awash with vapid interruption and, as I said, if they weren't having their thoughts interrupted they were *expecting* to have their thoughts interrupted, thus my students were sitting in *anticipation* of having their thoughts interrupted, either by the chirp, chime, or vibration of their phones, the nudge of their neighbor, or, who knows, a passing cloud, and this destroyed any clarity of thinking, anything resembling lucidity and sustained thinking, and I cross out my most recent title, *Montaigne, Mankind, and the Birth of Lucid Thought,* because *The Intrusion of Distraction* is so much stronger and less diluted; *The Intrusion of Distraction* has teeth, I think, *The Intrusion of Distraction* takes no prisoners and once again I see my essay as a powerful attack against the deterioration of sustained thinking and *mental Saharas.* My wife hardly dead a week, and my mind is lucid, my limbs loose and resilient; I feel my

mind grasping for powerful ideas, I sense my perception returning with verve and invention and immediately I caution myself
against celebrating as I only have a title, no doubt a glorious title
which is clearly superior to all of my previous titles, *Half-Gaze of
the Hyacinth* and *Faceless Tenants* for example, but I have to *support* the title and *lift* the title by an equally glorious essay, an essay like a decree, forcing the reader to recognize, by deft and
nimble analysis, the destruction of our modern world by the interruption of thought and the annihilation of *mental Saharas*.
I've done this before, congratulated myself when I'd only mus-
tered a title, patted my own back as if a title were all I needed, a
title, I told myself, more than enough for a book-length essay on
Montaigne, when a title clearly wasn't enough because once a
writer has a title, they still need a *book*. A title, I think, rather
useless by itself, because one needs a book that supports the title, and I consider all the books whose titles haven't measured
up to the book or, conversely, the books that haven't measured
up to their title and what a disappointment it must be for both
the reader and the writer, to have one but not the other, the title
but not the book, or the book but not the title, and I lift a legal
pad, glance at the second argument in my original thesis which
now seems tepid and mealy, begging to be improved, developed,
maybe removed altogether and, being a fervent and proper
Montaignian, a person unallayed by the meager infractions of the
world, a volume of Montaigne is always kept at arm's reach, and
I grasp my favorite, an assorted collection from the '70s, dog
eared, faded, and riddled with notes; I choose a random page

and read: *a useful saying or a pithy remark is always welcome wherever it is put. If it is not good in the context of what comes before it or after it, it is good in itself.* This quote, fortuitous and touched by sublimity, makes me realize the second argument in my original thesis is actually quite profound and should most certainly *stay,* and I underline the crux of my argument, chiefly the notion that all of us are prisoners to an enormous, unseen *idea-destroyer,* unseen because it's integrated into every facet of our world, simultaneously ubiquitous and clandestine, everywhere yet nowhere since it's built into the habits and routines of our daily lives, linked intrinsically to the bustle of the everyday and, as if to remind me of this, the phone chirps again meaning, I think, the person who called has left a message, probably of condolence, and I plan to listen to the message but suddenly remember I hate the chirp of the phone, have always hated the chirp of the phone and immediately I decide to change the chirp of the phone to something *less* pleasant since the pleasantness of the phone's chirp is deceptive, counterintuitive really, a sound designed to charm even though the news is guaranteed to be tragic or grim or, at the very least, *bad.* The more pleasant the sound of the phone's chirp, I think, the more unpleasant the news; the chirp of the phone with its tinny melodiousness is downright aggressive, surely the same chirp I heard each time my wife faced another grim diagnosis, as if the chirp of the phone was designed to make destructive and unbearable news palatable, and *fuck it,* I think, tossing the phone on the floor, deciding to approach these matters later, to put these matters off, and instead I look at the mound of unfinished ideas; had Montaigne faced these same challenges? Had Montaigne been plagued by self-doubt? Did Montaigne have a wife who died in the long, slow tedium of common misery? Questions I refuse to face without coffee, I decide, something Kenyan, single origin and shade grown, a roast possessing floral notes with hints of cocoa and melon. Just yesterday I'd written close to ten unbroken pages about coffee, its various geographic histories, brewing methods, and roasting techniques, which included the obligatory digression on Balzac, several thousand words regarding his death by coffee (caffeine overdose, some claim) while getting nowhere closer to my ideas on Montaigne as well as a rational life of solitude. In fact, those ten pages were a testament to *irrationality,* to bluster and gibberish, to the notion of writing words simply because one could. *Of course* coffee mattered. *Of course* coffee should be a minor subject touched upon in my essay about Montaigne. Coffee is an *idea creator* rather than an *idea destroyer;* coffee gives one mental lucidity and the confidence crucial for any intellectual campaign and not only coffee but the *ritual* of coffee, the ritual as important as the coffee itself, choosing the beans, grinding the beans, boiling the water, steeping the beverage, all the steps that seem trite and insignificant but are charged with meaning, steps that provide a soul with a sense of solace and routine. But ten pages? On coffee? I decide to *make* coffee in order to *not write* about coffee and *not think* about coffee, assuming I'd written so much about coffee only yesterday from a desire to *have* coffee, Kenyan, I think again, wet-processed, I think further, light-bodied but full-flavored, lithe and velvety, radiant and reassuring, only a cup though, I think, not an entire French press, like the day previous, a fatal mistake I now realize, hence I'd written not a single word, but instead *ten pages of unbroken text* which went nowhere, riddled with digressions about Honoré de Balzac, poor, tragic Balzac, who, in a pinch, would eat the crushed coffee grounds straight, at least from what I've read, drinking upward of forty cups of coffee a day in order to compose what, fifty-eight fucking novels? It seems preposterous and very likely untrue. Anyhow, I'd gotten tremors from drinking the entire French press of coffee and thus written *solely* about coffee although not before the coffee had me pacing the house in my pale-yellow slippers, wringing my hands, careful to avoid my dead wife's closet, making circles, taking laps, sitting before the rolltop desk, attempting to produce meaningful words about Montaigne but writing in fact nothing at all about Montaigne, only writing about coffee and Balzac, a goddamn maniac from the looks of it, and I'd nearly forgotten about those ten pages of nonsense I wrote yesterday solely about coffee, and the thought of coffee has triggered the recollection of those ten pages of drivel *about* coffee, ten pages of lunatic rambling resembling the half thoughts of my oafish students with their open mouths and bovine eyes and expressions of joyous anticipation at having their thoughts interrupted, and yesterday, as I circled the interior of the house, circumventing my dead wife's closet, I reflected upon those students, many of whom complained to the administration about my passion and disregard, yes, *both:* passion *and* disregard. I was either too involved, they complained, or not involved at all and, thankfully, the disparity in these grievances helped in their, meaning the complaints', not getting taken with much seriousness. I was a *passionate* teacher, I explained at the emergency review, a *devoted* teacher, I explained at the emergency review where I'd been ominously summoned, a frigid scene and a reminder Kafka was, more than anything, a realist. The infamous and compulsory emergency review, dreaded by every instructor at the community college because getting called before the emergency review meant a litany of complaints had been made (in my case more than a dozen from a single class) and at the emergency review the administrators gazed at me like unhappy statues, the atmosphere rife with cheap coffee and surrender. It was noon. Winter. The room silent. The assistant provost crossed her legs, cleared her throat, opened a folder. I waited. I considered urban modernity and the complexion of cities, how the temperament of a city shares traits with other cities, how Paris and Vienna for example, both landlocked with moderate skylines, enjoy an unspoken kinship, share aesthetics as well as an innate celebration of art and music, traits that encourage harmony and goodwill, while coastal cities, Sydney and Lisbon, or San Francisco for that matter, appear complacent and smug in their geography and these cities, if they were people, would be sworn enemies and, on a more granular level, I considered architecture, how the interior where one resides shapes one's mindset and behavior, be it Midcentury Modern or Soviet Brutalism, why not, and how these interiors must surely influence one's mindset and behavior, because living in a high-rise or a slum or a renovated barn *can't not* sway a person's mindset and behavior, every action and decision shaped by the narrow kitchen and bad plumbing and, conversely, one's peace of mind lifted by the transcendent views and bucolic touches, and I considered the high-rise resident, how, following a bad day, the high-rise resident might have the urge to jump or, at the very least, be *contemplating* the urge to jump, how the temptation might be overwhelming, jumping the easiest of all options, I reflected, the window being a constant attraction depending on the nature of the resident and their state of mind and if one were committed enough and the day bad enough, I thought, the window was always beckoning. I then considered the French countryside, the vineyards in Bordeaux which surrounded Montaigne's château in Périgord, the slow rolling hills, the flame of sunlight etched by trees, the gossamer shadows falling across the fields at dusk and then, for no reason, I thought of Cicero and ancient Rome. I considered the stoics. I considered Plutarch, Montaigne's favorite writer and thus my *favorite writer's favorite writer* and how Plutarch and Montaigne were never summoned to the likes of an emergency review or its equivalent because humanity was plainly going backward, of this I was certain, in fact all one had to do was read a book, a single book, written perhaps three or four centuries previous, to see we are plainly a species on the decline, a species that has quit its rapid ascent and is quickly sliding backward, one needed only to look around and observe, I reflected at the emergency review, one needed only consider the ceaseless, unremitting interruptions to deep thought, I pondered, the grimy screens and unending chirps that assail us every moment of the day, still waiting for one of the administrators to say something at the emergency review; how engrossed we are in a world of diversion, I thought, how we *seek* and *solicit* and *beguile* interruption, I thought, and therefore beg for *interruption* and, by default, mediocrity, anxious for anything to evade the slightest mode of contemplation which would yield sophisticated ideas, the sort of ideas that advance the world and enrich the soul. No, I pondered at the emergency review, in order to improve oneself and escape mediocrity one must have complete, unalloyed solitude, a *mental Sahara,* and society is the enemy and adversary of *mental Saharas* and evidently I was expected to speak first at the emergency review, thus I opened my mouth and spoke while a panel of weary faces gawked like vultures hungry and expectant for my demise, and as was my custom during my lectures I meandered, I spoke of virtue and obsession, I spoke of ethics and civilization. I described the soul of humankind as a rapidly rotting piece of fruit, an orange or a mango, I forget, all to demonstrate I was worthy of my position, thus the litany of complaints lodged against me were insignificant, invalid in fact, brought forward by dead-eyed, bovine-faced simpletons, oafs in fact, unschooled in *mental Saharas.* I invoked Aristotle and the savagery of Tiberius; I described the virtuous path of purity. I urged my peers to envision the solitude of a Buddhist monk upon a hill in Lhasa. I evoked the sublimity of imagination. I described the pale, luminous robe of Pliny the Elder. I was a *Montaignian,* I finally said in my defense at the emergency review, meaning a professor who knelt at the altar of Montaigne, who believed in ethics and philosophy, meaning humanism, a scholar who believed in preaching about the value of *mental Saharas,* meaning a scholar who preached *against* the obstacles to *mental Saharas,* and the dean—gaunt, angular, a touch reptilian—appeared sated, at least for the moment, because a conviction of guilt at an emergency review meant more eyes would be on them, the administration that is, and the one area where bureaucracies thrive is in inviting *more* bureaucracy, hence an act of discipline now meant a council or a tribunal later; a bureaucracy is hardly effective but its *ineffectiveness* is the point, a bureaucracy feeds on itself, gains its nourishment from the quality of its meaningless significance or its meaningful insignificance, I don't know the order, but the emergency review, if a verdict of guilt were reached, meant a litany of unpleasant steps would need to be taken, all of which required vigilance and effort, things my superiors had shed amid the bleak passage of their careers, indifferent to time, culture, the forces of history, each administrator shaped by the soft tyranny of repetition, and after a ruffle of papers and cleared throats, questions were asked about my personal life, as in what, if anything, was I *going through,* since the purpose of the emergency review, besides establishing a vigorous barometer of fear appropriate to any institution, is to ensure the community college is organized, meaning not running amok, making certain the staff, namely the professors, aren't unhinged or *becoming* unhinged or showing the slightest signs of becoming unhinged, because an institution of higher learning mustn't have teachers on staff who are *unwell,* as it would turn the community college into a circus and a spectacle, thus giving the impression of a lawless shitshow. And the dean, reminded of something, cleared her throat, said she'd recently heard about my wife's diagnosis and was there anything she could do and how long had we been married as if my wife were already as good as dead and luckily, due to the disparity of the students' complaints combined with the likelihood of my wife probably dying, the emergency review concluded with a dull thud, meaning a slap on the wrist, as well as instructions to be cognizant of the students' age, most incapable of appreciating the pain implicit in grief, the perverse anguish when a husband or wife or any partner of decades for that matter, has taken ill, and I left the emergency review feeling revitalized, though there were moments afterward where I was once more caught in the clutches of my book-length essay and found myself neglecting the students; I invented assignments out of thin air to manage those burgeoning dunces, and there I sat in front of the class, writing frantically lest the ideas escaped, lest my concepts evaporated, lest the inspiration were dashed by another interruption; pages upon pages about Montaigne, the inner life, the sublimity of knowledge, how he'd clutched the search for meaning and made it both the most common and profound act in intellectual history. I'd purchased an espresso machine, prohibitively expensive, colossal, and extravagant, installing it beneath my desk; I was on my third or fourth shot and the students were drowsy and sluggish, tapping their screens,

MARK HABER

texting or being texted, waiting to have their thoughts interrupted, when a shaft of sunlight burst through the window, not unlike the light one sees in a Renaissance painting, a light populated by dust particles with a suggestion of the divine, perhaps an angel or a halo or an angel *with* a halo, anyway, the light burst through and touched my arm and perhaps it was those four espressos or the students' silence, but I had a moment of clairvoyance or organic unity or mythical ecstasy, call it what you want, but I was suddenly uplifted from my feeble existence, an existence plagued by interruptions: the nursing of my sick wife, the endless intrusion of bovine-faced students as well as my son's implacable enthusiasm for dance music, *house music,* he constantly corrected me, the constant pleas for money whenever we spoke, whenever he displayed another musical contraption purchased online, so that my life became immersed in the constant struggle for peace, the peace that was downright essential to conceive a book-length essay on Montaigne, a book illustrating a life lived in isolation and devoid of interruption, but composed by *me,* a man thronged and attacked and besieged by interruption, by the hindrances and obstacles that ensue when one endeavors to make a deep, scholarly attempt at contemplation in the modern world, and the irony was not lost but heightened by the fact I was attempting an exhaustive, intellectual, pedagogic work of art about the man who defied interruption and the outside world, who politely told interruption and the outside world to *fuck themselves,* yet there I was, *riddled* and *assailed* by interruption and the outside world, by half thoughts and bovine thoughts, thoughts impeded by the chirps of phones; and one must withdraw from interruption and the outside world, I told myself, one needed to summon all the inner strength one had, namely the stamina, namely the fortitude, namely the mental audacity to accomplish this. And that day, sunlight bursting through the clouds, the third or fourth espresso coursing through my veins, possibility, yes, *possibility,* revealed itself in the form of a title: *Wisdom and Fate,* a simple title, but a title that captured the essence of Montaigne, and certainly an improvement over *Montaigne and the Lugubrious Cherubs* as well as the slew of other titles collected and amassed and which sat disorganized in monstrous stacks amongst ungraded essays and napkins, scribbled on scraps and receipts and slips of abandoned notes. Wisdom: the ability to know oneself. Fate: to reach the end of one's life and know one's diminutive place in the cosmos and, by that same extent, understand one's coda as the undeniable end to that self-knowledge. Life, a tedious and futile attempt to know oneself and for what? To essentially perish. Yet I'd asked myself that day, a day forever infused with the memory of that immaculate shaft of sunlight, what other choice did we have? Emboldened, I made a *fifth* espresso and the fifth espresso felt warm and bitter against my throat and, forgetting the students, I sought Montaigne or the ghost of Montaigne or, at the very least, the *essence of the ghost of Montaigne,* Montaigne, and his highly agreeable theories on life; I gazed lovingly at the title, *Wisdom and Fate,* the sum of all my present suffering. Later, of course, *Wisdom and Fate* was replaced with *Measuring Montaigne* then *Rippling River of Life* and soon after *In Parallel Devotion*, a title which felt fixed and enduring; shimmering on the cover of my manuscript in hundreds of fonts and sizes which varied depending on mood and inclination, and for several weeks I considered the title settled, one less thing to worry about, I thought, one less headache, the title fixed and complete, although not much later *In Parallel Devotion* was dropped for *The Exile of Self,* each title replacing the last, each title superior to the title that came before, until, several long years later, meaning today, I crossed out *Montaigne, Mankind, and the Birth of Lucid Thought* for the utterly flawless *The Intrusion of Distraction.* And I feel blessed by the simplicity of *The Intrusion of Distraction. The Intrusion of Distraction,* I think, grinding the coffee, heating the water, losing myself in the sensuous routine of making my single-sourced Kenyan coffee, will be the beginning of my intellectual campaign, and I'll dedicate the work to my late wife, of course, whose closet I've rigorously avoided since last week, the day after she died, when I made the mistake of stepping inside for something, I forget what, and the closet smelled, not of my dead wife's perfume or my dead wife's scent or my dead wife's being, but *all three,* it smelled of my dead wife *entire,* as if my dead wife hadn't died, as if she'd only stepped out for an errand and would be returning any second, and how could a person die but the essence of their existence remain, I thought, stricken by grief, my breathing shallow, panic rising, suddenly weeping, how could the tangible presence of my dead wife waltz about as if she hadn't ceased to exist? For that matter, how had the world—bland, dire, tediously complex—continued so stubbornly to exist in her absence? How were the neighbors getting dressed, leaving for work, returning from work, as if everything hadn't been shattered, depleted, and made worse? I was halted, stopped dead in my tracks, promising myself not to venture into her closet until the work, meaning my book-length essay, was complete because by then, I told myself, the obstinate, unremitting scent of my now-dead wife would certainly be gone and as the coffee steeps I pace and ponder, contemplating the relationship between French intellectuals and coffee, not only Balzac but Rimbaud too. Rimbaud, a pioneer in the coffee trade, something people don't know or forget about, people get sidetracked by the decadence and the gunrunning, but Rimbaud's introduction to the African continent was coffee; a young Arthur oversaw the export of the Harar coffee, a still-boyish Frenchman, an already retired poet, one of the first Europeans to conduct business in Harar and I picture Harar, see a vast desert, a stretch of low brown houses and squat palms, the awnings of the market, the outlines of the minarets, sporadic and tall, rising in the hazy distance; I hear the braying of donkeys, the afternoon calls to prayer, having no idea, of course, if this is what Harar resembles or even sounds like because every one of us brings our own ideas and preconceptions, or *misconceptions,* to a place we're quick to call exotic, yet what's exotic to a person born and raised in one place, who has never traveled and thus knows nothing more than the place from whence they came, Harar for instance? To them, Dayton or Newark is exotic. And I consider Rimbaud, wonder if he realized the African continent would consume him, wonder if Rimbaud realized that moving to Africa was courting an early death even by the standards of his day? But none of this matters before I have coffee, I think, single origin because I'm not a savage, and when making coffee one must consider every element, from the source of the beans to the roast of the beans to the water because even serious connoisseurs tend to forget about the water, disregard water entirely even though water is just as important as the beans, maybe more so, and why would a person who claims to love coffee, who spends prodigious amounts of time choosing a particular roast, brewing method, and grinder, squander it in the last minute by using bad water, tap or unfiltered water, hence water that ruins and defeats the coffee-making ceremony, and after pouring a steaming cup I enter the study, sit before the rolltop desk, and regard the scraps of notes, the endless typed pages and copious lists of abandoned titles that make up my unfinished work, all dead set against my success, each page refuting a breakthrough or a revelation and the chirp of the phone once again reminds me of wanting to *change* the chirp of the phone, that nefarious chirp that's pursued me for years, from the calls of my wife's doctors to Marcel's appeals for money, the same chirp that alerted me of the dean's voicemail mere weeks after the first emergency review essentially confirming a *second* emergency review, the voice in the voicemail asking in a tidy voice to please arrive on campus, meaning the community college, promptly at nine a.m. on a Saturday, *a Saturday* I thought, stomach dropping, panic rising, meaning I was forcing the administrators themselves to arrive promptly at nine a.m. on a Saturday, one of only two days administrators weren't expected to show up on campus, and without saying the words *emergency review* I well understood it was an emergency review, for the tidy tone in the dean's voice as well as her calm insistence to arrive promptly at nine a.m. on a Saturday meant it couldn't be anything *but* an emergency review and I considered the administrator's resentment at having to show up at nine a.m. on a Saturday on account of me and the cloud of complaints which had flourished since the first emergency review and, looking back, this was the beginning of the end, because not much later, shortly after the second emergency review where I was placed on administrative probation, came the *espresso incident,* that debacle with the espresso machine concealed beneath my desk which became quite the scandal, the *espresso incident* endlessly gossiped about, the *espresso incident* on the tips of both the students' and the faculty's tongues and walking the halls I felt the chatter about the *espresso incident* striking my back like tossed pebbles. It was Philosophy 102, a class overflowing with dullards and I'd asked one of those dullards to fetch a towel after a malfunction with the espresso machine because there'd been a rather large release of steam, more or less an explosion, while I'd been cleaning the machine, the Italian espresso machine hidden beneath my desk, a triumph of Italian workmanship, a *Nuova Simonelli* espresso machine no less, surreptitiously installed in my class because it was prohibited on campus, meaning the community college, and I couldn't bring it home either, couldn't let my wife see the machine and perhaps, in a rare moment of lucidity, have her inquire about the cost of that gorgeous contraption, undeniably a work of art, forbidding in its design, considered a *pinnacle* in Italian craftmanship with its shimmering silver-and-black exterior, an espresso machine costing more than my own car and it was a ridiculous expense, a whim which I decided instantly to return as soon as I'd bought it, until it arrived, and I figured I'd steal a glimpse before sending it back because I'd already gone to the trouble of ordering the *Nuova Simonelli* and paying for the *Nuova Simonelli* so I might as well *see* the *Nuova Simonelli,* a small caprice, I reasoned, a meager indulgence for a man whose wife was dying, yet one look and I knew I would *never* return the *Nuova Simonelli* espresso machine with its gorgeous curves, flat tray, and stunning receptacle, because the *Nuova Simonelli* was clearly the most beautiful object I'd ever owned and in order to devote the time necessary to cleaning the *Nuova Simonelli* I assigned an in-class essay about sadness and desire, but a pipe burst, released a cloud of steam, thus I spilled the espresso grounds while leaning my arm against the steam wand, botching the effort and burning my forearm in the process, and I instructed a student to race to the teachers' lounge for a towel, perhaps two, make it three, and the class was disrupted because I'd not only spilled the espresso grounds but scalded myself in the process and *motherfucker,* I shouted, *fucking Christ,* I barked in agony, the students staring in open-eyed alarm, their dull, bovine faces suddenly alert, more cognizant and aware than I'd ever seen because the burst of steam and my subsequent burn had given them a sudden and unexpected jolt; the water that went through these contraptions was inconceivably hot, something I learned from spending weeks studying the *Nuova Simonelli* manual that came with the *Nuova Simonelli* espresso machine, although it wasn't a manual in the typical sense, nor a booklet or brochure, but a compendium, a goddamn *codex* if I'm being honest, the weight and volume of the tome testifying to the gravity which these Italians took their coffee-making appliances and I both resented and respected the manual for its size and encyclopedic assiduity even though calling it a manual was an enormous injustice, for the *Nuova Simonelli* booklet that came with the *Nuova Simonelli* machine contained an index and a table of contents and a host of illustrations, all printed on highly expensive photographic-grade paper, glossy no less, weighed close to five pounds, and included an array of endorsements by coffee experts and celebrities alike, the longest and most verbose by Italian actor Enzo Giordano, who elucidated in great detail his personal experiences with the *Nuova Simonelli* espresso machines, one of which he'd purchased with his first royalty check from the studio as a professional actor, an older and retired model no doubt, but it spoke to the loyalty and devotion he had for the brand, and I studied the manual, underlined and highlighted the applicable portions of the manual, as in making a *cortado* or *café manchado,* as in the proper cleaning of the receptacle, yet none of it mattered if I couldn't master the basic task of removing the portafilter, meaning the espresso handle, and cleaning the machine without burning my arm, the skin beginning to blister, the injury becoming more dicey by the second, changing colors like mother-of-pearl, and *fucking shit,* I bellowed, suppressing a sob, the wound beginning to unnerve both me and the students who, normally sluggish and slow, stared in stunned silence, appearing to me suddenly as accomplices or antagonists, as if they themselves had ordered the *Nuova Simonelli* machine, as if they themselves had decided to clean and inspect the *Nuova Simonelli* machine during Philosophy 102 and, even worse, a student had activated the fire alarm seconds after the *Nuova Simonelli* detonated, although detonate isn't the right word when the machine really hadn't detonated or exploded as much as *combusted,* yes, the espresso machine *combusted,* and I tried calming the class, instructing the class to ignore the fire alarm, sending a student to the cafeteria for ice, cursing myself for cleaning the machine during Philosophy 102, a boorish class with tepid meditations on critical thinking and the analysis of logical arguments and blah, blah, blah, the entire curriculum overrun by trite and shitty platitudes, by kitsch, all which scarcely scraped the surface of true philosophy because I was intimately acquainted with the course, had been teaching the course for over fifteen years and, truth be told, burning my arm, despite the excruciating pain, was the most exciting thing that had ever happened during Philosophy 102 except for that day with the shaft of sunlight which produced the tentative title for my essay on Montaigne and even though my arm was burning, even though I'd likely have to visit the emergency room, I thought, placing a towel on the rapidly rising blister while urging my students to ignore the present quandary and work on their essays, consider sadness and desire, I instructed, for once in your lives reach for something higher than yourselves, still, I thought, it was worth a good cup of coffee, not dishwater, not swill, not the piss-brown drivel they served in the teachers' lounge for gratis because something as abhorrent and muddy as that couldn't be anything *but* free, that insult to coffee, that wretched affront to what coffee *should* be, a russet-colored concoction broiling perpetually in the teachers' lounge, a *lounge,* I laugh now, an affront to lounges everywhere, as if we, the teachers, spent our off-hours reclining in Voltaire chairs, legs extended, newspapers spread across our laps, the supple notes of Mahler fluttering in the air, as if we, the educators, were something other than instruments in some future flesh factory, and once more the phone chirps and I sip my coffee, considering if I should work on my book-length essay or deal with the phone and I pick up the phone, decide to finally change its chirp because not only is its chirp highly unpleasant but it brings back memories of all the times my now-dead wife called in a panic, to tell me either her food had been poisoned or wiretaps had been inserted inside her brain while she slept and, much later, her rants about *spaceships,* yes, *spaceships,* which she insisted were flying overhead, observing her, pursuing her, hovering above the dull suburb in which we'd chosen to spend our lives, and I didn't bother asking where they, meaning the *spaceships,* came from, as I only wanted to placate my now-dead wife, although she wasn't dead at the time, no, she was frighteningly alive, I only wanted to soothe and mollify my wife because the woman I loved, once so pragmatic and responsible, so vibrant and enamored with the world, was ranting about *spaceships,* insisting *spaceships* were outside the window, hovering and recording and soaring across the sky, and it was deeply unnerving because maybe my wife knew something the rest of us didn't? A small part of me suspecting there actually could be *spaceships* hovering outside the house, why not? So yes, I think, the chirp on the phone must be changed, suddenly determined to change the chirp, forgetting the jumble of pages before me because Montaigne or, to be clear, *Lord Michel de Montaigne,* father of the *Essais,* meaning the modern essay, can wait, has in fact already waited and can continue to wait, but the phone cannot. Pushing a button an array of choices appear and none of the choices have anything to do with changing the chirp or ring of my phone because what I need, I remember, is the *settings* feature, and I recall Marcel's explicit instructions weeks ago about the settings feature when I'd wanted to change some trivial function on the phone, Marcel sighing with impatience because the settings feature he explained, admonishing me as if I were one of my own students, was the easiest most conspicuous detail on the phone, the settings feature akin, he said, to a table of contents, the settings feature, he continued, like a compass or syllabus taking you anywhere you need to go on the phone, a phone Marcel insisted I buy in order for him to send me *links* or *downloads* of his most recent recordings, *mixes* he called them, replete with long-winded preludes describing the *mixes* themselves, justifying his long-held ambition for

LESSER RUINS [35]

making *minimal, underground* dance music, propulsive, pia-
no-driven *house music* replete with hi-hats and vocal samples
and complex bongo patterns edging into something wholly new,
those were his exact words, *wholly new,* not only music made for
the club or relegated to singles, he said, but entire albums with
narratives, with valleys and crescendos, encompassing entire
landscapes, containing the *aesthetics of rave* while invoking both
trance, ambient, Nu-disco, even *acid jazz,* and ultimately he
wanted to make an electronic album that could be listened to
from *beginning to end,* an album to either dance to or contemplate in solitude, or both at once: at a club with friends or alone
with a pair of expensive noise-canceling headphones, music like
bliss and euphoria, music like a vast and boundless plateau, he
said, where pain, sadness, hunger, and the insatiable desire to
placate the vacuum of existence were extinguished, and I remember thinking that sounded hyperbolic and ambitious, perhaps even dangerous, because no work of art, be it music or literature, even film, can be *everything,* I thought, no single work of
art can fulfill every need, succor each mood, placate each passion, and I considered how foolish the two of us were, how
Marcel had inherited his mother's open heart, boundless optimism, and kindness, but nothing at all from yours truly, meaning
his father, except of course his father's foolishness, a foolishness
palpable in the hundreds of pages before me, overflowing with
titles I once loved but later retired: *Tusk of Memory, French
Chimera, Origins of the Sire,* and hundreds more, none of them
harmonizing or conforming with the vision I have of my

book-length essay, countless titles showing a history of bad and unruly decisions, decisions taking me further from the truth instead of closer to the truth, until today with *The Intrusion of Distraction* and once again I nod, gratified by the title, a title I can spend my solitude working toward and for a moment I'm sated, the coffee smooth and bitter but not *too* smooth and not *too* bitter and I recall Napoleon who said *I'd rather suffer with coffee than be senseless* and the Marquise de Castro Gautreau, matriarch of the Auvergne region, a notorious coffee fiend who foolishly sent her minions scouring the Pyrénées for the richest, most distinctive, and best-tasting coffee; de Castro Gautreau enjoyed her coffee strong and, once it was consumed, liked to have the granules at the bottom collected in order to have her future read, seeing vistas and valleys and a better life there than she'd ever actually enjoy; and Harold d'Angoulême, the guillotine's blade glistening above his head, who claimed he'd contracted gout from drinking too much coffee and thus blamed the killing spree which followed, and for which he was being sentenced to death, on his coffee addiction, because the pain, he lamented, *the pain,* which, to me, seems valid, because Joseph Conrad, suffering from gout, described the pain as *walking on one's eyeballs;* so many stories infused by coffee, I think, Kafka for instance, delighting in the coffeehouses of Prague, who took his coffee black, lots of sugar, room temperature, a preference whose origins were rooted in the young neurotic burning his mouth on an espresso at nineteen and since then, pale and impish, courting tuberculosis like a vigilant lover, insisted on drinking his coffee only after it had sat for ten minutes and I imagined Kafka in the Café Arco, gazing at his watch, surrounded by friends who never suspected they would, in little more than a decade, be murdered by Nazis, Kafka waiting the allotted ten minutes he'd issued himself like a decree. Coffee preferences tell as much about the person as their tastes in fashion and literature and I consider these things and more; I consider anguish and longing, the precipice and the void, God and the eternal return as well as other spiritual subjects, the kind of subjects one ponders *while* drinking coffee and momentarily I'm content, glancing at the expanse of unbroken time before me, a nearly perfect plateau of continuous time in which to contemplate and produce, to meditate on Montaigne as any faithful *Montaignian* does, because I've begun to sense the stirrings of an inner-crisis, nameless and new, approaching fast, each time I walk by my dead wife's closet or consider passing my dead wife's closet, the inner-crisis clambering ever closer, and frankly I'm frightened, terrified of the silence which has assumed the proportions of a creature, announcing itself in the contours of her absence, a silence insisting my wife is dead, *reminding* me my wife is dead, as if I don't know, as if I'm not already avoiding my dead wife's closet, the nightstand too, the prescription bottles arranged like a tableau of madness, the purgatorial stench of illness, the echo of her rants, those rants about *spaceships* which, toward the end, illustrated how gone she was. *Jesus,* she'd holler, *the spaceships!* And me attempting to restrain her, struggling to stop my wife from hurting herself, both of us hysterical, both of us weeping, and no matter how ardently I insisted there weren't any *spaceships,* either in the sky or anywhere else, she wouldn't listen, me separating the curtains, lifting the blankets I'd secured over each window, obstinately pointing, insisting she look at a sky conspicuously absent of spaceships, as if getting through to her were remotely feasible, a stunning woman, hardly in her fifties, diagnosed with *frontotemporal dementia,* which is as bad as it sounds, a disease whose only outcome is death, sometimes fast, sometimes slow, but always the same, my now dead wife, once a passionate ecologist, an environmental scientist, whose decline, rapid in some respects, slow in others, felt like an endless war with a faceless enemy, and I realize the one thing I need, silence, is the thing that terrifies me the most because left alone, finally, with silence, I have only my own thoughts to guide or disturb, encourage or assail, and once again the phone chirps and I tell myself I have to deal with the chirp of that fucking phone which I will undoubtedly do, but not before I get to work, forgetting about the phone and my now-dead wife as well as the litany of titles concocted for my book-length opus and instead focus on the work, *the work,* I tell myself, and I stroke the pages of my draft, consider my favorite anecdote about Montaigne, not the grief he felt over his brother dying from a tennis injury (yes, a *tennis injury*), because Montaigne's brother dying from a tennis injury was surely a favorite anecdote, perhaps my second or third, not my favorite though, because my favorite Montaigne anecdote is Montaigne's brief acquaintance with Alexei Voznesensky, a Russian poet and fugitive, a relationship hardly discussed and which I discovered while doing research for my book after receiving a fellowship from the Zybècksz Archives at the Horner Institute, actually having taken leave for a semester from the community college, leaving my wife and young Marcel, escaping town in fact; three months I spent at the Zybècksz Archives at the Horner Institute researching everything available about Montaigne's life *outside* the essays when I came upon the brief association between Montaigne and Voznesensky, a relationship few knew or had written about and which I believed would separate my book from the hordes of minor works written about Montaigne which brought nothing new or original to the world of Montaigne scholarship. A poet of dubious renown in 1540s Moscow, Alexei Voznesensky was an instrumental member of the Sokolov Circle, an intellectual group of radical intellectuals, until he was expelled from the Sokolov Circle for writing outrageous sonnets scandalizing Ivan Grozny, known to many as Ivan the Terrible, obscene sonnets with a scatological bent, depicting the tsar and tsarina in fabulous acts of copulation which left little to the imagination, the tsarina especially, poems depicting the tsarina seducing drunk soldiers and slavish Muscovites not to mention illiterate villagers along the Volga, using the most colorful language imaginable, sonnets describing the tsarina exerting her well-appointed bosom to beguile hundreds of men, stanzas suffused with scenes of the tsarina shitting and copulating or, likewise, copulating and shitting, thus Voznesensky was forced to flee Russia and in his flight he'd developed a taste for dueling because every mercenary and musketeer Ivan the Terrible sent to kill Voznesensky, Voznesensky himself killed, the poet challenging his assailants to duels which no officer of the Imperial crown could refuse, and rapidly Voznesensky accrued a body count as he was excellent with the sword and could fend well with a dagger too, that is, stab a man at close quarters, contorting his body in serpentine shapes in order to kill the opponent, thus winning the duel, and Voznesensky was skilled with the musket too, although his preference was the sword or saber, staring into the eyes of his adversary amid his turbulent flight, in Gdańsk, in Munich, in Liechtenstein, always in some bucolic hamlet I imagined, but, eventually, entering France, Lyon to be precise, where he'd outwitted and assassinated a troupe of mounted archers by ejecting each from their horse and killing every aggressor, one by one, with the aforementioned challenge of a duel. Voznesensky had killed dozens of men in his exploits, for when he dueled he danced, his steps mimicking the illustrious *Barynya* of the Siberian Steppe, a folk dance the poet had mastered as a child amid those short, intense Siberian summers, the broad sky, the expanse of brown earth, the endless days charged with promise, and the *Barynya*, he discovered, when applied to a duel, guaranteed success. At the Zybècksz Archives I discovered this acquaintance in a facsimile of a diary belonging to Montaigne and hence spent weeks studying the history, minutiae, and finer points of duels, the history of appointing seconds as well as the *Code duello*, the code of duels, and when I returned home from the Zybècksz Archives I had dozens of pages about duels and dozens of anecdotes about duels, but hardly a word about Montaigne, in fact nothing at all about Montaigne, though that's not to say my time at the Zybècksz Archives wasn't transformative, undeniably so, the Zybècksz Archives at the Horner Institute, tucked away in the Berkshires, shrouded in virgin forest, a circuitous dirt path, overgrown and narrow, the only means of finding entry to that prodigious institution that, once unveiled, resembled an earthly paradise, its vast array of mid-century architecture and lavish pagoda, the *Bustamante Embassy* as well as the luminous *Pleasure Gardens*. The Zybècksz Archives at the Horner Institute represented the most vast, comprehensive, and invaluable collection of papers, diaries, lithographs, and primary materials in North America, works too priceless to be kept in ordinary archives, too brittle and frail to be left in the open air, hence the security, hence the hyperbaric chambers in the sub-basement, hence the exhaustive measures taken each time I took the elevator down to the *Tanner Room* where the archives themselves were kept, with its guards and metal detectors and ill-lit corridors surely meant to intimidate, the Zybècksz Archives finally my chance, I thought, to escape mediocrity, invited after years of sending letters and appeals—and subsequently, longer, more frenzied letters and appeals—to conduct research for my book on Montaigne. My letters paid off because, twelve attempts later, I received an acceptance from Director Pleva himself, the illustrious Franco Pleva, author of that peerless study on Schopenhauer and I'll never forget the day: late spring, cascades of tender light; Marcel was still in high school and my wife hadn't yet lost her mind, was still in possession of a gorgeous and brilliant mind, a mind both affectionate and sane, happy to support her husband in his escape from mediocrity, and after reading the letter of acceptance a third, fourth, and fifth time, hands trembling, pulse racing, I walked toward the house and for the first time truly saw the neighborhood in which I lived, the lawns and sidewalks, the slow-moving circles of nuanced light which, at that time of day, fell across the street in incandescent fingers and one could almost say it was beautiful. Yes, I told myself, it's almost beautiful. My breathing slowed and I felt as if I were finally escaping mediocrity, sympathizing suddenly with the petty dreams and petty lives of my neighbors, poor fellow travelers, I thought, poor petty dreams, I also thought. The perfume from the neighbors' garden, the flight of migratory birds, the half-hearted harmony of suburbia, it was beautiful *and* pitiful, a vital mixture which conveyed the smallest hint of our shared humanity, and I was carried aloft, over the hedges and sidewalks, the streets growing suddenly smaller, the lives beneath me growing smaller too, the neighbors' shrubbery, the small yapping dogs, agitated and unleashed, the yards partitioned by sidewalks, I was leaving it all behind, my neuroses and insufficiencies, my self-loathing and middling attempts at fatherhood, husbandhood, professorhood. Grasping Pleva's letter, I drifted into the cosmic sublime, floated for what felt like hours, held aloft by both my dreams and delusions, while the frivolous world, tired and petty, diminished below. In my more optimistic moments I saw myself as a visionary, yet those moments were few and fell easily apart, held together by thin webs of delusion; always I was overcome by a self-doubt instilled in me during my youth, forever discouraged by my parents and later my colleagues and department heads and let's not forget the bovine-faced simpletons waiting to have their thoughts interrupted, all of them skeptical that a book-length essay on Montaigne could change the world, that authoring such a book would lift a man from the bogs of mediocrity, and promptly I fell back to earth, collected myself, reread Director Pleva's acceptance, and walked inside the house, eager to share news of my admission to the Zybècksz Archives at the Horner Institute to stay in one of their guest cottages on a fellowship. Only the most serious scholars, artists, and soon-to-be-crowned geniuses were invited to the Zybècksz Archives at the Horner Institute, established in 1877, birthplace of numerous eminent works on Jung, Marx, Wittgenstein, and Plath. The Zybècksz Archives housed the original letters of Cavendish, Cromwell, Ibsen, and Sands; the sexually charged correspondence of Karel Kryl and Františka Goldblath, the Warsaw psychoanalysts, was also there, housed in the *Tanner Room* at the Zybècksz Archives at the Horner Institute, ceaselessly protected, a host of formalities, in fact, awaited the visiting fellow begging admittance to the *Tanner Room* in the sub-basement adjacent to the *Facsimile Closet*. Each time I requested access I was met with outrageous requirements, redundant and far fetched, the fingerprinting and invasive pat downs, a catalogue of interrogations, first by the sentries then, once permitted, by the custodian of the *Tanner Room,* a frail, bespectacled woman whose loose-fitting wig and sciatica suggested a soul from another era. Once inside the antechamber, a nameless official scanned my identification then proceeded by asking absurd questions having nothing to do with my studies, and my answers, though strange and vague, were no stranger or vaguer than the questions themselves. Everything was perfunctory and official, solemn to the point of distraction. Positioned across campus, bronze statues of past luminaries like Lukas d'Haussonville and Cynthia Nordau kept watch. Verdant plants punctuated the corridors of the *Bustamante Embassy* and the *Tanner Room* as well as the *Tanner Reading Room*, a capacious space, dim and sober, awash with history and one felt, at least I did, an allegiance to one's predecessors. Here, I told myself, is where Katarina Roth had written of Blake's nudism in *Elegy of Angels;* this is where Alessandro Costa had studied moral realism and gone insane, committing suicide among the hibiscus and marigolds of the *Pleasure Gardens,* found hanging from a towering oak with a note pinned to his pantleg reading simply: *weep for me.* Each morning I approached the *Tanner Room*, took the elevator down, suffered the frisking of the guards, the litany of absurd questions, walked the half-lit hall toward the *Bellinger Wing,* past the *Lithograph Room* adjacent to the *Facsimile Closet* which wasn't a closet but a large, high-ceilinged room adorned with Bauhaus architecture from the Weimar Republic; the *Facsimile Closet* contained facsimiles of every work ever conceived at the Zybècksz Archives including Sandra Vogel's study on the correlation between pulmonary infection and sorrow, *Tuberculosis and Grief,* which had introduced the world to this singular branch of research, a seminal work, still being taught, enjoying its seventh printing and what could only be called a cult following. These and more, researched and authored in the rarefied air atop the grassy hills of the Zybècksz Archives at the Horner Institute, nestled in the Berkshires, where one could hike or swim, meditate or rock climb, stroll the *Pleasure Gardens* in one's leisure or, like Tanner himself, birdwatch. The landscape, charming and austere, was matched only by the stature of its history. The biography of flautist Wilhelm Würfel had been composed in the very cottage where I would stay, the manuscript itself contained inside the *Tanner Room*, named after Desmond Horner Tanner, a Civil War veteran turned banker turned philanthropist turned avid ornithologist. Traumatized by the carnage at Vicksburg, Tanner, ashen-faced and dour, decades of alcohol addiction rippling in his wake, bought the hills and forests that would become the Horner Institute in 1873 as well as the accompanying lake in order to watch birds in solitude because even back then, meaning 1873, elevated individuals were looking for escape, meaning searching for *mental Saharas,* because already the world was becoming noisier and faster, already society was finding ways to encroach upon *slow thinking,* meaning finding ways to impair *slow thinking* or dismantle *slow thinking,* to intrude upon contemplation and discernment, meaning finding excuses to have one's thoughts interrupted. A handful of Montaigne's private papers, including a little-known diary, had found their way to the Zybècksz Archives at the Horner Institute, thus my countless pleas for a fellowship, year after year, filling out and sending applications in the hopes of escaping mediocrity and, at long last, I'd been accepted and, with Pleva's letter creased in my hand, I entered the house to the clamor of Marcel on the Steinway, recently purchased, his playing barbed and unruly, not my intention when we'd purchased the piano, Marcel, a high schooler, already obsessed with dance music, *proto-house,* he recently explained, meaning *post-disco,* meaning *house music* at its inception, before it had been divided, minced, and labeled into a hundred different micro-genres, before it became *progressive house* and *minimal house* and *downtempo trance,* and *left-field electronica,* the endless directions in which it had inevitably gone and just last year, after walking inside the house and looking in on his sleeping mother, Marcel had sat across from me and given a sermon on an upcoming set he was planning to play as well as his thoughts on *club culture* and *dance culture* in which he seamlessly moved from meditations on *trance music* to *breakbeat* to *underground techno* to the various trends of *minimal house* and, more recently, the seismic shift to more euphoric disco-infused party tracks not failing to describe the infinite micro-scenes and fads and let's not forget, he stressed, the latest obsession with invoking tropical music into deep house, an obvious throwback to the early '90s, artists from as far away as Norway excelling especially at this new trend, in which tropical house, using tropical sounds and jungle rhythms, made the music warmer and more humid and you'd think, he opined, it would be the Latin American DJs who'd really shine at this, but no, he said, it's the Danish and the Swedish and the Icelandic who truly eclipse all the other DJs at *tropical-infused house* and who knows, he said, me on the couch, listless and peeved, waiting for Marcel to stop talking, something I found myself doing whenever he *began* talking, and I loved the boy, but I had a wife, just as he had a mother, dying in the next room, a woman who saw *spaceships* everywhere, insisted she saw *spaceships* hovering outside the window whenever she was awake, and who knows, Marcel conjectured, maybe it's the Nordic DJs' appetite for these sounds that helps them exceed at this genre, living all the time in those arctic conditions so they're desperate for the sounds of a toucan or a macaw, desperate for whatever kinds of birds live in the Brazilian rainforest that *exude* the sounds of a jungle, something lush and rippling, green and balmy, though I honestly don't even know what the fuck a jungle *sounds* like and, turning his head, Marcel's profile suddenly resembled my soon-to-be-dead wife's, something I'd never noticed, and my heart sank, realizing that once she was gone I'd continue to see her, meaning my sick, soon-to-be-dead wife, in the face of Marcel, each time he turned and laughed, smirked or cried, even raved about *electronic music*, I would see *her*, and it would be a loss that would never end, a death that would never die. *Underground dance music*, Marcel bemoaned, is getting perverted and diluted, getting hijacked by mainstream audiences, kidnapped by the masses, he said, who've always had the worst taste, so now we have the posers and pretenders celebrating *goddamn* EDM which is short for *electronic dance music*, he explained, but EDM is also shorthand, he said, for *terrible* and *pretentious dance music*, the posers getting all the attention with their atrocious and god-awful EDM, but instead of bringing me down it's only going to make me stronger and my set is going to change the *landscape*, he exclaimed, my set will be a prelude to what my album will be, soft and cathartic, gurgling and shape-shifting, but harsh and challenging too because, he said, I want the album to incorporate *everything* and with great tenacity, with a look of resolve which consumed his face whenever the subject was music, he gushed about his album, how it, meaning the album, would be loyal to *dance-music diehards* as well as the casual listener; he talked of *calypso* and *found sounds, basslines* and *synth chords, handclaps* and *vibraphones,* tracks of disembodied voices flickering like ghosts, hovering over the track, *dipping into* the track only to be *flushed out* then disappearing again, hints of jazz-inflected piano too, he said, but visionary and euphoric, voices mixed with drum patterns, drum patterns gaining velocity, drum patterns becoming simpler and more complex, both at once, drum patterns that would make the listener, likewise the dancer, go *out of their fucking minds,* drum patterns like the beating of a thousand human hearts and I looked past Marcel's shoulder, down the hallway to the bedroom where my wife, heavily medicated, was likely dreaming of *spaceships,* of extraterrestrials recording her thoughts. Meanwhile, Marcel had hastened into a discourse on *dub music and its influence,* an entire sermon on *dub music and its influence,* a subject Marcel especially loved, and whenever *dub music and its influence* were brought up it was a sign to either interrupt Marcel or drift because Marcel could talk about *dub music and its influence* for hours, and that's exactly what I did, drift I mean, I ventured past the kitchen toward the rolltop desk where my book-length essay on Montaigne was waiting, large portions conceived at the Zybècksz Archives at the Horner Institute when I received a scholarship as an *artist-in-residence.* Leaving the community college, I brought along all the books I needed as well as my countless coffee-making accoutrements: the Moka pot, the grinder and the gooseneck, the filters and filter brush, the double-lined borosilicate French press, a backup French press (just in case), a porcelain single-cup pour-over and a subscription to my favorite coffee roasters which a clerk at the Zybècksz Archives assured me would arrive like clockwork because without my coffee I was useless, I explained over the phone, or worse, not only useless, but *dangerous,* not dangerous to others, I quickly clarified, only to myself, a danger to myself and the work I planned wholeheartedly to dive into with a fervency unrivaled and which I already envision, yes, I said, I *envision* the fervency with which I'll create my masterwork, I see it approaching from the horizon, ascending a small hill, let's call it a hillock or better yet, a *bluff,* yes, I said, I see my work clambering up a bluff through a field like a brilliant and beautiful explosion, and the clerk who picked up the phone at the Zybècksz Archives at the Horner Institute, a person who no doubt dealt with the anxieties of writers and artists, in short, *serious thinkers,* all the time, assured me that my coffee would arrive unmolested, that the mail delivery at the Horner was nothing if not reliable, the mail delivery at the Horner, in fact, was a *zenith of consistency,* and the focus, she said, should be the stretch of unbroken time before me not to mention the *priceless resources* at my disposal, *unbroken time,* she stressed, and *priceless resources,* she also stressed, and indeed, at the Zybècksz Archives at the Horner Institute I discovered those *priceless resources,* chiefly a facsimile of a copy of Montaigne's diary which had never been fully scrutinized, detailing subjects ranging from the care of his vineyard to his near-constant suffering from kidney stones, as well as other minor details and historically it was a terrible time, especially when one considers the plagues and religious wars and lack of basic hygiene and sure, one might *believe* the French countryside of the 1500s was bucolic and enchanting, a land of pastures and vineyards and majestic days stretching into the golden horizon, but that's a stupid belief, in fact that belief is the pinnacle of stupidity because the French countryside of the 1500s was a cesspit, savage and repellent, immersed in revolts and religious wars in addition to endless plagues, endless because once one plague ended another began so if you weren't sick you'd be sick soon enough, meaning if you avoided one plague while everyone else around you, friends and neighbors, sisters and cousins, the old and young alike were struck down, you only had to bide your time because another plague was always right around the corner and if *that* plague was avoided (unlikely though this would have been) the next plague *after that* was already snapping at its heels, so that life, in short, was simply one long process of waiting to die from the plague and, making matters worse, I thought, was the presumed stench of a person in the French countryside of the 1500s and though I didn't know the stench personally, I could well *imagine* what the typical stench of a person in the French countryside of the 1500s was like, in short, I thought, like shit. Montaigne's diary didn't refer to how he or anyone else smelled in the French countryside of the 1500s, though he did write about his brief meeting and subsequent acquaintance with Alexei Voznesensky, a man unbeknownst to Montaigne, who'd murdered dozens of mercenaries, imperial guards, and professional musketeers, henchmen called *streltsy*, vicious and unrestrained in their barbarity, all sent from the tsar with the express orders to bring back Voznesensky's head as retribution for the obscenity of his poems as well as justice for the men the poet had killed in his flight from Russia, mostly by duel but also entrapment for it was discovered that Voznesensky, sensing the tsar's agents on his heels, would not only challenge these men to duels but, if feeling outnumbered, lie in wait, setting up elaborate and fiendish traps, as he had done in Łódź and Baden-Baden and Austerlitz, afterward arranging the corpses in lavish displays mocking the Russian crown, the murders in Limousin for example, what became a rather well-known massacre, where Voznesensky staged the bodies in a tableau: a cordial game of cards, four dead musketeers, their ribbons and insignia replaced by crude stanzas penned by Voznesensky, such as the one in Baden-Baden, which read:

I knew a little tsarina
Whose teats were filled with milk
And every Russian man
Of every rank and ilk
Dreamt of lapping those abundant breasts
Of soft, heavenly silk.

Sophomoric and vulgar and left for the *streltsy* to chance upon in their pursuit, the poet no doubt recognizing the *streltsy* for who they were, meaning barbaric and insatiable, men the imperial crown had charged with finding Voznesensky and killing Voznesensky, but slowly, instructed the tsar, make the poet pay and once he's paid, meaning once you've found, captured, and killed Voznesensky, bring me his head, no one better suited for this than the *streltsy* because the *streltsy* had fought in the Siege of Kazan, had witnessed warfare of outlandish proportion, battles the likes of which humanity had never seen. Inside the *Tanner Room* I clutched the facsimile of a copy of Montaigne's diary, translated from Montaigne's original diary, and each day I checked out the facsimile from the *Tanner Room* to study inside the *Tanner Reading Room*, returning to the *Tanner Room* every thirty minutes since it was a well-known stipulation that books must be returned to the *Tanner Room* every half hour, a rule I respected and begrudged in equal proportion because the value of the books, a subject beyond reproach, was eclipsed by the draconian regulations of both the *Tanner Room* and *Tanner Reading Room*, since the works removed from the *Tanner Room* were forbidden to be taken anywhere *but* the *Tanner Reading Room,* and for no more than thirty-minute increments before the scholar, in this case me, had to return to the *Tanner Room* in order to check the book back out anew, consequently I could only do research in thirty-minute segments, even less, since the tangles of halls dividing the *Tanner Room* from the *Tanner Reading Room* were convoluted and complex, complete with two flights of stairs (one up, two down) thus, once I returned from the *Tanner Room* to the *Tanner Reading Room,* a trifle agitated, a touch breathless, five minutes had elapsed, hence of the thirty minutes given, only twenty-five remained, consequently I researched and studied and transcribed with the weight of ticking time pressed upon my shoulders and I admired these venerated works being kept, as it were, on a short leash, however couldn't the rules be improved, I thought, couldn't the circulations desk at the *Tanner Room* find a way for the books inside the *Tanner Reading Room* to be accounted for? Didn't the technology exist, I wondered, to withdraw a book from the *Tanner Room* and thirty minutes later have the book accounted for in the *Tanner Reading Room* simply by notifying the *Tanner Room* with the use of pneumatic tubes or walkie-talkies, because the librarians stationed at the circulation desks in both the *Tanner Room* and *Tanner Reading Room* often seemed, if not exactly bored, a bit idle, and I found myself forced to set an alarm in order to return to the *Tanner Room* or, likewise, the *Tanner Reading Room,* depending on the order, to make sure I was on time, meaning not late, thus avoiding having my privileges or membership, even fellowship, nullified and revoked, in short, quashed; every twenty-five minutes I returned to the *Tanner Room* after vigorously studying a translated copy of a facsimile of Montaigne's diary in the *Tanner Reading Room* to once again check out the facsimile in the hopes of returning to the *Tanner Reading Room* with my mind aflame, fixated on Montaigne and 1500s France and kidney stones too, and I couldn't let my concentration wane, I told myself, couldn't let my mind wander from my book-length essay, a book which would allow me, finally, to escape mediocrity, no, I reassured myself, I mustn't let the constant treks from the *Tanner Room* to the *Tanner Reading Room,* or vice versa, depending on the order, hinder my work, yet inevitably this was exactly what happened because instead of thinking about my book I became overwhelmed with solutions, all of them simple, as in extending the allotted check-out time from thirty minutes to forty-five, even an hour, why not, or placing both Tanner rooms beside one another since the original *Tanner Room* and the subsequent *Tanner Reading Room* both neighbored large, open-aired rooms with high ceilings and well-appointed windows, ideal for a library or media center, rooms with the advantage of natural light where one could sit for uninterrupted hours, research and write or, likewise, write and research, allowing the grandeur of the settings to placate the frustrations of the soul and the chaos of existence, and lastly, I also thought, knocking down a wall, inserting a desk, something small and unimposing, facing both Tanner rooms at once, used simultaneously as a circulations desk for both the *Tanner Room* and *Tanner Reading Room,* because a desk servicing *both* Tanner rooms would eliminate the need for *two* librarians, saving the Zybècksz Archives at the Horner Institute, in the end, thousands of dollars a year. There were infinite solutions, I thought, all of them simple, all of them begging to be established, and this consumed my mind while going back and forth between the *Tanner Room* and *Tanner Reading Room,* or vice versa, the order was immaterial, what was, indeed, *material* was the fact that I was getting sidetracked and impeded when what I needed were long stretches of unbroken time, meaning *mental Saharas,* the unbroken time promised when I received the acceptance from Director Pleva as an *artist-in-residence,* allowing me three uninterrupted months secluded in the Berkshires, because I was still young enough to escape mediocrity, I told myself, young enough to compose a book-length essay about the *inventor* of the essay because this was years before all of the bad things started, years before the first and second *emergency review,* before I'd retired or was fired (there are different versions), before my wife lost her mind and began seeing *spaceships* everywhere, not just outside the window but hovering over the city, *spaceships* filled with what she called *dark beings* and, simply put, I was flustered and vexed, no different than the other scholars I passed in the halls and stairwells, harried like me, amid the ceaseless sequence of laps between the *Tanner Room* and *Tanner Reading Room,* or vice versa, depending on the order, all of us addled and agitated, nodding at one another, suspicious we were actors in some macabre farce, because it was an extraordinary route between both Tanner rooms, quite torturous, and it was incomprehensible that the Zybècksz Archives at the Horner Institute, one of the most illustrious and revered institutes of research and scholarship in North America, would knowingly impose these pointless ordeals upon its scholars; the hopeless treks, the constant traipsing between the two Tanner Rooms, when we, meaning the *artists-in-residence,* should've been occupied, meaning indisposed, meaning working inside one of the two Tanner rooms, either the original *Tanner Room* checking books out, or the *Tanner Reading Room* studying the aforementioned books checked out from the initial *Tanner Room* itself, the *first* of the two *Tanner Rooms* conceived in 1912 with the aim of containing all the significant artistic and academic works conceived in the United States, and later internationally, singular and priceless, either purchased for the Collection or original works produced at the Horner Institute itself, and I cursed the flights of stairs, the narrow halls, the picture windows facing the *Bellinger Wing* which lent one a vague sense of exile and sorrow, not to mention, if one refused the stairs, the precarious elevator that took an eternity though there were only two floors in the unnamed building housing both the *Tanner Room* and the *Tanner Reading Room,* a low, elongated structure, unassuming at first glance, spread across campus and divided in half by the luminous *Pleasure Gardens* which, at twilight, minutes before both Tanner rooms closed, felt touched by the divine. The ceaseless trips between the two Tanner rooms a contest to keep one's attention on their work, I thought, a contest to remain calm, I also thought, and the entire reason I'd taken leave from the community college was for unbroken time, not *broken time,* not time cleaved into twenty-five-minute fragments, not even fragments, I thought, but *vestiges* of time, *whiffs* of time, the *detritus* left when time had dissolved, and, making matters worse, one also needed to fend themselves from the *scholarship poets,* a gang of juveniles admitted each season, I was told, for tax purposes, hence the *scholarship poets* weren't invited based on the quality of their work or talent, nor the *future promise* of their work or talent, but because they'd once published an essay or a poem or guest-edited some regional journal, the vetting of the *scholarship poets* feeble at best, and it was obvious they had no interest in *mental Saharas* nor the fragile inner world nor the sustained time required to create art, but were, I'd heard, all cases of nepotism; some relative tenuously connected to the Horner, a distant aunt or uncle who'd once made a not-so-small donation, though no one seemed certain how the *scholarship poets* arrived, only that there they were; young, cackling, tramping the grounds in their combat boots, rolling cigarettes, roving in small packs, asking anyone to be audience to their latest verse or begging for a ride down the mountain to the gas station for alcohol, laughing under their breath, entangled in countless melodramas, and though small in number, the *scholarship poets* seemed to be everywhere, boasting an array of multicolored hair, smoking joints, lingering in the corridors of the *Rare Manuscript Room* or loitering outside the *Tsypkin House of Holocaust Research* and avoiding them was futile because anywhere I looked I observed a duo or trio or tetrad of *scholarship poets* emerging from the woods, ambling raucously across the *Pleasure Gardens* and passing them it was impossible not to be reminded of my own bovine-faced students who wanted, more than anything, to have their thoughts interrupted, and once again my phone chirps and I can't tell if it's a call or a message, because the phone, or the chirp, doesn't differentiate between the two, at least not the sound, and I curse Marcel who, in his good-natured enthusiasm, bought me the phone, a *smartphone,* he bragged, handing me the sleek gray apparatus, smiling as he boasted of everything the phone could do when all I wanted was a phone that could do *next to nothing,* a phone that hardly worked, namely an old-fashioned phone, a phone which took a person *away* from people, not *closer* to people, a phone which allowed me to escape from people, because all I wanted, in short, was solitude and peace, the *smartphone* the antithesis of solitude and peace, the *smartphone* an adamant fuck-you to solitude and peace, the *smartphone* an invitation to *join* society even though I *abhorred* society because society was undeniably on a downward slope, inundated by mediocrity and half thoughts, hindrances and interruptions, namely the ceaseless chirps of phones, and the chirps of my phone, I think, are likely calls or messages of sympathy, genuine concerns about the state of my health, meaning my *well-being,* friends and colleagues of my dead wife, or perhaps the rabbi, a dour man with dark, thinning hair and a somber scowl, because I alienated most of my friends by the time I was fired or retired, there are different versions, and what would I even say assuming I picked up? I'm fine? Things are good if I avoid thinking about my deceased wife or avoid passing by my deceased wife's closet in the house we shared for close to three decades? Because there's her nightstand, which is bad, and there's her closet, which is worse, and last week, when I walked into her closet for something, I forget what, a pair of socks or a shirt, I was consumed by panic, felt terror radiating outward, racing through each limb with no focal point, and I stumbled, I gasped, I fell to my knees, and since then I've avoided both the nightstand and the closet, not to mention a host of other areas which do nothing but remind me of my dead wife because I sense a terrible storm advancing, and the only way to keep the storm at bay is to focus on my book-length essay, and coffee too, and I forget about the chirps of the phone and my wife who's gone forever, meaning eternity, meaning in perpetuity, meaning I'll never see her again, and I muse upon Balzac and Voltaire, consider who drank more coffee, because both were rapacious coffee fiends, gluttonous when it came to coffee, and supposedly Voltaire, swayed by his own intuition, believed coffee promoted digestion and fortified the stomach; coffee, considered at the time to be an *intellectual drink*, the drink of philosophers and writers, painters and great thinkers, coffee known to benefit the body's humors; there were countless opinions and Voltaire ignored the noise around him, meaning the arguments both for and against coffee, and did what he wanted, meaning drank dozens of cups of coffee a day; he also enjoyed mixing chocolate in his coffee either at home or at the *Café Procope* in the sixth arrondissement, a café still in existence, only a teaspoon though, not too much or it's ruined, stirring ever so tenderly, leaving the thinnest patina of chocolate on top; coffee, a drink Voltaire indulged in as early as five in the morning and continuously throughout the day, cup after cup, as friends, strangers, and curious pedestrians looked on, and under the scrutiny of those Parisian eyes Voltaire, his love for coffee fervid and unabashed, his passion for coffee a statement of his own selfhood, happily dismissed the mediocrity around him. Coffee became my drink of choice when, one long-lapsed afternoon in my teens, I said to myself, *I think I'll try a cup of coffee,* heavy and black, and quite promptly felt my mind tremble, my heart resonate, sensed the margins of my imagination break free and shake the dust gathered since youth, not a particularly *bad* youth, just a moderately unhappy youth fenced in by mediocrity, mediocrity celebrated and longed for, mediocrity talked about as if mediocrity were something to aspire to, but that first coffee, a pungent brew, whispered the possibility of something *other,* because I'd always been different, always contained what some might call a mystic yearning, a desire for philosophy and music, literature and art, in short, *transcendence,* hence I always felt I had both coffee and Montaigne to thank for helping me escape mediocrity or, at the very least, *instilling the desire* to escape mediocrity, because in a sense coffee *introduced me to myself,* coffee confirmed the intuition of something *other,* because I'd always believed the things I saw or felt were invisible to everyone else or, worse, nonexistent. My education was a *standard education,* meaning an education of omission not inclusion, thus my knowledge was limited; in fact it wasn't a case of what I knew (which was paltry) but what I *didn't know,* which was everything else, hence I amassed a rich interior life, all of my experiences *inner* experiences, falling in love with books, thinking ceaselessly of books, books more real than people: literature and philosophy, poetry and art, the moderns, the classics, everything I could get my hands on, Horace and Petrarch and Euripides; Romanticism, then Modernism, Byron and Shelley, Borges and Woolf, Nabokov and Stein, then Montaigne, although long before Montaigne and my *Montaigne phase* I'd read Kafka and thus gone through a Kafka phase, which led to a Walser phase then a Wittgenstein phase followed by an Arendt phase, thereupon leading to my Rousseau phase which inevitably lead to my *Montaigne phase,* a phase I've never really left. Yes, a profusion of phases before I'd met my now-dead wife at the *3rd International Conference for Social Sciences, Aesthetics, and Disaster Management,* a slew of different disciplines converging under a single roof due to an asbestos outbreak at several of the hosting city's original venues, a fortuitous occasion, both of us hardly out of school, she attending a symposium on biotrophic fungal pathogens and me, two auditoriums away, at *Tendency of the Sublime,* a discourse on Plato, and later we shared a drink, she speaking of *water pollution* and *hybrid energies* with the same passion in which I spoke of Montaigne as well as my recently completed thesis, *Montaigne and the Lugubrious Cherubs* which, even then, I envisioned as a book-length essay and I told her as much. An opus, I declared, a shout from the void, I added, to underscore my book-length essay being, as I'd just described, a shout from the void, yes, I said, looking into her radiant eyes, my work will castigate the modern world which denies every living soul the *breathing room* required for unfettered thoughts, and I was fervent, sharing two or three of the newer titles at which I'd lately arrived because already I'd cooled on *Montaigne and the Lugubrious Cherubs,* already felt *Montaigne and the Lugubrious Cherubs* was pompous and overblown, and my eventual, soon-to-be wife was not only beautiful but funny, passionate, bright, all the things a person seeks, or at least what I sought, and she didn't find my obsession with Montaigne dubious or off-putting or something she'd one day have to worry about, but instead found it clever and endearing and though neither one of us cared much for the other's fields, we admired the other's passion, and this became an unspoken understanding, a love both tender and tolerant, and through the years she never failed to ask me about Montaigne, faithfully inquiring about the progress of my book-length essay, even amid the vexing years of parenthood and mar-riage, often a day-to-day drudgery, my years at the community college, hers dedicated to various environmental concerns: de-forestation, the thawing permafrost, enormous islands of plastic choking the oceans, each year getting worse, *it's a losing battle,* she'd say, *time is running out,* she'd say, coastlines are eroding, she'd tell me, meaning, I'd think, *we're good and fucked,* all before she began to decline, before she began forgetting necessary and fundamental things, forgetting to eat or get dressed or ask Marcel about his music, *house music,* he'd correct her, and certainly be-fore she became a shadow of her former self, seeing things that weren't there, *spaceships* for example, yes, I had many literary and philosophical phases before my *Montaigne phase,* my longest phase and a phase that shows no signs of stopping, and I reflect on both my *Montaigne phase* and my *coffee phase,* both permanent phases, phases which assisted me in my flight from youth, away from my family who loved me in their own way, as best they could, but loved mediocrity more, and decades later, meaning now, little has changed and I sip my coffee attempting to ignore the fact I've been widowed, reflecting instead on my time at the Zybècksz Archives at the Horner Institute, the months spent racing between both Tanner Rooms, trying to transcribe a facsimile of Montaigne's diary, all while attempting to clutch long spans of unbroken time and I recall Kleist, my only friend at the Horner Institute, an acclaimed Viennese sculptor occupying the neighboring cottage, whose subject was rapture, not *the* rapture, she'd insisted, not a religious or holy rapture, *God no,* she scoffed, but the *divine,* meaning rapture itself, rapture like a first kiss, rapture like euphoria, rapture the reaching for something higher than oneself, all of this illustrated in her thick Austrian accent, spitting on the ground, shoulders hunched as though anticipating an attack, her calloused hands, like gnarled talons, her rigid posture, smoking a pipe from another era, a pipe resembling a musical instrument. It was Kleist's third fellowship, having been at the Archives in the '80s when Alessandro Costa killed himself, she'd seen him swinging from the towering oak in the *Pleasure Gardens* before the police arrived and sure, she said, I felt bad, but not *terrible,* because

Costa's work was unmitigated bullshit, she proclaimed, his work drenched in affectation, she added, and the time I have for sympathy is finite, no time at all for frauds and phonies and Costa was the textbook definition of a fraud and a phony, she said, the textbook definition of a con man, all that drivel about *perception* and *moral subjectivity* and the *impossibility of objective truth,* and she laughed, spat again, lit her pipe, no, she said, I only have so much time, meaning, I inferred, not a lot. Fluent in English, Kleist favored cursing to make her point promptly because, she explained, her feelings ran hot, thus she had no time for the *tame* and the *fatuous,* the *anemic* and *half-assed* emotions, and I'm stating the obvious, she said, but we have only a single life, no rehearsals, no dress-up, and I won't dance around people's feelings, she said, I won't kowtow to assuage sensitive hearts, especially about Alessandro Costa, that *hack,* that *charlatan,* that *upstart* who borrowed ideas and claimed those ideas as his own when the only good idea he'd ever had, she said, his *best* idea in fact, was killing himself, and we tend to make martyrs of those who are gone, she said, but we must reckon with the truth, the unscrupulous truth, the afflictive truth, the truth which burns like a conflagration because the truth is as dazzling as it is ugly, as seductive as it is repulsive, and the *undeniable truth,* the truth more pure than a blazing nebula, is that some people are phonies, meaning, I inferred, Alessandro Costa, and simply because they're gone, she said, it doesn't change who they were, in Costa's case, she said, a shameless fraud, an intellectual crook, a feeble-minded swindler. Kleist called Costa's work *spiritual kitsch,* called it a *perversion of philosophy,* said it was redundant and superfluous, and what could be worse, she asked, than the superfluous, her answer being nothing, nothing worse than the superfluous, nothing worse than Alessandro Costa and his *intellectual pamphleteering* and with deep mirth she called his work *pseudoscience* and with even deeper mirth described Costa's *pathological need for approval* as well as his *rapacious and unquenchable thirst for accolades.* Costa was a vampire, said Kleist, Costa thought he'd befriend *real artists* and *real thinkers,* Costa believed he'd soak up the *residue* of their talent and make it his own but that's impossible because one must possess a *poetic consciousness* to create authentic work, a *poetic consciousness* absolutely indispensable for an artist because without a *poetic consciousness* one is merely planting seeds in a desert of impotence, a desert as vast and barren as the Atacama, and one can only do that, she said, meaning graze the gifts of the *talented adjacent others,* for so long before falling short or getting caught and one can only fool the public as well as one's contemporaries for a finite time, she said, and killing himself doesn't make Costa a saint and Kleist, gazing into the tremulous sky, exhaling puffs of fragrant smoke, gently wheezed. All of this expressed at our first encounter, me returning from an afternoon dashing between both Tanner rooms, exhausted and spent, walking past the quadrangle as ribbons of plum dissolved into the shroud of night. I'd walked past the *Bustamante Embassy* through the *Pleasure Gardens,* climbed the slope where the fellowship cottages, arrayed like a Russian village, sat in silence, and there stood Kleist, sturdy as a statue, a smirk of contempt, like a wedge of dirt, smudged across her face. Kleist's first name was Alma but she went by her dead husband's surname to retain a vestige of Ernst, her life's only love, a naturalist who'd specialized in orography which, Kleist had to explain, was the study of mountains, and Ernst had written extensively on the Bavarian Alps, the *history* of the Bavarian Alps as well as the *future* of the Bavarian Alps and his life's work was establishing, after centuries of erosion, were the Bavarian Alps growing or shrinking? That was the question which plagued Ernst his entire life, said Kleist, and were the Bavarian Alps and the assorted mountain ranges that made up the Bavarian Alps still climbing because of seismic activity or, conversely, ebbing due to weather and erosion and this is what obsessed Ernst, said Kleist, producing a photograph of a thick-mustached man in a Tyrolean hat and the sparkling eyes of an autocrat. They'd fallen in love and consequently for one another's passions, Alma falling in love with the Bavarian Alps and the question of whether they were growing or shrinking and Ernst, likewise, falling in love with sculpture and the feeling of rapture Alma was attempting to attain, though she was only a novice at the time, two decades younger than Ernst, the man who nurtured and supported her passion for finding rapture through sculpture, a man from the Salzkammergut, near Salzburg, in the Alpine region, bordering shimmering Lake Hallstatt, who, since adolescence, had been seduced by the Bavarian Alps and the question of whether they were growing or shrinking and he'd studied the ice age and ancient glaciers that long ago covered all of Europe, the ancient glaciers that helped *create* the Bavarian Alps, the stretch of mountains Ernst cherished and spent his life climbing, asking himself, are they getting higher or lower, meaning were they growing or shrinking, and he died, she said, in that selfsame chain of mountains, lost his foothold near the *Krottenkopf peak* in the Ester Mountains of the Bavarian Prealps, slipped into a crevasse along the *Michelfeld Ridge*, and his assistant, a young understudy from Brussels, the only witness, and yes, she said, a part of me died then, a part that could never be recovered and Alma mourned Ernst and mourned as well the part of her that died along with Ernst but, within a month, was back to work, meaning sculpture, meaning the steadfast attempt to find and ensnare rapture in limestone, marble, sandstone, even steel, all of this explained as the shadows lengthened and the blue blades of grass trembled in the growing dark, and soon the two of us began meeting outside our abutting cottages while Kleist smoked her tobacco, vigorously packed in a churchwarden pipe, a pipe from another century, a pipe like a toboggan, her heavy boots, her ossified face which retained the faintest wisps of lapsed beauty, yes, I was mesmerized by Kleist, her self-posses-sion, her artistic certainty, the stubborn understanding of her own soul. Alma possessed a staunch limp, a smoker's cough, and an affection for cold weather, something I noticed mere weeks after my arrival when winter made its swift advance into the Berkshire foothills and Kleist's spirits visibly improved. Despite her advanced age, Kleist could be found either inside her cottage sculpting or exploring the surrounding woods collecting sticks because she had no need of the materials in either the *Tanner Room* or the *Tanner Reading Room,* not to mention the *Bellinger Wing, Lithograph Room,* or *Facsimile Closet,* and very rarely was she seen anywhere near the quadrangle because Kleist wasn't *writing* about sculpture or *studying* sculpture or even *researching* sculpture but was, in fact, sculpting herself, with works celebrated across the globe, with collections exhibited from the *Rijksmuseum* in Amsterdam to the *Sorolla* in Madrid, as well as permanent exhibits in the *Whitney* and *Tate,* sculptures of seething holocausts and cityscapes asunder, of arms in ecstasy and deranged visages with the aspects of primitive howls, works of great depth, she explained, works as powerful as they are alarming, she said, because the search for rapture, human rapture, always meant destruction because a history of human rapture was, of course, a history of human destruction. Rapture, she insisted, came with the risk of destruction and if one claimed they were passionate about rapture but refused to consider destruction then they were no better than *you-know-who,* meaning, I inferred, Alessandro Costa, and when anyone described her work as the embodiment of *destruction,* not *rapture,* they were not only perceptive and astute, she said, but souls possessing the most innate and meticulous understanding of art. Kleist's sculptures dealt with genocide and bliss, warfare and morality, in short, she explained, the pursuit of human rapture, as well as other fundamental questions, for instance: was a person, her sculptures asked, allowed to search for joy in a world afflicted by suffering? Also, for instance: could an individual have a clear conscience when the crimes of their ancestors hadn't been atoned for? Was this, her sculptures asked, akin to committing the crimes oneself? Was this, her sculptures asked, akin to *collaborating?* These questions haunted her work, they lay at the marrow of hundreds of emaciated arms reaching through the flames, the long-perished arms of Europe, she said, of Germany, of Austria and Romania, the arms of the *vast historic tormented* beset by our *own diseased humanity* and occasionally, after a day bustling between both Tanner Rooms, I'd arrive at the fellowship cottages, observe Kleist's silhouette near a copse of trees, and without preamble we'd find ourselves chatting, Kleist always obstinate, always roused by a variety of subjects, from divine light and formal ambivalence to the tragedy of knowledge, and sometimes the Bavarian Alps and whether they were growing or shrinking, a question that had yet to be answered, she'd say, and I would talk about Montaigne and human friendship as well as human folly and my lifelong attempt to escape mediocrity by finding long swathes of unbroken time and Kleist, with a rare tenderness, admitted she liked me, *tolerated* was the word she used, yes, she said, I *tolerate* you, because at least you're genuinely trying, and chances are you'll fail, but you try anyway, despite yourself, and unlike Alessandro, who held the pretense of being a *serious thinker* and an *important thinker,* but who was only an exemplar of utter baseness, you at least have a certain authenticity, gullible no doubt, but endearing nonetheless, despite the fact you may possess no talent because one is either a *genuine artist* or a *phony artist,* there's no in-between, she asserted, no middle ground, and a *phony artist* can never become a *genuine artist,* however a *genuine artist* can always become a *phony artist,* in fact a *genuine artist* is always at risk of becoming a *phony artist,* always at risk of losing themselves, because the world tempts with its detours and diversions and moronic fanfares, the world is literally begging for the *genuine artist* to succumb and descend and thus become a *phony artist,* so the artist is taken down a notch, so the world can celebrate and declare the artist is no different than the rest of them, meaning the *non-artists,* and has always been like the rest of them, because a creative life, an *artist's life,* makes no sense to the rest of the world, an *artist's life* makes the world uncomfortable; to an outsider an *artist's life* is nonsensical. Why aren't they serious about the things we're serious about, the world asks, the things they're *supposed* to be serious about? Why are they, the world asks, moved by the ineffable, by things we neither see nor feel, because quite frankly the rest of the world is dull and torpid meaning, she said, hardly alive, alive in the scientific sense, sure, with blood and viscera and beating hearts, but they possess souls which have been anesthetized, she said, the rest of the world all numbers and sharp corners, the rest of the world ceaselessly organizing against the inevitabilities of death, the world obsessed with building fruitless bulwarks against the inevitabilities of death, never realizing the only thing that endures, the only thing that *refutes* death, is art, hence any time the world turns a *genuine artist* into a *phony artist,* through money or exposure or the surrender of the artist's beliefs, the world celebrates because another one has joined their ranks and Kleist would continue in this vein, preaching about history and sculpture, *genuine artists* versus *phony artists,* or the time Alessandro Costa, petulant and drunk, shared his shitty poetry at *bonfire night,* a ceremony held each season at the Horner Institute, where the fellows gathered in the *Pleasure Gardens* to dine and socialize around an enormous bonfire, and it was the most vile and pedestrian poetry I'd ever heard, said Kleist, garish and sentimental too, and Costa should've had the sense to be embarrassed but of course he wasn't because men without scruples are seldom embarrassed, unscrupulous men always oblivious and unaware, men like him too self-absorbed to realize when they're making fools of themselves, which he was, and it was that night, she said, *bonfire night,* a night encouraging fellowship and community, a long-established Horner tradition, where the fellows gathered, sometimes for the first time, but not for the purpose of pompous readings, she said, not for the purpose of beating one's chest, and it was an enormous miscalculation on Costa's part because *bonfire night,* she said, was an occasion celebrating *all of us,* not *one of us* and Costa's ridiculous reading of his banal poems, what he called *dramatic pieces,* was the last indignity, a self-inflicted indignity, because the next morning Costa hanged himself and this he did at the scene of the crime, the *Pleasure Gardens,* where he'd read his so-called *dramatic pieces* only hours before, deranged concepts about the human spirit replete with ruminations on, of all writers, Madame Blavatsky, a writer with whom Costa felt a kinship but a writer for whom Costa didn't know the first thing, and we were all there, Hannah Gömbrich and Martin O'Dell, a few fellow sculptors as well as Diego Gabezón, the Oaxacan literary theorist, celebrated for his scrutiny of Sosa's mystic visions in the Chihuahuan Desert, Gabezón's theories on the Mexican Plateau utterly unsurpassed, but *Jesus fucking Christ* those poems, and all of us sitting there, paralyzed and aghast, witnessing the birth of some terrible darkness and Costa, lit from behind by the pulsating trees, distorted and dim, resembling some sort of ridiculous conjurer as he read his God-awful *dramatic pieces,* and none of us stopped him, none of us knew *how* to stop him, a man painfully ignorant of himself and only the next morning did he realize, he *must've* realized, those preposterous *dramatic pieces,* plagued by platitudes and sophistry, ruminations about cosmic order and ancient wisdom, works that never seemed to end because they were truly *epic,* not in *quality* of course, but in *length*, dramatic pieces epic in *perversion* and *bombast,* yes, he must've seen himself as he truly was, a clown, a dunce, an asshole phony, because the next morning he'd acquired a rope, likely stolen from the caretaker's shed, and Alessandro Costa, ultimately disgraced, ended it all and Kleist, roused by the memory, tamped her pipe, locked eyes on mine, and without pretext began discussing sculptors, specifically Jewish sculptors and, more specifically than that, Jewish sculptors rounded up and massacred during the Second World War, most of them Polish, taken from their families and imprisoned, no doubt tortured and summarily executed, snatched from their future work as well as endowing the world with their future work and her current project, the *pinnacle of my career,* she said, was a collection of sculptures never created because the wholesale slaughter of those Polish sculptors, works conceived in her imagination and sculpted by her own hands but, in essence, made by those murdered Polish Jews, Jews collected and killed at the hands of men with anesthetized souls, men frightened by the *possibility* and *expanse* of art, frightened by art's *amplitude,* and she was doing this, she explained, to purify and absolve her *sullied European soul,* to balance the scales of history and *fill the vacuum* borne from their annihilation, yes, she said, to speak for the *hordes of invisible dead,* to atone for their decimation and she went on to speak of Primo Levi and Chaim Kaplan and the generation raised by Holocaust survivors to which she belonged, an entire generation raised by the remnants of ghosts because of the *plague of stupidity* which had conquered and annihilated the continent of Europe; she spoke of Elias Canetti and *Crowds and Power,* and had I ever read *Crowds and Power,* she asked, because *Crowds and Power* must surely be read by anyone interested in the *barbarity of human nature,* yes, she said, Canetti understood, Canetti perceived the *hordes of invisible dead* because the *invisible dead* are everywhere, pleading with us to avenge the stupidity of their deaths, because it's sheer, unadulterated stupidity, the only explanation, and if you came from where I did, meaning Austria, with parents like mine who somehow survived the stupidity of fascism as well as the murderous stupidity of the death camps, then you'd know, and after the war my parents saw entire cities suffering from *rigor mortis,* can you imagine, whole cities crippled and inert, and if you survived the odious plague of fascism, a continental wail of stupidity and horror, then you would know, and my parents witnessed the faces afterward, faces like skeletons, and cities with *rigor mortis,* Berlin and Vienna and Warsaw, and pictures don't do justice, she said, firsthand stories don't illustrate the stupidity and the horror, the extravagant stupidity and the wretched horror; entire cultures with families and rituals, stories and synagogues, wiped off the planet, *no,* crushed into dust, left to seep into the soil; as a child it rippled through my life, my mother's disengagement from the world, putting herself to bed in the afternoon and me, a child of six or seven, not seeing her until the next day or the day after, the way she'd disappear inside herself, flee the shore of her soul, the way, as a teenager, I'd put my ear to the ground and hear the boots of stupidity, always mounting, always marching, even today, I put my ear to the ground and hear the boots of stupidity because they're never very far, they're never *not marching,* and my current work, she said, my most *important* work, she clarified, is to speak for the *hordes of invisible dead,* because the dead aren't finished with us and never have been, and it's on my shoulders, she said, the ancestors of the murdered and the children of those ancestors, on my shoulders to balance the scales of injustice, to have their grievances answered for, and I was moved by Kleist's words, felt a connection because after all I was a Jew, at least tenuously, meaning I was a *cultural Jew,* a common enough way of avoiding having to confess being a *bad* or a *lazy* or a *nonchalant Jew,* which I was, with a synagogue never attended, with parents and grandparents who'd never been mindful much less devout in regards to worship, who never lived in Europe and hadn't seen firsthand the cost of being Jewish; my grandparents remembering at most stories of *their* parents arriving from Hungary or Russia or Romania, nebulous and half-remembered accounts of ancestors in shtetls, fleeing pogroms, nothing handed down, no rituals or relics, certainly no generational trauma. My own parents practicing the religion of work and money, of holy capitalism, anything remotely more mystic tossed aside. My attempting to sit shiva after burying my wife, unsure if I was doing it correctly, whatever sitting shiva correctly *meant*, nodding awkwardly at my wife's friends and former colleagues, glancing at the taciturn rabbi with no more presence than a puff of air, patting Marcel's knee, sporting the blazer I hadn't worn since the community college, wanting more than anything to be left alone with my grief, unable to face the grief while a group of strangers and a rabbi who felt more like an intruder sat around eating pastries, postponing the grief until I could cry by myself or circle the house in my pale-yellow slippers, perhaps both at once, and if this was what being Jewish meant—the delay of grief, the deferment of mounting heartache—then I'd satisfied the requirement, I'd fulfilled my duty admirably, sitting shiva for a week, keeping the grief at bay until the rabbi, knees cracking, stood to leave; all of this though was years away, I think, my wife's dying I mean, so Kleist's words carried some weight but not the weight they have now. And Kleist said some other things about shame, disgrace, and the wail of stupidity, reiterating it was on her shoulders to expose this in her *final work*, gazing into the hazy afternoon and concluding with a cough. This was Kleist's fashion: to discuss art and sculpture and the burden of history while smoking her pipe and quite happily I listened and sometimes Kleist offered me coffee and without fail I'd decline because she once mentioned in the most unceremonious manner her habit of drinking *ersatz* or *instant coffee,* I forget which, and thus I felt free to refuse since I wasn't a savage nor an imbecile and *ersatz* or *instant coffee* shouldn't even be allowed to invoke the word *coffee* because *ersatz* or *instant coffee* is swill, worse than swill, it's swill's bastard cousin, in fact there's nothing in my mind more diabolical and repulsive than *ersatz* or *instant coffee,* nothing more demeaning and distasteful than the belief that *ersatz* or *instant coffee* has any relationship to coffee itself and simply because the word *coffee* is in its name, doesn't, in any way, mean that it *is* coffee, my feelings about this long and complex, probably stronger than they should be, but I kept this to myself, politely declined and instead went inside my own cottage to make a single-sourced Bolivian espresso containing the softest, most aromatic hints of caramel and orange, subtleties dispensing small jolts of bliss so that when I sat down to consider Montaigne and humanism and the notes I'd taken from a translated copy of a facsimile of Montaigne's diary, I was filled with optimism, the facsimile of Montaigne's diary taken from the *Tanner Room* and ceaselessly studied in the *Tanner Reading Room* at twenty- to twenty-five-minute intervals, depending on how nimble I was feeling, the diary translated by an anonymous scholar in the 1890s, the original enclosed in glass inside the *Tobar Pavilion* directly behind the quadrangle beside the *Rare Manuscript Room,* visited by me each week to gaze upon the original scrawl of my hero's handwriting. Besides Montaigne's brief contact with the Russian and some offhand descriptions of minor household affairs, the diary spent several long-winded pages lamenting his valet and manservant, Jean Brismontier, known later in many circles and the subject of more than one posthumous biography. Boasting a lineage dating back to the nobility of Dordogne, Brismontier's parents had fallen on hard times and Jean, intimate with the world's comforts since youth, suddenly found himself plucked from well-being, tossed into the tedium of poverty and there's nothing so humdrum and slow as poverty, Brismontier later wrote in an introduction to his book on wigs, nothing so lacking in taste and tact as indigence. His father, a Republican and minor civil servant, had been aide-de-camp to Charles de Guillemot, a retired diplomat and notorious shipping magnate, and through this connection secured work for his eccentric son at a tiny pâtisserie in Bordeaux where Brismontier met Montaigne amid one of my hero's casual Sunday strolls where, after a brief conversation, he was hired. Due to inclinations both eccentric and deviant, the young Brismontier was ahead of his time, anticipating trends a century before they were fashionable, seduced as he was by fabrics and adornments, wigs especially, the larger the better, the curlier the better, and whatever income Brismontier earned attending to Montaigne's horses and cleaning Montaigne's stables as well as assisting Montaigne in an array of everyday affairs, Brismontier spent on his ever-growing collection of wigs, wigs which arrived from Paris in opulent boxes of pale pink and azure and upon delivery Jean would disappear to bequeath his most ardent attentions upon them, modeling for himself before floor-to-ceiling mirrors or powdering his wigs while exercising the caution of a queen's servant dusting bone china and this he did while donning spangled doublets and scarab-green capes, his buckled shoes immaculate in their luminosity. In the diary, Montaigne bemoaned Brismontier's passion for wigs and if the boy concerned himself as much with the service of my horses as he did with his vanity, Montaigne wrote, I read, I'd have no complaints because what I most desire is a manservant not so swayed by fads, unless those fads include philosophy, art, and the study of the human soul because the trends of popular society, Montaigne wrote, I read, only prance across the surface of life, rejecting what's most mysterious and profound, the trends of today, wrote Montaigne, only serve to take man further from himself. Not many scholars had given this diary the attention it deserved, I reflected in my cottage, sipping a *café con leche,* the brisk Berkshire air suggesting winter had arrived and meanwhile Kleist, mere yards away, sculpting the imagined works of dead Polish Jews, somehow sated my soul, enough for me to forget myself and revisit the subject of titles and though I hadn't yet found a concept or a premise for my book, a fact I blamed on sprinting between both Tanner rooms, I had at least arrived at several agreeable titles, *Splendor at Night* and *Penumbras of Bordeaux* for example, both conceived on the brilliant grounds of the Zybècksz Archives at the Horner Institute, and even though the ever-elusive theme or concept, the one ingredient necessary to anchor the work, the element required to truly begin, was tenuous, vague, fluttering just beyond my field of vision, over a month remained of my fellowship which, I felt, was more than enough. And the chirp of the phone once again removes me from these reveries, the coffee no longer warm, the tangle of pages gaping like discarded relics, and I'm certain the chirp is notifying me of another voicemail, someone concerned with my state of mind, meaning my well-being, and there were no phones in Montaigne's life, I'm reminded, hence no voicemails, hence no intrusions on long swathes of undisturbed time, and I wonder if it's Marcel because Marcel's voicemails are extraordinary, some lasting well over ten minutes where Marcel, accompanied by the distant clamor of his roommates, dispenses muddled soliloquies on the *culture of dance music* and *turntablism* as well as the *vibrant tenacity of dub*. Months ago he left his longest message yet, the message solely concerned with the *ideal length of a house song*, how the length of a house song was the first requirement of a *serious house track* and a *serious house track* could be no less than five minutes, he asserted, because a *serious house track* lasting less than five minutes was impossible to take seriously, he said, since it didn't take itself or the tropes and traditions of *house music* seriously and no self-respecting dance song is less than five minutes, he said, it's impossible, because it's the *repetition* that creates a good dance song and what can be repeated in the span of three to four minutes? Nothing, he answered, not a fucking thing, he continued, because the perfect length, the *ideal* length, the *sweet spot* of a good house track must be between seven and eleven minutes, and a track less than five minutes I won't bother listening to because a dance track less than five minutes refuses to take itself seriously, at least in observing the custom of a *traditional house song*, because *house music*, he went on, is the practice and celebration of repetition, finding a hook, a melody, a *powerful piano chord* and riding one, or all three, until bliss is attained, he actually used those words, *until bliss is attained,* and I remember rolling my eyes as he continued raving about the *ideal length* of a dance song, still no idea why he'd left the message, seven to eleven minutes, he continued, the sweet spot of a *respectable house track,* adding flourishes along the way, small, incremental touches, muted basslines, hi-hats, handclaps, faux congas and more, so the song isn't just about melody and movement, which is a necessity, but the *journey* too, and once the song ends the listener, courtesy of the song, is nowhere near the place they were when it began, so if the listener is at a warehouse or a club or, shit, by themselves at home they're no longer where they were when the song *began,* no, they've been taken somewhere *new,* somewhere *other.* Marcel's monologues about *dance music,* its capaciousness and warmth, its blurring of genres, its soft suggestions of sex, its plasticity and ability to meander, were something to behold, and it works in the opposite direction too, he continued, a house song can also be *too long,* it can wear out its welcome because it's a delicate balance, he said, being too long or too short, and what's more, he said, a DJ or a producer, meaning a *musician*, must appreciate this delicate balance, must find the perfect, most impeccable length, meaning the ideal running time so the song ends when it's *supposed to end,* the ending of the song natural and organic because the listener knows, or at least *senses,* it couldn't have ended any other way, yet these rules don't apply to *jungle* or *techno, dubstep* or *breakbeat,* no, those genres all have songs ranging from two to seven minutes and anywhere in between, those genres much more flexible when it comes to song length, it's strictly *house music,* meaning *deep house* or *minimal house* or *progressive house,* whatever anyone wants to call it, yes, it's *house music* which is so concerned with song length due to the *aesthetics of house* and without pause Marcel held forth about his favorite labels which, he pointed out, were dictated by geography: *Kompakt* and *Smallpeople* in Germany, *Defected* and *Shall Not Fade* in England, *Studio Barnhus* and *Smalltown Supersound* in Stockholm, *Full Pupp* in Norway, and *Apparel Wax* in Italy, there's so many, he said, veering suddenly into specific artists, *Bjørn Torske* and *Todd Terje, Will Saul* and *Prins Thomas, Crooked Man* and *Maurice Fulton,* and *Four Tet, fucking shit,* he said, interrupting himself, don't get me started on *Four Tet,* because there's no one in the world of electronic music more complex (and badly imitated) than *Four Tet* and going back further, he said, to the beginning of *rave culture* and *acid house,* there's *808 State* and *Moodymann* and, going back even further still, to *classic Detroit techno,* there's *Derrick May* and *Juan Atkins* and *DJ Aakmael,* and for the downtempo and hypnotic, *Kruder & Dorfmeister,* whose soul-infused influence is still being felt in the sense of *mood, mood* something you can't *phone in,* meaning something you can't *half-ass,* meaning something you can't *bluff,* and I recall his epic voicemail about *mood* and the *respectable length of a house song* and me suspecting he was going on like this in order to coerce money from me for a new instrument, a Korg mixer or Yamaha synthesizer or a Roland drum machine, brands long ago forged in my brain, and meanwhile me, holding the *phone-preceding-the-smartphone* away from my ear so I could consider ways of handling my wife who would soon be waking up and that's when the shit would really start because by then she was approaching the end, I'd been fired, or retired, years earlier, had already spent copious amounts of money on nurses, most of my time attending to her needs, making sure she wasn't a danger to herself, assisting with her medicine and meals and I returned the *phone-preceding-the-smartphone* back to my ear, listened as Marcel cataloged more labels like *Pampa* and *Domino* and *Ghostly International,* and then, in a tone of deepest solemnity, as if confiding a long-held secret, Marcel confessed his most cherished allegiance was to *house music sans vocals,* although, if done well, he conceded, there's nothing sweeter in the world than good *house music with vocals* and me conflicted, wanting nothing more than to wake up my wife and play this ridiculously long voicemail, to share the absurdity of our son, because I loved him, terribly so, the same child I lifted in my arms countless times as an infant, whose piano recitals I always attended without fail, whom I comforted as an infant in the middle of the night when he was agitated or sick, holding him as I walked the very same rooms I'm pacing now, but this message about the *ideal length of a house song* was demented and outrageous, even for him, and I was convinced the message would've advanced unabated if his roommates hadn't wanted to go *crate-digging*, meaning looking for obscure and secondhand vinyl, because Marcel relished *crate-digging*, especially at secondhand stores, finding albums made decades before he was born, records he would sample or simply listen to for inspiration, but I mustn't wake her up, I thought further, because she was long gone by then, having essentially stopped recognizing us, meaning Marcel and me, or if she did it was fleeting, a few minutes at most, and she was happier asleep anyway, or at least better off, because, once awake, she'd begin ranting about the *recorders* and *spaceships* and *villainous plots of dark beings,* and the nurse from hospice, who came twice a week with an expression of *you should start making arrangements* was really too much and the futility and heartbreak of life, I think, the unavoidable pain of loss, I think, the pain of loss always approaching, at any time and any age, besieged by grief, or grief's approach, the assault of grief with no means of escape, no means of avoiding grief's ever-inescapable reach, the fingers or flames of grief, fingers or flames, depending on how one feels, and navigating the *aftermath* of grief worse than the grief itself, the *wake* left by grief no different than a knife in the chest, I think, and how to keep one's soul at bay from the goddamn grief like a stab wound or an unscalable black wall, and I never finished listening to that exceptionally prolonged voicemail about the *ideal length of a house song* because Marcel never brought up the reason he called, no, he simply began debating on the voicemail whether or not to go *crate-digging* with his roommates, arguing with his roommates about the best record shops, hence I tossed the *phone-preceding-the-smartphone* on the couch because I'd heard her, meaning my now-dead wife, stirring from the bedroom and I try to forget about all of it, try to put it in the back of my mind, sip the luke-warm coffee and gaze at the rolltop desk with a sense of shame and disgrace, the desk I felt was necessary to write my book, convinced my book-length essay was impossible without the rolltop desk, the rolltop desk, I believed, utterly indispensable for composing my book based on my decades-old thesis, *Montaigne and the Lugubrious Cherubs,* as well as the research gathered from the Zybècksz Archives at the Horner Institute, only a rolltop desk, I thought, capable of giving me the strength and insight to complete the task, in addition to the dozens of filing cabinets contained *within* a rolltop desk, repositories ideal for storing excerpts and titles, so many titles I considered writing a book made solely of titles, *Resinous Solitude* and *Ambivalent Stowaway,* for example, because following my return from the Zybècksz Archives at the Horner Institute I was obsessed with the rolltop desk, an object which consumed me and a subject I refused to drop, making my wife quite miserable because every conversation we had I'd find a way to turn it into a conversation about the rolltop desk, any comment she made about Marcel, the weather, her job, I'd coerce it into a discussion about the purchase of the rolltop desk, a perverse notion, but one I couldn't shake, and my wife had her own life and its attendant affairs and did I care? Did I ask how *she* was? Did I inquire about the things she wanted? No. I stressed the importance of the rolltop desk in order to galvanize my thoughts for the plummet I was preparing to take into deep thought because little did I know my wife would vanish, be diagnosed with *frontotemporal dementia,* little did I know I'd eventually be left alone, staring at the rolltop desk, purchased and placed in the third bedroom, my wife's office before I'd taken it over, commandeered the third bedroom for my own needs, and occasionally I'd shrug and half-heartedly apologize for confiscating the third bedroom, but I wasn't really sorry because even while I was half-heartedly apologizing for taking over the third bedroom with the rolltop desk, a room always meant for my wife's career in environmental science, her work as an ecologist, I was thinking only of the rolltop desk, the rolltop desk and endless titles, *Dark Hemispheres, God's Trifles, The Naked and the Sacred,* and hundreds more, titles produced at home and later at the Horner Institute and later still at the community college on slips of paper as I lectured to those sluggish buffoons who wanted, more than anything, to have their thoughts interrupted, and after a first and then a second emergency review regarding both my passion and disregard I tried curtailing my behavior, that is lessening the *severity* of my passion and disregard, to make my passion and disregard less conspicuous, but I was having a mystical crisis concerning aesthetics. I'd stopped eating, was thinking ceaselessly of my book-length essay as well as possible *titles* for my book-length essay, and the students, doubtless frightened, hardly spoke. Once more I assigned essays about sadness and desire, Armageddon and utopia and, if I were up to it, I'd lecture about the divine and the radiant and damnation too, don't forget damnation, I'd tell myself, reading passages from *Paradise Lost, The Divine Comedy,* and, if time permitted, the Greek tragedies, really anything that dealt with hell and human decay; I fumed over Henry James's preposterous notion that *Sentimental Education* was a lesser novel than *Madame Bovary,* cackling irrationally, sipping endless lattes, explaining the worst literary critics in the world were writers, a writer knowing perhaps how to write but nothing at all about *judging* or *thinking critically* about a book and if I wanted to know the worth or merit or *artistic purity* of a literary work the last person I would ask would be a writer because a writer knows one thing, I said, how to write, and nothing else. I was despondent. Distracted. I was suffering from insomnia. My return from the Berkshires coupled with resuming what I called the *humdrum everyday,* not to mention Marcel's frantic appeals to me for *samplers* and *Moog synthesizers,* extraordinarily expensive instruments for a child, downright exorbitant for a tenth- or eleventh-grader, all of it had me glum, chafed, and not long after, perhaps a year or two, three at most, the changes in my wife, vague, nameless, hardly remarkable at first, all began spinning a skein of foreboding the way a spider spins a web. The way she'd begun to stop midsentence with a blank expression or would suddenly forget certain words or the threads of conversation, particularly strange for my wife because my wife never lacked for things to say, never forgot the subject at hand nor misremembered or misplaced a name or detail, no, my wife was rational, temperate, and circumspect, an exemplar of memory and fluency until she suddenly wasn't, until she began exhibiting aberrant behaviors I found deeply unsettling, as in asking which car was hers and me thinking it was a joke, discovering only later she'd taken *my* car by mistake. Her hostility about the rolltop desk vanishing entirely though she'd spent months upon my return from the Horner Institute arguing about the need to keep her office in the third bedroom, an office we'd agreed was hers when we bought the house twenty years before, the third bedroom where she worked on all of her environmental projects, maps of soil contamination, of fetid swamps and vanishing coastlines, sustainability spreadsheets tacked across the walls showing what she despairingly called *red zones* as well as the deforested regions of the globe and, alternately, large swathes of the oceans which were effectively dead, *oceans of morgues,* she called them, and me not taking it with much gravity, never having taken it with much gravity, because I'd always believed the end of the world, and by our own hands, was a foregone conclusion, so why all the fuss, I thought, why the ranting and strife, I also thought, why the struggle for a *better* environment and a *better* world when our own natures would never allow it? Anyway, I'd become edgy, harried, felt my work was slipping away. I played Stravinsky in class, quietly at first, but later at louder and louder volumes, gently humming *The Rite of Spring* as I composed titles for my book or *ideas* for titles for my book, jotted across legal pads and scraps of paper which quickly developed into small mounds littered across my desk and soon enough complaints were being made by the neighboring instructors regarding the *volume* at which I played Stravinsky and *The Rite of Spring*, the *volume* of Stravinsky and *The Rite of Spring* hardly suitable for a community college, meaning a junior college, our campus not highly regarded, notorious in fact for accepting anyone with a beating heart, and was I, the administration asked, teaching Music Theory or Humanities 102, knowing full well I was a humanities instructor who sometimes digressed, who sometimes lectured on Hegel and Mallarmé or the sex lives of failed revolutionaries and through these digressions, I believed, was instructing those slow-witted dullards about the yawning maw of existence and this was either before or after the second emergency review and subsequent administrative probation, I can't remember, but it was a terrible time; me home from the Berkshires with no book-length essay, my wife losing her mind, trapped once more at the community college, glumly observing the dim-faced oafs perpetually scrolling their *smartphones* during Philosophy 101 or Ethics 302 or a survey course on moral anxiety, anyway I'd stopped troubling myself with the *earthbound,* as Kleist called them, those afraid of radiance and splendor and the triumph of the soul, those afraid of drinking seven Turkish coffees in the middle of the afternoon because coffee, strong coffee, I'd begun to believe, was a conduit to the divine, and after my time at the Horner Institute and my friendship with Kleist I found myself changed. I dismissed those who before I would've happily humored, stopped kowtowing to the *earthbound* and instead ingested cup after cup of *Turkish coffee,* a recent fetish, fashioned in the teachers' lounge by boiling the most finely minced grounds of coffee along with sugar and cardamom in a brass *cezve,* ignoring the looks of those *earthbound* instructors, and with a circular motion, stirring ever so slowly, ever so lovingly, adding a second spoonful, stirring once more, adding perhaps a third spoonful, the water shivering, boiling, turning bronze, eventually chestnut, and I'd remove the spoon, absorb its fragrance and after four or five of these Turkish coffees felt I was ready for Humanities 102 or Philosophy 103, and if I were feeling up to it I'd lecture about *Madness and Civilization* because Foucault always terrified the students, the students always anxious when I brought up Foucault and *Madness and Civilization* because reading or discussing or even thinking about *Madness and Civilization,* I lectured, was akin to looking into the depths of the darkest mirror and seeing reflected back the engorged pupils of our own destruction, a galaxy of death, a universe of doom, an abyss that hungers for annihilation at the dead-end street of nothingness and when one reads or studies or contemplates *Madness and Civilization* one is meditating upon the corpus of their soul and if one does this, meaning studies or contemplates *Madness and Civilization* while also listening to Stravinsky's *The Rite of Spring,* it's the equivalent of losing a limb or getting executed, but in a good way, meaning, I said, the moment *preceding* the loss of the limb or the execution, not the execution itself, no, of course not, but the moment before the blade drops or rifle fires, Dostoevsky for example, I said, those seconds before Dostoevsky was to be executed, where Dostoevsky felt time itself expand before him, those fleeting moments where he, he being Dostoevsky, fully convinced of impending death, suddenly experienced two, three, four lifetimes, moments infused with God and the divine, time charged with an understanding which only comes from believing death has arrived, and once he was pardoned Dostoevsky was never the same, largely because of those three or four minutes *preceding* certain death, a lifetime in minutes, and could *Notes from Underground* have been penned by a man who hadn't suffered and glimpsed the end, I asked, I think not. My lectures meandered, veering as readily into Tennyson and Blake as Shelley and Spenser, Diderot and Wittgenstein as well as descriptions of Nabokov's butterflies or Yiddish fairy tales or the little-known chess match between Paul Bowles and Clarice Lispector, a chess match seldom publicized, the two writers never having met in person, each move made via the post, letters sent back and forth, between Tangier, where Bowles lived, and Rio de Janeiro, where Lispector grew up, her family fleeing Europe to Brazil because of the pogroms, meaning anti-Semitism, meaning Jew-hating, each move on the chess board taking weeks, even months, to arrive, until Bowles eventually forfeited, blamed meddling Moroccan youths for stealing his mail, Lispector convinced it was an excuse, certain Bowles was a lesser player, something she boasted of until she died and I was untethered, or becoming that way, conflating passages of all the books I'd ever read, sometimes in a single lecture.

Returning to the community college from the Berkshires I was stricken, morose, having come back with hundreds of possible titles, *Xenophon's Regret* and *Torment of Cicero,* but no finished work, no working manuscript either, and despite the disappointment at not having completed my work I felt both troubled and inspired, felt myself approaching something vast and ineffable, and while preparing my *Turkish coffees* I'd feel the eyes of my colleagues upon me, each of them perplexed by my transformation but incapable of pinpointing the disparity, a brave few inquiring about my time at the prestigious Horner Institute, asking if I'd finally completed my work but having no idea *what* my work was, likely no idea *who* Montaigne or *what* a book-length essay was, others mystified by my reverence for *Turkish coffee,* a drink enjoyed, I happily pointed out, by Victor Hugo, yes, I explained in the teachers' lounge, Victor Hugo famously enjoyed the *Turkish coffee ceremony* which exemplified, he felt, all that was refined in society and Hugo was known to lambast his maids for *more coffee like the Ottomans' drink!* Yes, I'd continue, nerves aflutter, stirring the brass *cezve,* adding more coffee grounds because one can never have enough coffee in their coffee, one can never truly make a *Turkish coffee* too strong, and my *Turkish coffee* phase was later eclipsed by the delivery of the *Nuova Simonelli* espresso machine and my subsequent *espresso phase* leading to the *espresso incident* and consequently my getting fired or retired (there are different versions) but all that was ensconced in the murky, unforeseen future, my wife not yet having lost her mind, Marcel obsessed with making a *dance record* which, he declared, would *transform the landscape of electronic music,* spending nights at dance clubs, hovering around DJ *booths,* fervidly asking questions, stealing tricks from the resident DJs, he'd boast, though at the time I was merely in the teachers' lounge expounding to the three or four accredited dunces present that Victor Hugo was known to adore *Turkish coffee* along with the *Turkish coffee ceremony,* Hugo having no qualms abusing his maids about the rigorous preparation of his *Turkish coffee,* yes, I said, facing my colleagues, even in exile, hiding from Napoleon in Guernsey, Victor Hugo would curse his many *femmes de ménages* in the most explicit fashion to go easy on the cardamom or, conversely, make the cardamom and, by default, the coffee, more robust, hurling insults while writing novels and political tracts and really I have no idea, I confessed, no inkling if Hugo preferred his *Turkish coffee* strong or weak, no idea if the *Turkish coffee* soothed his nerves, bestowing a sense of well-being, or if the *Turkish coffee* riled his nerves, promoting a narcissistic dread, the way I often feel after six or seven *Turkish coffees,* I explained, feeling my chest tighten, my throat constrict, feeling myself skirting the void, but still I endure, indeed, *force myself* to endure, because my panic, my disquietude, my misgivings about life and art are constantly skirting the abyss, hence verging on genius, yes, I said, I feel most alive, most *at home* when I'm trembling with dread because the more palpable the dread the closer I am to genius, the closer to oblivion, the nearer I am to clutching genius and, following this logic, I said, the more *palpable* the dread the more I've successfully *eluded* mediocrity, yes, I continued, one must risk their own well-being, indeed, one's own sanity, for the cause of wisdom and is it genius or oblivion, I asked, a revelation or the void, I also asked, one doesn't know, one *can't* know, unless one crosses the quivering precipice, and my colleagues were startled and mute, resembling more and more my own bovine-faced students, dull-visaged and bland, and more than a little troubled by my declarations, and the chirp of the *smartphone* returns me once again to the third bedroom where I must face the long-postponed moment of finally learning how to silence the *smartphone* because an exemplary work of single-minded boldness, of irrefutable artistry which aims to embody the spirit of Montaigne, is unthinkable with the constant assault of the *smartphone*, easily the most ironic name for an object in human history, I think, sipping the coffee which is no longer warm, hardly room temperature, because there's nothing *smart* or *clever* about an object that cripples, nay, *eviscerates* one's concentration, an object causing a person's thoughts to be no more intelligent than belches or hiccups, and this I must do, meaning silence the *smartphone*, and without Marcel's assistance, because calling Marcel would be a mistake, Marcel sure to bring up *Krautrock* or *tribal house* or *Dutch techno*, whatever the fuck that is, I think, laughing, picking up the *smartphone*, the *smartphone* chirping like a desperate bird, noticing the blinking red light of the *smartphone*, the blinking red light representing the outside world, I think, the blinking red light informing me the outside world is trying to reach me even though I want nothing to do with the outside world, and I unlock the *smartphone*, the screen notifying me of *eleven unheard messages,* friends of my wife perhaps or the sullen rabbi whose name I've already forgotten, old colleagues or perhaps Marcel proselytizing the euphoria contained inside *jungle* and *dubstep* and if I leave it for long enough, I realize, the phone will exhaust itself, eventually the battery will drain because despite Marcel's boasts regarding the *considerable battery life* of the *smartphone,* a battery can't last forever, I think, and if I want I can simply walk away from the *smartphone,* indeed, walk away once I manage to silence the *smartphone* because these goddamned chirps are impairing my concentration, chirps alerting me of another message from the outside world, messages removing me from my reveries and my attempts at *slow thinking,* returning me once again to this house pungent with the specter of my now-dead wife. Even with the distractions Montaigne faced, the upkeep of his vineyards, his kidney stones, Montaigne didn't have the ceaseless assaults of a *smartphone* and its relentless attacks, a *smartphone* whose *settings* feature is as slippery as an undisturbed thought in this ignoble world and, careful to avoid my wife's closet, I approach the kitchen in hopes of finding the *smartphone's user manual,* the *user manual* tossed aside, never studied because Marcel was only too happy to share his knowledge of the *smartphone,* insisting I disregard the *user manual,* disparaging the *user manual,* demanding I ignore the *user manual* completely, Marcel instructing me with no uncertain glee on the ease and convenience and benefits of the *smartphone,* gliding his finger across the glass surface which shimmered like a counterfeit God, Marcel awed by the *smartphone* and its *endless capabilities,*

Marcel showing me clips of movies then a video of his friend, a fellow DJ, spinning at a festival in Glasgow, and see how fast it moves, he said, you can skate along the surface of the *known world,* one second showing me a dance club in Hamburg then aerial shots of the Argentine *Pampas* then Machu Picchu, next Saint Basil's Cathedral, next a portrait of Montaigne, because Marcel, knowing well my passion for Montaigne, understood Montaigne was a selling point in my agreeing to accept the *smartphone* bought with my own money, yes, Marcel declared, it moves effortlessly, you can conduct research for your *French book* too, he said, Marcel always referring to my work-in-progress as my *French book,* conduct research for your *French book,* he said, and keep me up to date on Mom, research your *French book* and tell me how Mom is doing in addition to *photos* and *texts* and my *latest mixes* which you'll be able to *download and play,* yes, it'll be able to play all the songs I produce and whatever mixes I send. Marcel was delighted, ecstatic even, scrolling through the *smartphone,* explaining the ease with which he'd be able to send me his *latest mixes* and on he went, expounding upon the utility and majesty of the *smartphone,* the magnificence of the *smartphone's battery life* and when he stopped by I'd been trying to put her, meaning my now-dead wife, meaning his now-dead mother, to sleep, the same day in fact the doctor had paid a visit, making a small, almost imperceptible gasp, claiming the *severity* of her degenerative condition was so *acute,* so *chronic,* he was shocked she was swallowing food and hours later Marcel was standing before me, handing me the *smartphone,* selling me on its *capabilities* and *speed* and the litany of things the *smart-phone* could do and I wanted to cry, and Marcel, I suspect, wanted to cry too, Marcel ranting excitedly about the *smart-phone* to avert talking about his mother dying in the next room, because he'd always been sensitive, always kindhearted and tender and there's no way to prepare a person like that for the world, I thought, no way to equip a child for the catalogue of grief that's steadily advancing, grief advancing ceaselessly from the second one is born, no, I told myself, it's impossible. Marcel and his tenderness and his benevolent and open-hearted approach toward the world, and me incapable of explaining how the world breaks a person, sometimes fast, sometimes slow, but no one is exempt, no one immune, because the world is always triumphant, the world in fact enjoys an unblemished record at breaking people, and his mother, withering a bedroom away, was always closer to Marcel, always understood his gentle nature whereas I had no idea what to do with a boy who loved a world that would only punish him, his mother insisting he take lessons on the piano at the age of five or six, recognizing what she called the *delicacy* of his nature, and I find no *user manual* in the kitchen, every cabinet and drawer bereft of the *user manual* and once again, avoiding my wife's closet, I return to the study, sit before the rolltop desk, sip my coffee, hear another chirp and curse the outside world. Montaigne had no such distractions, I think. Besides his brief acquaintance with the Russian fugitive, Montaigne's diary was chiefly concerned with the frustrations of Jean Brismontier, complaining of the young man's growing quirks, his deep affection for clothes and jewelry, his obsession with wigs even though wigs were a hundred years from being fashionable. Adorned in velvet waistcoats, Montaigne wrote, I read, purple capes and lately his preposterous beauty marks affixed to his face based on some cryptic schedule I've tried but cannot decode, the mark always of a varied size which fluctuates depending on the day and mood, emerging on the left cheek one day as easily as the right on the next, I find myself perplexed and mystified. Montaigne had forbidden Brismontier from wearing wigs around the château, particularly on rides due to their height, wigs which seemed to ascend with each excursion and Jean's slender shoulders, in Montaigne's view, were ill inclined to sustain the grandeur of such atrocities, atrocities which arrived punctually from Paris days after Jean was paid, alabaster wigs, golden wigs, red-wine wigs with riotous curls fashioned from the scalps of unknown Parisians and I know when a wig is expected, wrote Montaigne, as I observe Jean parading outside the servants' quarters in frantic expectation of the cabriolet. Brismontier and his baby-blue frocks, Montaigne wrote, I read, an assemblage of bizarre ensembles that push the boundaries of common taste, and those cursed beauty marks which advance across the boy's face like islands drifting across a dull and placid ocean, it's simply too much, moreover the way he clicks his heels which, cloistered in my citadel, chronicle his vain wanderings. On a recent excursion, Montaigne wrote, I read, Jean's wig was caught on the lowest branch of a tree and, beside himself, rivulets of tears cutting paths through his snowy makeup, he was useless for the rest of the day, and it was then I forbade the wearing of such trappings. I care for Jean, Montaigne wrote, I read, but he's been attending lectures, getting ideas in his head, senseless opinions about clothing and coiffures, notions that the way a man looks reflects what's inside his soul, and the boy asks my opinion on the height of his lifts, heels he calls them, and yesterday I found him in the forecourt modeling for himself, primping his collar, pursing his lips, winking at his reflection like an exotic bird. I knelt behind the planter for fear of being seen, my embarrassment for the boy extending well beyond my own exasperation and I worry for his future, worry he'll disoblige himself among the locals for he contains a stubbornness in his bones, a dumb belief that others will one day share his interests. Everything I've tried, Montaigne wrote, I read, from archery to philosophy, fails to stir his soul, it merely sends him off to powder his face and garnish his livery whilst humming to himself in wide-eyed oblivion and do you know the origin of the paisley he recently asked and I told him the origin of the paisley interested me no more than the cost of beef in England, meaning not a whit. When I'm left alone, when the clicking of the boy's heels finally recedes, I begin to write and I stopped reading, trembled inside, for it was the first time Montaigne mentioned his own writing in the facsimile of the diary, a diary I swiftly ceased reading because my twenty-five minutes in the *Tanner Reading Room* had elapsed. I'd become acutely cautious, practically paranoid, about the stringent regulations of both Tanner Rooms; earlier that week I'd exceeded my thirty-minute slot and, returning to the *Tanner Room* from the *Tanner Reading Room,* was reprimanded by a clerk who extracted the book from my hands, studied it for defects before I was tersely dismissed. By the time I reached my cottage a letter, stamped and notarized, had found its way beneath my door, explaining it was not the Horner Institute's responsibility to *oversee the fellows,* that an absence of trust was a *slippery slope,* that the pricelessness of the books in both Tanner Rooms demanded *complete and unequivocal accountability* and thirty minutes meant exactly that, not thirty-one, thirty-two, or, God forbid, thirty-three, because thirty-three minutes was cause for complete expulsion. I'd been issued five demerits, of which another ten, it read, would see me banned from both *Tanner Rooms* for a week not to mention exclusion from *bonfire night.* It was essential I sign and date the note, returning it to the solicitor's office beside the quadrangle within the hour, the word *hour* underlined with ruthless severity, and the letter, charged with officialdom, a touch draconian, felt unnecessary because I, more than anyone, was devoted to the well-being of the books inside the *Tanner Room* as well as the safekeeping of those books while under my twenty-five minute charge in the *Tanner Reading Room* and what other artist-in-residence stumbles into the halls of each Horner complex in a state of delirium, I wondered, half mad with reverence and wonder? There was Yannick Verhoeven, the Dutch novelist, and Francisca Araújo, the landscape engineer from Brasília, whose hours of research often mimicked my own, thus we passed one another in the course of our daily commutes between the two Tanner rooms and in a gesture of silent comradery I'd often display my fingers to indicate how much time remained or how many minutes had elapsed since we last passed, and neither appeared grateful but *put out,* neither in fact seemed touched by the smallest sliver of reverence, neither seemed humbled by where they'd found themselves either, as if one were simply *invited* as a fellow to the Zybècksz Archives, simple as that, no different than being invited to a birthday party or a cookout. Most mornings, while heating the water and grinding the coffee by hand, performing the rituals that had mollified my addled soul for decades, I would pause, astounded at the fortune of finding myself on such hallowed ground, a fellowship cottage at the Zybècksz Archives at the Horner Institute, nestled in the Berkshires, walking the same paths as Sandra Vogel and Františka Goldblath and my dilemma, I felt, was the *ease* with which the other fellows occupied a *space of creativity* whereas I with my slew of misgivings and struggles could attain no *space of creativity,* was at a loss at having been bequeathed with the time to nurture a *space of creativity,* and the trouble, I felt, was my complex relationship with time, both my *lack* of time as well as my *inability* to do anything once I had fought, struggled, and *found the time* or, in this case, been *awarded* the time, because here I was, I thought, with nothing *but* time and doing nothing but squandering it, because I was unschooled at making the most of creative time, ignorant as to which direction I should proceed, only titles, unending titles, accosting me as I circled the *Pleasure Gardens* or the *Bellinger Wing,* eating alone in the *Ferdinand Schönburg Commissary,* portraits of past luminaries positioned above the exits and the salad bar, each regarding me with shame and chagrin, long-dead masters adept at lulling the world around them, skilled at locating the *mental Saharas* necessary to create towering works, portraits which intimidated more than inspired and apart from a notebook bursting with promising titles like *Pastures of Affliction* and *Underling's Lament,* I'd found no thread or theme for my book-length essay, in fact I found myself studying obscure books in the *Facsimile Closet* more than what I should've been doing, meaning studying Montaigne's diary at twenty-five-minute intervals, looking for the most favorable angle at which to approach my book-length essay. I was altogether lost. Did I sit and reflect as I'd seen others do? Camp myself, Buddha-like, before the vacant page and wait for the essay to appear? Stroll the woods like Kleist, collecting sticks, provoking ideas to take shape, watching the contours of impending work gain dimension with a diligence and fortitude I lacked? With typical mirth Kleist laughed at the letter, claimed Ernst had received plenty in his day for sundry offences: overstaying his welcome in various academic complexes as well as threatening a groundskeeper with a knife for losing one of his bocce balls. What matter? she asked. Who gives a shit about the artlessness of the world when what you need is *here,* she said, poking my sternum with the lip of her pipe, let the trifling distractions of the world be just that, trifling and petty, and she cackled like a bird of prey, insisting the voice I'd heard for years demanding I write a book-length essay was the only voice worth listening to, the only enlightened voice, she said, the only voice, in fact, worth a good goddamn, and if the voice turned out to be irrational or false or who knows, she sighed, dull, dim-witted, or *fucking deranged,* that was the risk one took, the only risk *worth* taking because ignoring one's inner voice was akin to suicide or death or a fate *worse* than death, Kleist pausing, clearing her throat, knocking her pipe on the sole of her boot and though I welcomed her words I was daunted and ill at ease, felt all the years preparing to take the slow descent into artistic creation were a self-induced fable, a scam I'd sold myself so often and for so long I simply believed it. What's more, a winter storm was swiftly advancing toward the Berkshires, thus the delivery of my coffee had been suspended indefinitely. I had enough coffee for a week, maybe more, but my reserves were dwindling. More and more I found myself thinking about coffee or, to be precise, a *looming lack of coffee,* a nightmarish scenario causing untold amounts of psychic distress; I paced the lengths of my cottage immersed in visions, odious and bleak, rife with physical dread, a tightening of the throat, dull and indiscriminate aches charting paths up my legs, extending to my arms and chest and what would I do if I ran out, perish the fucking thought, I thought, what if I exhausted the coffee necessary to make a *café au lait* or *cortado,* used up my Yemeni and Ethiopian and Indonesian beans, beans roasted in small batches, dark brown with a tawny head, humming to myself while seeing the world with an optimism both tremulous and frail, an optimism emboldened no doubt by the coffee and the coffee-making ritual, a ritual downright necessary to which I'd accustomed myself over the past two decades, my one indulgence, I told myself, a single luxury, the sole expense in fact while teaching those dullards, because my wife's career as an ecologist, though important, and *heroic-sounding,* paid little, and combined with my own, hardly enough to sustain a small family, meaning one child, and yes, being alive for most meant this, meant the constant menace of homelessness and hunger, of destitution and indigence, all of it hovering ceaselessly over one's head like a shaky ceiling fan, unable to pay a doctor or repair a car and weren't most of us a minor misstep away, I often thought, a small hiccup from this very fate, and the distractions never ended, I thought, besides the chirps of the phones and the dullards pleading to have their thoughts interrupted there was poverty to contend with too and how, I wondered, does one conceive a luminous work of philosophic mastery in a culture designed to usher people to the depths rather than lift them up? Anyway, coffee, I felt, was my one indulgence, but a blizzard was drawing near and the notice from the post office advising me to *expect delays* was akin to a death knell because reaching the Zybècksz Archives at the Horner Institute was no easy task, precarious on the best days, the roads notoriously intricate, teeming with narrow, arterial paths ending abruptly in dense scrub or spitting out the driver on the side of a remote highway and one wasn't certain they'd chosen accurately until the moment one beheld the golden-green meadow, espied a pair of ancient oaks boasting the Horner insignia on an unassuming placard which welcomed the driver with supple dignity and, going a bit farther, the sound of gravel beneath the tires, the heady scent of gardenia, the narrow road hugged by jasmine and sweetbriars, the oblique roof of the *Bustamante Embassy*, a tribute to modernism and the *Frankenhoff School* with its decorative pools and innovative statuaries, that one finally felt a sense of relief, that one felt free to gaze at the grounds with wonder and bliss, the entire expanse presenting itself without pretense or pomp, the enlightened visitor knowing the risk had been worth it, realizing they'd survived the barbarous maze of erroneous paths that even an experienced postman, say one delivering Indonesian coffee, would miss, the most capable driver gladly forgiven for confusing any of the assorted trails for the main road, although *road* was a generous description since the sole passage dispatching a visitor upon the Horner grounds was especially narrow, and everyone knew the story of Amanda Nissen, the performance artist, lost in '52 en route to her first fellowship and only in the spring was her body found, a grim reminder of the dangers these paths presented. Historically, every administration of the Horner felt the same, believed these paths were an argument for themselves, a natural protection against anyone visiting unannounced, imposing to strangers as well as sightseers, solicitors, and ne'er-do-wells alike, a blessing, they felt, as the paths winding around the mountain in rings both arduous and illogical enforced the isolation of the fellows as well as the integrity of the grounds, gratifying to me on arrival no doubt, but becoming increasingly worrisome because this difficulty, a difficulty I'd recently welcomed, was the same difficulty keeping me from my coffee. I felt trapped, cornered; I began contemplating a future of coffee rationing like the survivor of some catastrophic war, wandering the bleak and battered streets with a tin cup. Agitated, I gazed at the last bag of beans, weighed it in my hand, felt its contents dwindling. I thought of Constantinople and Mecca, considered their shameful histories of banning coffee, something I'd read in a book once, felt a comradery with their citizens because if the delivery of my coffee was halted my lifeline to art and philosophy, my entire outlook on humanism and the creation of my book, I thought, would be destroyed. Daily I visited the mail room where Linda shook her head and looked heavenward as if to say, *what do you expect,* which, in fact, she often *did* say, what do you expect, Linda said, I don't control the weather, the mail gets delivered once a day, not twice, I sort what comes in, dispatch what goes out. Since word of the blizzard's approach our interactions had taken on a vague, threatening tone, I saw it in her smile, her laugh like a wood chipper, the cynical ease with which she creased the blades of her eyes and Linda wasn't above subterfuge, I suspected, Linda had dark regions in her soul. A retired electrician who'd decided to work at the Horner mail room half of the year, I saw hazard in Linda's eyes, saw the longing for something which had always eluded her, joy, ardor, perhaps a vague sort of serenity, something she believed the grounds of the Horner would offer, and she relished nothing more than the narrow domain of her power, the mail room, a ramshackle hut with a Dutch door whose lower half remained forever shut and sometimes her son Aiden stopped by, a stick-thin juvenile with a face designed for petty crime, immersed in his *smartphone,* its reflection illuminating the boy's bad skin and overbite, all while Linda condescended, explaining the mail was delivered *once* a day, not twice, and, in fact, she said, never in her experience as a human living in America had it, meaning the mail, ever been delivered twice in the same day, as if I didn't know, as if I hadn't stopped by from desperation and dread, for the smallest possibility my coffee had made it through, even as the snow began to fall, turning heavy and abundant, my flesh accosted by a piercing cold as well as the certainty the blizzard had finally and irrevocably arrived, lurching through the wind, retreating to my cottage, contemplating the terror of the void as well as the soundlessness that forever accompanied the terror of the void.

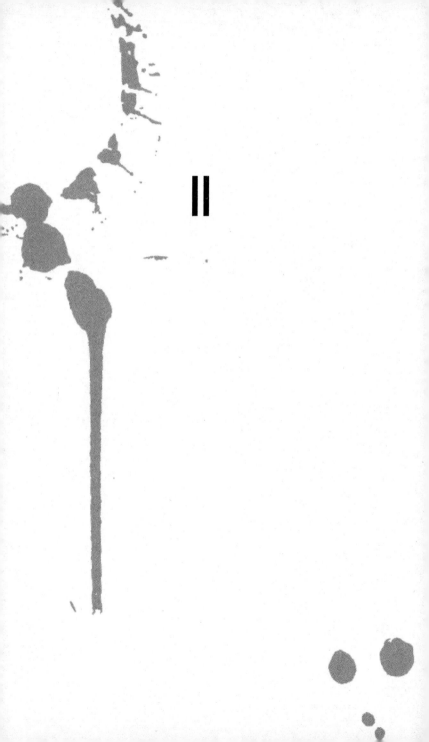

II

During the storm's approach, before the lone path became impassable, before the Berkshires lay beneath what I was later told was a *historic* amount of snow, I'd begun suffering visions of *coffee-less* days, thus I began making small concessions: drinking three morning cups instead of the traditional four, nervously administering more frugal amounts of the Ethiopian grounds in the pour-over as well as denying myself the traditional afternoon reprieve where, liberating myself from both Tanner rooms, I'd scramble to the cottage for an *Americano* or *cortado,* whatever I had the time to make, feeling rushed but likewise knowing there was nothing *worse,* nothing more *barbaric* than rushing a cup of coffee, approaching the cottage, pondering the exultation coffee afforded, the nut-brown granules, the aroma, the sensuous dignity of the custom and as I passed the *Bustamante Embassy* and the *Bellinger Wing,* the walls of the quadrangle, strident and untainted, blanketed by virgin snow, an attitude of self-reproach arose, bothered by the belief I had no idea what to do with large swathes of unbroken time and sitting here now, the coffee no longer warm, I decide the thing I need most is music, specifically Stravinsky, more specifically *The Rite of Spring* and, more specifically than that, "The Adoration of the

Earth," that rhapsodic introduction to *The Rite of Spring* which I'd repeatedly tell my students was the *soundtrack to the apocalypse,* "The Adoration of the Earth," I'd say, the *music of the end-times,* the music *best suited* for the end-times, optimal and ideal, in fact, for the end-times, and one must embrace the trembling hooves, I implored, the collapsing stars, I pleaded, turning up the music, making the music nearly unbearable, because Stravinsky captured the music of *Satan haunting the soul* or perhaps the *soul being haunted by Satan,* the order irrelevant, because all that mattered was the music captured Satan and the soul as well as haunting and it didn't matter who was haunting who, meaning who was doing the haunting and who was being haunted. And the students were terror-struck and mute, the coffee was humming in my veins and the euphoria I felt was the harbinger of things to come, calamity or rapture, solace or heartbreak, who could say? This was toward the end, following both emergency reviews and administrative probation, and it may have been the strength and quantity of coffee, but I felt immaculate, unassailable. I assigned essays about sadness and desire, a personal favorite, as well as *George Eliot and the Dilemma of Virtue* because returning from the Berkshires I found myself drifting away from philosophy and *entering literature through the back door,* an expression I'd grown fond of using, *entering literature through the back door,* meaning being self-taught, an autodidact, because a person who *entered literature through the front door,* I believed, was a person unduly influenced, force-fed literary theories as well as having their opinions molested by the gatekeepers, no, *entering literature through the back door,* even the *side door,* was surely superior to *entering literature through the front door* which, to my mind, was akin to being spoon-fed tropes and ideologies as well as being corralled by the myriad movements: Modernism, Romanticism, Postcolonialism, all the different *isms* mere fences, I felt, unscrupulous fences, I also felt, fences erected solely to keep the literary livestock placated and as a youth I preferred literature over philosophy and only later did I prefer philosophy over literature, felt philosophy was *superior* to literature, even went to school to study philosophy, becoming a humanist, meaning a *Montaignian* and soon thereafter wrote my master's thesis, *Montaigne and the Lugubrious Cherubs,* and in the ensuing years I taught philosophy and regarded myself as a practitioner and an instructor of *philosophy,* saw myself as a *philosopher* in the deepest pith of my soul but, returning from the Horner, I felt my bearings rearranged, sensed my priorities swapped; I began seeing myself as I once was, that is, *a reader,* nothing more perfect and pure, I felt, than a reader, especially a *serious reader* because a *serious reader* was the most immaculate creature on earth, and by *serious reader* I meant a reader with romantic sensibilities, one who approached books with hope in their hearts and no concern at all for *schools* or *disciplines,* the *serious reader* seizing each book with wide-eyed possibility because *serious readers,* I felt, were utopians and every book an attempt at transcending oneself. I began teaching *literature* in my philosophy classes instead of *philosophy* in my philosophy classes, assigning essays like *The Abiding Sorrow of Sancho*

Panza or *The Galactic Expansion of Virginia Woolf* as well as *Auden and Anxiety,* another favorite, and when not besieged by the cacophony of possible titles for my book-length essay which arrived with ever more ferocity, often while drinking an espresso or finishing an espresso or kneeling beneath my desk in order to make another espresso, I'd lecture on the poetry of Brodsky or the works of Charlotte Lennox because, quite unknowingly, Kleist had transformed my soul. I began seeing Montaigne not only as the greatest philosopher and humanist in history, but also the greatest *writer,* and I recalled my early love of Jules Verne and later Stendhal, and a serious reader's interest in literature follows a nomadic path, I suddenly think, finishing my coffee, a path which winds through a person's life leaving a trail of imagined events more *palpable* than the supposed *actual,* invoking both history and geography, perspective and sentiment, because my *Montaigne phase* was due to my interest in Jules Verne, meaning France, meaning French literature, which later meant Flaubert and Duras and Zola, all in conversation with one another, whether they knew it or not, whether they wanted to be or not, the entire literary firmament illuminating the dark vault of existence, Baudelaire, for instance, or Machado de Assis, also for instance, Iris Murdoch or Joseph Roth as other instances because they go on and on, the instances I mean, they never stop, *passionate reading, ecstatic reading,* a tree with untold branches, and Fernando Pessoa, I think, a reluctant angel, Gogol with his religious manias and epileptic Dostoevsky, all those nineteenth-century Russians in fact, each more obsessed with their suffering than the last, all in conversation and all, to quote Kleist, *building bulwarks against the inevitability of death,* and later my obsession with literature of the shtetl, chiefly Isaac Babel, poor tragic Babel, getting executed for being an intellectual, which was bad, as well as being Jewish, which was worse, declared a non-person by the Soviet Union and murdered in Stalin's purges and Bruno Schulz, I also think, shot in the head by the Gestapo while holding a loaf of bread and suddenly I'm disheartened pondering the agony of existence and the cruelty of man, as well as the goddamn *needlessness* of this cruelty, and instead of brooding on the bleak affairs of humanity I decide to play some Stravinsky, specifically *The Rite of Spring,* more specifically than that "The Adoration of the Earth," preferably by the Royal Liverpool Philharmonic, a version performed with the utmost fidelity, but not before a second cup of coffee and, avoiding my dead wife's closet, I return to the kitchen and prepare a second cup, Kenyan and shade grown, heating the water, moistening the filter, humming "The Adoration of the Earth" while grinding the beans by hand, perhaps the sole moment of peace I'll allow myself before beginning work on my book and, ten minutes later, careful to skirt the aforementioned closet which conjures the scent of my now-dead wife, a closet that evokes the scent of grief with a pungency too strong to ponder, I return to the third bedroom, sit before the rolltop desk with a fresh cup of coffee, and attempt locating Stravinsky and *The Rite of Spring* on the *smartphone,* something Marcel instructed me on when showing it off, the entire history of recorded music, he bragged, can be *streamed* through this device, explaining how to *download* music and *play* music, specifically his most recent mix, a forty-five-minute mix he'd worked on for months, he said, stopping by to talk about the *progress of his mix,* the songs he sampled, the beats he made, the openheartedness of dance music, its hedonistic nature, its playfulness and sense of wonder, all illustrated for the ump-teenth time and the mix he promptly downloaded onto my *smartphone* was sun warped and drunken, he boasted, dappled and bright, with hints of static making it feel warm and human, tiny imperfections, along with squelches and soft, thudding pat-ters, visited later by beats both smooth and punchy then beats both punchy and smooth, yes, he said, each trading with the other until, fifteen minutes in, layers of *'80s synth* arrived like ka-rate chops along with great blocks of heavy keyboard and hints of voices, not really voices, just *hints* of them, meaning voices, more specifically, *samples* of voices, voices taken from an ob-scure 1974 pop hit or borrowed from an old gospel song, then, minutes later, supple hints of organ indicative of *leftfield disco* and *Balearic house,* hovering over the song while the song builds, as the percussion gains velocity and complexity, bongos, hand-claps, drum machines, all of it *almost* syncing up, but *not quite* syncing up, *approaching* syncing up but not syncing up *quite yet,* and any listener knows, any dancer losing themselves on the dance floor knows, at least unconsciously (meaning their body on the most primitive level knows), that the song can't be doing anything *but* building in preparation for syncing up; the synco-pated drums, the flickering voices, the keyboards and the cadence, all of it heading toward one irrefutable conclusion, a climax as expected and satisfying as it is *necessary,* yes, Marcel explained, because a *mix* is nothing like an *album,* a *mix* is meant to show off the DJ's impeccable taste at *mixing* as well as *crate-digging,* the DJ's flair for finding the purest beats and melodies and using them intuitively in the mix or, alternatively, using a well-known hook familiar to everyone, a *fashionable* and *trendy* hook, a hook everyone and their sister knows, but speeding it up, slowing it down, mincing it, using it in new and unexpected ways, and weaving these textures of different songs or *snatches* of songs, borrowed from hip-hop, grime, jungle, new wave, K-pop, truly any and everything, and making them flow together *seamlessly,* making them merge into something wholly new, sometimes on purpose but just as often by chance, whereas an *album* is another creature entirely, an album a showcase of one's own ideas, an album involving production, songwriting, a focus on the songs as well as the *sequence* of the songs, yes, he said, the pillowy synths, the patter of drum machines like distant rain; and aesthetics too, that's where my lessons on the piano paid off and Marcel, whose sidelong glance more and more resembled his mother's, looked in the corner where the Steinway once stood, the upright I'd begged him for years to play, just a small piece, I'd say, something from Schubert, the *Trout Quintet,* for instance, modest but eternal, or Debussy, I'd say, yes, play a morsel of Debussy, something which embodies the human spirit and Marcel refused, Marcel always obstinate in his designs and that night, following the monologue in which he highlighted the differences between DJs and musicians, mixes and albums, he sighed a sigh of infinite gloom and peered past my shoulder toward the bedroom where I'd sedated his now-dead mother after a day spent placating the woman I'd spent decades talking, laughing, and arguing with, my lover and mainstay, now a lunatic, a woman unable to feed or bathe herself and vividly I recalled our first night at the *3rd International Conference for Social Sciences, Aesthetics, and Disaster Management* where we'd had too much to drink and the lights of the lobby were incandescent and cloying, lights which gained in intensity the more we drank and she was dauntless and unafraid, something I discovered over time was intrinsic, because unaided by alcohol my now-dead wife was still fearless, my now-dead wife staring unflinchingly at the things in life which frightened me and when the bar closed she invited me to her room and once inside it was like breathing underwater, each of us taking large strokes through the boundless depths, and we did this blissfully and ardently as if a connection had always existed, something unspoken but understood, both of us swimming in unison while also independent of the other, our lungs vast and expansive, a whole host of clichés to describe our first night where blissfully we made love then fell in love and stayed that way, meaning in love, for decades, which is as rare and unique as it is *difficult,* often growing tired of the other, *exhausted* by the other, yet locating that thing, whatever that thing is, which compels one, as well as the other, to stay, because staying is as much of a decision as leaving, staying a much harder decision because the reward for staying is never immediately apparent (if it ever is) and even when the attraction and the eroticism faded (hers toward me and mine toward her) she still possessed a generous and forgiving nature, always reassuring me about my work-in-progress which amounted to hundreds of titles for a book-length essay but no book-length essay, nothing *resembling* a book-length essay, hundreds of titles and not much else, a few paragraphs appropriated from my master's thesis, tame observations about Montaigne's *influence* and *relevance,* things I'd read in a dozen forgettable books which all said identical things; Montaigne was the *first modern thinker,* a *profound* and *original* thinker, things any academic could've written and which offered nothing new or original in the study of Montaigne and she, meaning my now-dead wife, was always encouraging, especially about my acceptance to the Zybècksz Archives at the Horner Institute, boasting to her friends and colleagues, Marcel especially, about the *prestige* of being invited to such an illustrious artists' colony while he tinkered with the piano or skulked to his bedroom, young and sullen, still a teenager, none of us knowing I'd return three months later with nothing but titles, *Gardens of Anguish* and *Mute Pavilion* for example, three months in the Berkshires not without their drama, but returning with only a renewed love for literature and additional titles for my book-length essay but, again, *no* book-length essay. And it wasn't long after my return from the Berkshires that she began showing signs of losing her mind which was very slow until it wasn't and I recall the moment when the shit with the *spaceships* began, the first time she'd said the word *spaceships* in fact.

One afternoon before I retired, or was fired, depending on the version, she parted the curtains and mumbled the word *spaceships,* repeated the word *spaceships* and *Jesus,* I thought, what a cliché, as if my wife were a caricature of someone losing their mind instead of a person who was, day by day, hour by hour, truly losing their mind, and she said the word *spaceships* in a tone that left no question of the seriousness with which she believed there were *spaceships* floating in the sky, and I stood behind her, placed my hands on her shoulders, peered into a sky so empty it felt like an affront, a sky literally absent of everything, *spaceships* especially, no planes or satellites, no clouds either, and the calm of her face betrayed the lunacy of her words as well as the conviction with which she'd said them, and I can't languish like this, I suddenly think, sipping my coffee, can't brood anymore on the losing of my wife's mind and, hardly a week ago, the loss of her forever, me sitting shiva, trying my best to be a *Jew in mourning,* knowing all the while I was a bad or a lazy or a *faithless* Jew, sitting shiva to keep up appearances, sitting shiva in order to defer the moment I'd walk into her closet and feel the earth opening its throat, an enormous fissure beneath the floor, me choking on sobs, trembling vigorously, and I consider how to hear Stravinsky on the *smartphone,* specifically *The Rite of Spring,* more specifically than that "The Adoration of the Earth" performed by the Royal Liverpool Philharmonic, a towering interpretation with the deepest understanding of Stravinsky as well as Russia's pagan myths, surely more robust and faithful than those other renditions which always struck me as sappy and maudlin, those other renditions merely half measures, renditions *grasping* at the truth but not *reaching* the truth, and there's nothing so contemptible as *grasping* at the truth and not *reaching* it, meaning the truth, one might as well abstain from attempting to reach toward the truth at all, just give up *seeking* the truth, I think, avoid any semblance of truth-seeking, abandon the pursuit altogether, leave the truth for the *truth-seekers,* I think further, those able to *grasp* the truth and *touch* the truth, Montaigne for example or, in this instance, the Royal Liverpool Philharmonic, whose peerless interpretation of Stravinsky's *Rite of Spring* is unrivaled in its devotion and lack of gratuitousness, because those other versions are unseemly and coarse, versions *immune* to the truth, versions which take the listener *further* from Stravinsky and Russia's pagan myths, instead of *closer* to Stravinsky and Russia's pagan myths, and I recall discovering *The Rite of Spring* in college, I forget how, surely by accident, and it was like a veil had been lifted, an upheaval in my soul; the premiere in 1913 causing an uproar I later learned, Stravinsky hiding in the wings at the Théâtre des Champs-Élysées after the curtain opened, Picasso and Proust and Gertrude Stein all in attendance, and a riot quickly ensued, factions formed, vegetables were thrown, audience members ejected, and afterward the critic Henri Quittard called Stravinsky's masterwork a *laborious and puerile barbarity,* Puccini considered it *the work of a madman . . . sheer cacophony* because no one had ever witnessed such dissonance, no one had ever seen ballet dancers stomp the stage in earthly ritual and it must've seemed like madness and bedlam, especially in 1913, but it's the founding work of all modern music, I think, with its refutation of typical elegance and traditional ballet, invoking Lithuanian folksong and disarray and lest we forget, I think, the notorious *sacrificial dance,* something which ushered in a new sensibility, a new vision, something met at first with anger and denunciation, and again, I think, how to do this, meaning find Stravinsky's *Rite of Spring* on the *smartphone* when I'm incapable of silencing the device, a goddamn loathsome device, I think, the screen now alerting me to *thirteen unheard messages,* as if the grief alone isn't enough, as if the odious weight of mourning isn't enough, as if avoiding the closet which smells of my now-dead wife isn't enough, a closet that lies in wait, and last week, the day after she'd died or perhaps the day after, I walked past her closet, caught an enormous waft, and I was transported to a moment long before she was sick, a sliver of sun, a nape of neck, her walnut-brown hair, the way she tied it behind her head without a thought, like scratching one's elbow, and I was bewitched every time and, carried back further, I recalled some indiscriminate morning, waking up beside her, observing the shape of her unconscious back, the slow rise and fall of sleeping breaths, knowing one day she, us, *this,* would be gone, and how delicate and swiftly obscured those rare moments of naked clarity are, I thought then, and think again now, the seconds which are solemn and good, like that anonymous morning God knows how many years ago, one of thousands, where I awoke and knew enough to observe the passing tremor of time, like the flutter of wings, the finite nature of all of us, it comes and goes in a flash, and I remembered our single trip abroad, to Europe, and was that memory, I wondered, still inside her, did that memory—depthless, intangible—exist somewhere outside of us, or had it gone the way of her mind, that dark grotto before words existed, and last week, standing outside her closet I was halted, felt a convulsive shudder course through my body, felt the air leave my lungs, felt my insides collapse and I wept like I hadn't wept in years, perhaps decades, and eventually, *thankfully,* fell asleep on the floor outside her closet and fuck the *smartphone,* I suddenly think, once more tossing it on the floor, fuck Stravinsky and the Royal Liverpool Philharmonic too, I also think, the *smartphone* the cruelest instrument ever devised, I think, sipping my coffee, my bovine-faced students so enthralled by their *smartphones,* having no interest in anything but their *smartphones,* staring perpetually at the screens of their *smartphones* while I held forth about Virgil and Diderot, and later, after my return from the Horner Institute, Milton and Hawthorne, meaning those who *entered literature through the back door,* those who'd declared to the world, or at least themselves: *literature or life,* because for them there was no other choice, *literature or life,* I admonished the class, Philosophy 101 or Humanities 103, I forget, raising my voice, gliding between the desks, meaning, I said, the *vocation of practicing literature,* the only path that presented itself to those with a *spiritual calling,* at least without the deadening of one's soul, no different than joining the priesthood or becoming a monk or walking the plank over a tempestuous sea swollen with peril and do you think Alexander Pushkin had a choice, I asked, do you think Pushkin could simply turn his back from the calling that was literature, the yearning which throbbed through every fiber of his being demanding he practice *the vocation of literature,* all before he died in a duel? Anyway, I continued, *entering literature through the back door* is as beautiful as it is hopeless, a tragic decision no doubt, but the pious see and recognize and understand and still they continue because choosing literature over life is a revolutionary act, unrivaled and sublime, opposed to those who *enter literature through the front door,* I almost spat, because those types are careerists, a chromosome removed from being engineers or bankers and certainly not authentic writers, no, they like the *idea of books* more than books themselves, the *front-door types* choosing literature for any number of reasons, poverty of spirit, ambition, lack of imagination, who knows, endless reasons a person chooses to pursue literature by taking the cleanest, most manicured route when this is the *opposite* of literature, it's literature's *antithesis,* because literature, I ranted, is a chaotic devotion, horribly disheveled, literature is diving headfirst into the maelstrom, it's lighting oneself on fire, I proclaimed, it's covering oneself with a thousand leeches, in short, I said, literature, *literature with a capital L,* reflects the human heart and, pardon my French, but the human heart is a *goddamn mess* and sure, anyone can find a book nowadays written by those who've *entered literature through the front door* and these books are clean and clever, tempting and tidy, but where's the blood, I asked, where's the viscera, I also asked, because those who *enter literature through the front door* confuse *intelligence* with *passion,* confuse *knowledge* with *soul* and a few students yawned, others shifted in their seats and while I lectured about the *front, side,* and *back* doors of literature, I kneeled beneath the desk and turned on the *Nuova Simonelli* espresso machine in order to give myself an afternoon respite by means of a jolt of espresso. This was weeks before *the espresso incident* and my standing at the community college, though not exactly good, wasn't strictly bad, although I'd stopped making my Turkish coffees in the teachers' lounge following heated arguments with the literature professors vexed at me for concentrating on the very subject in which they specialized, the literature professors easily the lowest, most loathsome cohorts of an already dubious profession, the *Nuova Simonelli* purchased precisely to avoid the teachers' lounge and the dull-eyed literature professors chafed at me for teaching Sterne or Stein, Thackeray or Byron, instead of philosophers like Montaigne whose portrait, incidentally, I'd hung on all four walls of my class so whichever direction I turned my hero's countenance reminded me of my cosmic purpose, meaning the completion of my book-length essay. Each portrait was framed in the *Palazzo* style, gold leaf with bronze accents, cheap imitation frames but they got the job done. Anyway, these literature professors, without coming right out and insisting I *stay in my own lane,* were essentially insisting I *stay in my own lane,* demanding I stick with Erasmus and Hegel and I'm sorry, I said, incapable of hiding my contempt, I didn't realize you owned the rights to *Pushkin,* no idea you and your *cohorts* owned the intellectual rights to *literature entire* because I teach *humanities* and what could be more *human,* I asked, more *democratic,* I also asked, than the vocation of literature and its elusive abstractions? Yes, I admitted, I've discussed Alexander Pushkin in my classes, and yes, I conceded, I've assigned *projects* about Alexander Pushkin too, though not his work, which is fine, but the circumstances surrounding his fatal duel because introducing the *philosophical aspects* of dueling is supremely astute, the timeless principles of honor, bravery, passion, and true love, yes, I said, my breath tepid and stale from the fourth or fifth Turkish coffee, I stopped keeping count, not only dueling's history, I said, or the myriad cultural and topographic attitudes regarding distance, seconds, weapons, and so forth, but questions of fate and honor, bravery and virtue, you understand, *philosophical concerns.* For instance, is getting cuckolded reason enough to challenge someone to a duel, reason enough to risk one's life, I asked, and on that same note, have any of you ever received a letter of cuckoldry like the one Pushkin received which prompted the infamous and tragic duel dispatching the still-youthful poet, *Russian's greatest poet,* from our earthly realm, have any of you, I went on, ever gotten an anonymous letter suggesting your husband or wife was fucking around? This provoked raised voices and heated exchanges, the literature professors more readily inclined to take offence than I anticipated, and fine, I yielded, lifting my arms, I'll keep my hands off *Eugene Onegin* and the short stories too, but the duel itself is fair game, I thought, because I'd already assigned Ethics 102 and Intro to Philosophy projects concerning the duel, staged reenactments with the possibility of extra credit equal to but no more than the final exam, depending on the credibility of the dialogue and quality of the costumes; original letters of cuckoldry could also be written and read aloud and just imagine yourselves receiving an anonymous letter, I told the mob of young knaves sitting impatiently waiting to have their thoughts interrupted, imagine a letter implying your lover or spouse was sleeping around and, worse, *everyone knew it,* because the betrayal is only half as bad as the *public knowledge of the betrayal* and picture it, I said, my heartbeat rapid, temples throbbing, everyone in Petersburg slandering you, the rumors of infidelity quickly becoming fact, an unproven fact, but once enough people gossip about something it becomes that way, meaning a fact, yes, the betrayal on everyone's tongue and making things worse for Pushkin, perhaps *intolerable,* the author of this so-called anonymous letter was none other than Georges d'Anthès, a real shit-stirrer, a French officer in the Russian Guard, and imagine this dirty Frenchman saying, without actually saying, he was sleeping with Pushkin's wife, fucking her in all sorts of sundry positions, the ample-bosomed Natalia Pushkina, a notorious hussy in my opinion, hardly deserving of the poet's matrimony, and who knows the positions of carnal fervor described in the letter: on all fours, slapping and barking, eating plums off each other's bellies, mounting one another like troikas, one can only imagine, and one *must* imagine, because the letter, setting into motion the downfall of Russia's greatest poet, was lost to the sands or hands of time, is it sands or hands, I can't remember, point is, the letter was anonymous, *suggesting* infidelity without coming right out and *saying* infidelity, so consider this when working on your projects: the wooded hills, the bleak winter, the glimmering lights of Nevsky Prospect and I kneeled once more to make a *ristretto* or *cortado*, ardently in love with the newly purchased *Nuova Simonelli* machine beneath my desk which I felt ashamed for coveting, but Jesus Christ, I thought, staring at the gorgeous contraption, its silver exterior mirroring back my own agitated reflection, a goddamn work of art, I thought, an instrument unparalleled in design, it was Humanities 101 or Intro to Philosophy, I can't remember, *immerse yourselves,* I howled from beneath the desk, dosing the grounds, tamping the grounds, standing back up, reminding the class Pushkin's duel was a duel of *close range,* meaning ten steps, despite Europe agreeing to twenty-five steps, although dueling, for all intents and purposes, had been outlawed and, as a consequence, Pushkin and d'Anthès, as well as their seconds, as well as the witnesses, all of them were knowingly breaking the law, but envision Pushkin shrouded in the misty dusk, I said, and beyond, a vast sea of darkness, the poet's breath curling skyward as he put his affairs in order, conferring with Arthur Magenis, his second, yes, I continued, and consider a cold unlike any cold you've ever known because all of this occurred centuries ago when the earth was colder and the ice caps hadn't begun to melt and we, meaning humanity, hadn't begun hastening the world's demise with lunatic glee, I'm kidding, sort of, anyway it was the kind of cold no one experiences anymore and I laughed to myself at something, I forget what, chuckled again thinking of it, then stooped to make the *ristretto* or *cortado,* one more in an afternoon rife with *ristrettos* or *corta-dos,* addled by the sheer array of Italian-style coffees available from the *Nuova Simonelli* espresso machine, me flipping the switch, begging the students to hear me out, to *bear with me,* because let us look at what we know, I said, standing back up, Pushkin was not afraid of a duel nor was he afraid to die, I said, this we can ascertain simply from reading his poetry, for instance, take the opening of "The Prophet" and lifting a tattered anthology, I cleared my throat: *My spirit was athirst for grace / I wandered in a darkling land / And at a crossing of the ways / Beheld a six-wing'd Seraph stand / With fingers light as dream at night / He brushed my eyes and they grew bright,* yes, I whispered, strangely moved, momentarily altered by my own recitation, does this sound like a man afraid to meet his maker? And let's also remember that Russian translations do not lend themselves to English because of tone and register, anything of Slavonic origin to be honest, I pointed out, and what's left, if we're lucky, is the best *appropriation* of a masterful Russian poem, a mere glimpse, a timid shadow, not the poem itself, the poem merely a frail flower we must tiptoe gingerly toward, *shh,* I told the students, we must not alarm the English translation of Russian Romantic poetry, *shh,* I repeated, we must be gentle with the English translation of Russian Romantic poetry, Pushkin especially, the *Nuova Simonelli* beginning to tremble and convulse, and from this frail shadow, I said, this gentle flower (I'm still talking about the translation of the poem), the reader must ascertain the holy, biblical *atmosphere* of the work, one must *invest* in it and *infer* from it, because even the most accurate and astute translation can unwittingly betray, each syllable, every stress and stanza, just another opportunity for the English translation to betray the Russian original, the betrayal practically begging to happen, betrayal hovering over every translation like an enormous raptor, translation itself an enormous monster fashioned for the express purpose of betrayal, but "The Prophet" is a solemn, liturgical work, I went on, which on its best day, and even by a skilled translator, still risks sounding bombastic and mawkish, especially in English, and any reader, even a reader with the *teensiest* brain, can see "The Prophet" couldn't come from the pen of a Romantic poet afraid of death, or a Romantic poet afraid of dishonor or shame, things which Pushkin was willing to die for because, remember, Pushkin was still young, hardly in his thirties, and meanwhile the motherfucker managed to invent an entirely new stanza, I said, *iambic tetrameter!* Pushkin alternating rhymes between the masculine and feminine, exemplified in his greatest work *Eugene Onegin,* what some call an *Onegin Stanza* or a *Pushkin Sonnet,* invented by Pushkin, and rapturously I went on about Pushkin and the challenge of Slavonic translations, the disparity of Pushkin translations into English, the Deutsch translation versus the Elton, the Johnston versus the Arndt, the Arndt versus the Falen, whose translation incidentally, deeply influenced by Nabokov's, was considered the most faithful to the spirit and atmosphere of the original, the students becoming anxious and fidgety, the *Nuova Simonelli* trembling to a standstill, the bouquet of my Brazilian roast lifting like a florid curtain.

I was suffering from emotional fatigue. When I wasn't frightening the students, I was frightening myself, perfectly obvious my mind was amiss, my nerves in crisis, my heart in shambles, every part of me really, words and gestures, alarming facial tics, stretched too thin for comfort, hardly stable enough to get through the day. Even the joy I found from making the espressos, then drinking the espressos, contained a certain hysterical desperation, as if each cup inched me closer to some invisible chasm only others could see. Yes, I continued to lecture, one could write an entire book just about the demands of translating Pushkin's *Eugene Onegin* into English, which, indeed, I've considered, and I said a few more things about melody and rhyme versus exactness and faithfulness as well as the duel in *Eugene Onegin* which prophesied the real-life duel in which Pushkin lost his life, requesting the class to work in silence because the palpable approach of possible book titles was hastening toward me, *God's Incense* and *Flanks of the Vagrant* for example, titles which intoxicated and exhilarated and convinced me I was capable of completing my book-length essay and I circled the class, sipping a *ristretto,* the name of the drink translated from the Italian as *short shot,* though there was nothing short about my version of a *ristretto* since I'd used the equivalent of a quadruple espresso and sipping my bitter concoction, Montaigne's four portraits peering down with profound ceremony, I became ecstatic about the possibility of titles that would one day accompany my essay but meanwhile aggrieved at myself because, titles excluded, I had a dozen decent pages at most, much of them appropriated from my decades-old thesis, none of it remotely succinct in capturing Montaigne's melodious essence, a pair of pages discussing Montaigne's brief encounter at a Bordeaux café with the fugitive Alexei Voznesensky, an anecdote I'd transcribed in a notebook in the *Tanner Reading Room*, the Russian entertaining Montaigne with tales of escape as well as the bounty Ivan the Terrible had put on Voznesensky's head and my hero insisting the Russian stay at his château, at least for the night, and they talked into the morning of literature and honor, of Stoicism and the sublime, the potential of man and certainly Plato's dialogues, and though this was never mentioned I felt certain, saw it all like a vision, and Montaigne sent him off with food and blankets and this tale, this diversion concocted almost entirely from my imagination, for what? Two meager pages. A pale anecdote. What was the use of these digressions, I wondered, what purpose did they serve for a luminous work of groundbreaking humanism, I also wondered, because I found myself feeble and impotent, unable to approach Montaigne in any meaningful way, terrified of thinking and thus writing about the only subject I cared about, meaning Montaigne, as well as my thoughts and feelings *about* Montaigne, no, instead I had pages upon pages of nonsense, bizarre tangents meandering into peripheral topics like dueling, thousands of words dedicated to the etiquette and formalities of dueling, from the *offense* to the *challenge* to the *satisfaction* while also giving special attention to the description of swords and sword-making and, bizarrely, a fifteen-page digression about the Viennese coffeehouses of the 1930s, a subject that appeared from

God knows where, likely from one of the magazines in the doctor's waiting rooms into which I had endlessly ushered my now-dead wife, terrible rooms with fluorescent strip lighting, solemn to the point of discomfort, rooms in which everyone avoided making eye contact because making eye contact meant conversations like *how long* or *when did you find out* or *what are the side effects,* endless questions shared by the ill and the family of the ill, the family infinitely afraid of being mistaken for the ill because a line divides the sick from the healthy, nowhere more pervasive than a doctor's waiting room, because a doctor's waiting room is where the sick and healthy coexist, separated by no more than a chair or a small table, and the healthy hate the line, nothing frightens them more than crossing the line or being reminded of the line or, worse yet, being mistaken for having crossed the line, that is, getting mistaken for being ill. Years spent in waiting rooms where the line dividing the sick from the healthy was as frail as it was despotic and sometimes my wife saw *spaceships,* but on the good days she was occupied with a book or a magazine and in one of these I found an article about the Viennese coffeehouses of the 1930s teeming with writers and thinkers like Stefan Zweig and Arthur Schnitzler and Sigmund Freud, and I'd ripped the article from the magazine, stuffed it in my pocket, and brought it home, a tiny article about the culture of the Viennese coffeehouses in the 1930s, the zenith of intellectual commerce at the time, the *Café Griensteidl* in particular, frequented by the brightest thinkers of 1930s Vienna, and I found myself writing about the smell of the Viennese coffeehouses and the architecture of the Viennese coffeehouses, especially *Café Griensteidl,* patronized by the likes of Hermann Bahr and Karl Kraus, the great satirist who loved and loathed the literary scene of Vienna in equal measure, whose essay "The Demolished Literature" castigated writers like himself and Alfred Polgar who'd famously said the Viennese coffeehouse's sole purpose was *to kill time before it killed them.* Thousands of words I'd written about the enchanted coffeehouses of 1930s Vienna, an artistic culture that celebrated ideas and lionized art beneath the odious weight of the Habsburg Empire, a whole continent on the cusp of fascism and Jew-hating which was nothing new of course, in fact Jew-hating was downright *ancient,* but suddenly Jew-hating wasn't only accepted but encouraged and soon enough *state sponsored* which was the beginning of the end, so along with the decline of those wonderful Viennese coffeehouses awash with Jewish intellectuals and non-Jewish intellectuals, meaning *gentile* intellectuals, came the fleeing and the hiding of these Jewish intellectuals and if these Jewish intellectuals failed at fleeing or hiding they were captured and eventually murdered and soon enough there was the burning of their Jewish intellectual books riddled with Jewish intellectual words and ideas and one of these Jewish intellectuals, Stefan Zweig, having fled Europe, found himself in Brazil and later killed himself in Petrópolis, along with his wife, unable to continue because, as he'd once said, one's language is one's identity and without it, meaning one's language, a person loses track of themselves, just as I've lost track of myself, even though a wife isn't the same as a language, I think, it's close enough, and I've become adrift, un-selved, because without her who am I, I think, ignoring my own question, returning once more to the subject of anti-Semitism and nothing has shaped modern Jewish thought more than anti-Semitism, I think, sipping my coffee, because a Jew's identity is inextricably linked to the way Jews are seen by others, hence shaping the way Jews see themselves, and there's nothing *more* Jewish, I think, than anti-Semitism, the subject of course, not the hating, yes, anti-Semitism a subject Jews love to contemplate and ponder, something Kleist elaborated on when I found her outside her cottage amid the blizzard, celebrating the completion of what she vowed would be her *final collection,* works meant to speak for the *hordes of invisible dead,* murdered Poles who *spoke through her* or she *spoke through them,* I forget which, point is I found her outside in nothing but a bathrobe and boots, knee deep in snow, hands aloft, one grasping an empty bottle and the other her ubiquitous pipe. Save some pockets of light, day had ceased, and Kleist's wails, resounding for hours, hadn't registered, it simply hadn't dawned on me the cries were from a person, certainly not Kleist, because my mind was muddled; days spent endlessly pacing the single room of the cottage in my pale-yellow slippers, rationing my coffee, looking over legal pads riddled with notes on Bordeaux and Montaigne and Montaigne's footman Brismontier, as well as the copious titles accumulated like mounds of rubble and I felt myself becoming unraveled; the inflexible winds, the banality of my own mind, all of it prompted an agitation I hadn't anticipated and what was I even doing at the

Zybècksz Archives, I wondered, who was I to think I could write a book about Montaigne? Clearly, I was an *imposter,* an *intellectual grifter,* a *counterfeit scholar,* a host of terrible names all amounting to *phony,* and I reminded myself this was only the *looming lack of coffee* talking, that indeed the greatest artists throughout history had been tormented by insecurity and self-doubt and why would I be any different, I thought, and wasn't my self-doubt perhaps a sign of unrealized genius? I had as much a right to occupy a fellowship cottage at the Horner Institute as anyone, Kleist included, and my book, I thought, once complete, would be a towering wall of scholarship, difficult to approach, harder to ascend, wholly original in its design, but once admitted, a universe would emerge like a solar flare or the birth of a galaxy, yes, I thought, *the birth of a galaxy* and sure, only the strong would survive, but deep inside a colossus burgeoned, and just because I *envisioned* the book but hadn't yet *written* the book, hadn't in fact even begun *writing* the book, didn't mean the book didn't exist, I thought, because the groundwork had been laid, the seeds planted, and to conceive *hundreds* of titles for a book but *no* book seemed the pinnacle of cruelty. These were the arguments I was having with myself: one moment a fraud, the next a genius on the brink of revelation, pacing in circles, attended by the soft padding of my pale-yellow slippers, my thoughts dark and defeated, and that very morning, nursing my last cup of coffee, all of my beans exhausted, savoring every drop, I considered Kleist, wondered if she were safe in her next-door cottage and likewise should I escape the confines of my own to see about borrowing some ersatz coffee, should I stoop so low as to drink that muck, the grounds themselves never smelling of coffee but of sorrow and surrender, and I'd yet to meet a person who claimed to enjoy ersatz or instant coffee and not feel a sense of unmitigated pity, and merely *entertaining* the notion of asking to borrow ersatz or instant coffee reeked of indignity and defeat, and the cries outside suddenly registered, muffled moans peppered with German and I peered through the window to observe the figure of Kleist waving a bottle, howling supplications (or denunciations) to the heavens, furious gusts hissing along the window as squalls of snow, like impatient galaxies, spiraled past. Kleist attempted to stand in place, her frame slumped against the wind in solitary battle. I slipped on my boots and ventured outside, quickly realized hers were not cries of anguish but celebration. It's complete, she howled, finished! Kleist shaking the bottle over her mouth attempting to root out the last drops of schnapps, brandy, vermouth, whatever she'd imbibed, you hear me, she said, finished! I congratulated her, pulled the sleeve of her bathrobe, suggested we go inside and Kleist, her face like a condor, her nose dignified and pronounced, smiled, and it was the most knowing smile I'd ever seen, a smile which declared: *I've seen the abyss and returned from the abyss,* a smile which displayed an endurance of something I'd never understand. Again, I insisted we go inside, and her eyes sparkled in defiance. I can finally escape, she declared, crying then laughing, laughing then crying, perhaps both, I can finally leave *all of this*, Kleist hurling the bottle which was instantly consumed by the encroaching dark, and I was certain in Kleist's mind, *all of this* meant North America or the Horner Institute but she swiftly corrected that notion, explained *all of this* meant the world, the universe, existence entire. Kleist cackled. Kleist grunted. Kleist inquired, apropos of nothing, if I knew what the strongest element in the universe was and I, not giving it much thought, said marble, corrected myself, said steel. Kleist guffawed as snow gathered around our ankles, both of us absurd in our identical Horner-issued bathrobes which bore, upon the right breast, the profile of Desmond Horner Tanner, and Kleist reached into the pocket of that selfsame bathrobe for a pouch of tobacco and again I proposed we go inside, urged her to show me her new sculptures because really, I said, the winds were staggering. *Stupidity,* shouted Kleist, attempting to pack the pipe which to my mind was an exercise in madness, her ancient claws trembling while flakes of tobacco fluttered skyward and she was undeterred because she was prouder and more zealous, more entrenched than anyone I'd ever known, and Kleist somehow managed to get enough tobacco into the pipe to pursue *lighting* the pipe, an evident success because, after being crouched over, she faced me, exhaled a wisp of spicy smoke, and happily retorted, *stupidity,* stupidity is the strongest element in the universe. She smacked her lips: idiot dreamers might say *beauty* or *art* or the *human spirit,* but no, she moaned, stupidity is by far the strongest element in the universe and my *final collection* is my definitive assault against stupidity which, I realize, won't do anything (how can it?) because stupidity is unrivaled, unequivocally so, and my sculptures will do nothing more than *acknowledge* the stupidity and *denounce* the stupidity, no more than point out the *fundamental* and *grotesque absurdity* of stupidity, and perhaps that's enough. Art is not the cure, she said, art is merely a respite, a narrow island in an ocean of horror, a million paintings or poems or sculptures, none of them enough to hold off the torrent of stupidity growing every day, none of them enough to bring a shred of justice, none of them enough to avenge even a single one of those murdered souls, Jakub Witkowski, for example, from Vilna, or Wladyslaw Nowak from Danzig, whose sharp and minimal works I've sculpted *for* him or *through* him and are, I hazard to believe, created *by* him, yes, she said, her eyes sparkling, her lips purple and pale, the dead spoke and I listened. *Me,* she said, the *artistic surrogate* to those young murdered Poles all killed by stupidity. And while creating this, my *final collection,* I finally understood that rapture was not the subject of my work and never had been, it was stupidity, stupidity all along, because one of stupidity's tricks is its ability to cloak itself, often as its opposite, and people like to dress it up, call it fascism, capitalism, communism, whatever rotten conviction they can muster a name for and which they're either staunchly for or against, in short, whatever dogma they're able to categorize and label, and all of them amount to the same thing which is *stupidity,* all of them mere spokes in the wheel of *stupidity* because stupidity isn't simply *not knowing,* no, stupidity is the *pretense of* knowing which is arguably worse, stupidity is *feigning* knowledge while knowing nothing, perhaps *less* than nothing, because a stupid person's knowledge is a *negation* of knowing, a *willing disregard* of knowing, a knowing *in deficit* and this *affectation of knowing* is the main ingredient of the *most successfully stupid* and naturally someone who *pretends* to know will never make the effort to *truly know* because *pretending to know* is so much easier than *knowing* and the subsequent energy it requires in order to actually *know*, whereas stupidity is *so easy* it practically requires nothing at all and stupidity is the opposite of truth; stupidity is hubris and audacity, it's unbridled cynicism and the enemy of good and it, meaning stupidity, plagues the ghouls of this world who want nothing more than to rule all of us and this has never changed and never will and Kleist, unaffected by the roaring winds, pulled on her pipe. Hours ago, she said, I completed my collection, *Die Stiefel der Dummheit*; my final *assault,* my final *insult,* she added, laughing at the ridiculousness of the English language, loving the English language, she said, for its ability to bend shapes and, if one wanted, a person could justify virtually anything they said simply by speaking in English. In any case, she continued, my final *assault,* my final *insult* to stupidity is complete and I gazed at the imperial breadth of Kleist's face, the scythes of her eyes, the ravines which spoke a thousand nameless trials and I couldn't help but think of my last cup of coffee, the notes of citrus and rose, the way I'd prolonged and stretched that last cup in order to enjoy it as much as possible, and how long had it been since savoring that cup, I wondered, five, perhaps six hours, surely longer than I'd gone in years without coffee and simply considering this a sharp headache, cloaked in dread, emerged. Meanwhile Kleist was elaborating upon the *paradox of stupidity*, how stupidity was the most powerful force in the universe, not because of any inherent strength, she pointed out, but in fact the opposite, stupidity's strength lay in its *weakness* and *deceptiveness* and really, she asked, raising her voice above the gusts, is there anything more underhanded and fraudulent than stupidity, the *elusiveness* of stupidity, the *chimerical nature* of stupidity which is, of course, the *paradox of stupidity*, because one is never sure if it, meaning stupidity, is actually as stupid as it portends and thus one relaxes, one lets down their guard, one's self-belief grows, all the while stupidity musters its strength for the final assault and with this stupidity wins, as it will always win until the end of days because, as I've said, she said, stupidity is the single strongest element in the universe. I heartily agreed, reiterated the need for warmth, the pressing need to get inside, because, I said, *look at us*, nothing more than bathrobes and boots, ill equipped for the current conditions, conditions getting worse by the second and Kleist, drunk and aloof, licked her thin lips, explained *this*, meaning the current conditions, was no worse than where she'd grown up in Austria, in Liezen, near the foothills of Hochwildstelle, where the winters weren't especially brutal but they weren't anything to shrug off either, colder than this here, she said, unfolding a hand, allowing the snow to fill her palm and oddly this reminded Kleist of stupidity or her mother or perhaps both, because her mother's animosity of stupidity, she said, was the wellspring from which her *own* animosity of stupidity had been born, and this animosity, meaning my mother's, she said, was a silent animosity, rigid and unspoken, which is no doubt stronger than an animosity wielded with words because an unspoken hatred finds ways to conduct itself in more wicked ways, she said, in my mother's case the contempt she felt for the outside world, her contempt an extension of her physical demeanor. She had me late in life, Kleist confessed, expelling a cloud of smoke, my parents had tried for years, had gone to doctors and finally given up, then suddenly my mother was pregnant and soon enough I was born, a miracle and a curse, a curse because what kind of parent can someone be who's survived the endless breadth of horror that was Europe in the twenties, thirties, and forties and by this I mean a Jew born in Europe between, say, 1920 and 1945, and what rotten goddamn luck that was, and Kleist laughed and spat, a span of close to thirty years, she said, where it was the pinnacle of misfortune to be born a Jew anywhere on the continent of Europe, and if you happened to have been afflicted or cursed, that is, a Jew born anywhere on the continent of Europe between the years 1920 and 1945 and couldn't find a way to *leave* the continent of Europe you were doomed, meaning fucked, and Kleist, simulating the blade of a knife, ran a finger along her throat, laughed again, added that none of this was exclusive to Jews of course, but applied as well to homosexuals, Romani, Communists, and plenty of others too, and if I had any advice, she said, it'd be to simply not be born on the continent of Europe as a Jew or a Gypsy or any of those countless others between 1920 and 1945, simple as that, because Europe, during those years, was collectively worshipping at the altar of stupidity and my contempt for stupidity was the greatest lesson my mother bestowed because she failed terrifically in every other area and I was trembling from the cold, grinding my teeth; snow had found its way into my boots, glacial rivulets running toward my feet and still Kleist wouldn't budge, the winds in fact hadn't impaired Kleist but inspired her, inciting her to speak on an array of topics like goodness and virtue and how can a person contain goodness or virtue, she asked, how can someone contain any respect for the sovereignty of life when they've seen life molested, watched the *ease* with which life is molested? Something inside my mother was dislodged before I was born, said Kleist, my father too, hence I grew up with a mother and father who contained enormous fissures inside of them, fissures which grew with time until they were more fissure than human, and ultimately the fissures swallowed them whole. They were both prisoners during the war, she said, drawing on her pipe, in *Gusen II,* a subcamp of Gusen I, which was a subcamp of the larger death machine of Mauthausen, camps for Austrian Jews but also Italian and French Jews, and my mother watched both of her parents worked to death in *Gusen II,* the life expectancy no more than six months. My father was lucky in that his parents died fast, killed at the start of the war; a lineup one day in the Leopoldstadt ghetto for a head count, a typical custom to humiliate the Jews, line them up, bark their names before having them clean the pavement, and some ss officer who'd had a rotten day shot my grandparents with no more thought than wiping the mud from a loafer, and five long years later their son, my father, was liberated from *Gusen II,* along with his wife, my mother, yes, somehow they survived the forced labor, the rampant disease, the constant threat of death and together they weighed no more than eighty-one kilograms, can you imagine, both my parents weighing no more than a pair of dogs? Behind Kleist, I watched the smoke leave her chimney, nudged my head toward the warmth and she paid no attention because she was rummaging the past, combing the landscape for shards of glass amid the rubble of her youth. Growing up, the way my mother endured her grief, said Kleist, coming home from school I'd find her sitting in the kitchen attempting to take up as little space as possible, attempting to collapse inside herself, seeking to become an absence of space. And the mood swings: the ecstasy, the anguish, her feeble smiles at life's joys replaced with seething contempt for everyone and everything with nothing in between, no *room* for anything in between, her detached tyranny, her exorbitant memory lapses, one moment berating Europe's *loss of innocence* and *black destiny,* the next asking how my dinner was, was it warm enough, did I need more bread, her docility scarcely masking her rage, her meekness unable to disguise her hidden torrents, because my mother had existed for decades *inside herself,* a wilderness populated by ghosts or devils, probably both, and my father was soft spoken and meek, a machinist by trade, he attempting to calm my mother during one of her *spells,* mollifying her any way he could, making tea, escorting her to the bedroom where she wouldn't emerge for days, my father not too rational himself, no better or worse, simply a different assortment of traumas, and both died in the span of months, she said, not long after I'd gone to university to study art, as if they'd held off long enough for me to leave Liezen and begin my life and, like so many others, I'd read the stories of survivors leading perfectly *normal* lives, *happy* and *successful* lives, and was baffled, even suspicious. What war had these people been in, I'd thought, in which camp had they been prisoners, because surely no one ever *survives* these things, you *survive* a car accident, I thought, you *survive* a mugging, because even if one walks out, meaning *escapes* or *is liberated* from a place built with the sole purpose of collective murder, they're merely the husk of who they were, every conscious moment suffused with the certainty of what a monstrous species we are because donkeys possess more decency, apes and dogs too, the sheer banality of death, no, of *murder,* because there's nothing more abhorrent and banal than the indignity of murder, she said, of someone choosing your death for you, because the purpose of life is to *elude* death for as long as possible, life in its purest form is the act of *not dying,* and for someone to force your own extinction upon you, negating your existence simply by snapping their fingers or barking a command to some square-jawed minion who never hesitated believing himself a part of something larger and greater than himself, is vile and incomprehensible, yes, she said, murder is despicable, *despicable* not nearly a strong enough word, but they haven't invented a word in any language powerful enough to describe the repugnance of murder because the world is already fraught with peril, the world all sharpened edges and trapdoors: drowning, disease, madness, exposure, the *needlessness* of murder is its most loathsome aspect, because staying alive is arduous enough, dreadfully arduous, and wordlessly my mother instructed me on the stupidity of our species, a stupidity inscribed in the cosmos, in the architecture of our souls, thus a stupidity which can't be escaped nor avoided since it's the most innate aspect of our natures, stupidity etched into each chromosome, nestled inside our bones, and only art or charity or a willingness to *admit* one's own stupidity can lift us above the muck of ourselves, can wage anything resembling battle against the *curse of our species*. Kleist sighed, emptied her pipe, suggested I follow her inside for another bottle of brandy and perhaps a look at *Die Stiefel der Dummheit*, her final collection, which translated as *The Boots of Stupidity*, and nothing prepared me for the immensity of her collection, nothing hinted at the work created mere yards from my cottage, works so colossal I suspected the roof would need to be removed to extract them. Crossing the threshold, I faced enormous works of granite and marble, two smaller sculptures of metal, steel I think, and without even trying I noticed the can of *instant coffee* sitting on the shelf of the kitchenette and I felt hope rise, felt a surge of joy pierce my soul. *Sit*, Kleist instructed, shaking the snow from her boots, poking her pipe in my shoulder, forcing me into the only chair inside the cabin while she excused herself to *take a piss* and swiftly she disappeared and though Kleist's sculptures interested me, coffee interested me more, hence I stood back up, negotiated around a massive creature boasting scales and talons, advanced toward the can of coffee to make a quick audit, simultaneously heartened and repulsed, because lifting the lid I saw the can was untouched, completely full, but it reeked of swill and sorrow, prompting memories of all the terrible cups of coffee I'd suffered in my life, the coffee I'd settled for when nothing else would do, and *fucking Christ,* I thought, *of course* I would drink it, I had no choice, but the grounds were darker than the darkest shit, blacker than a starless night, coffee grounds frozen and defrosted in transit, I imagined, lingering endlessly somewhere on a store shelf, grounds lacking nuance and grace as well as the diligence and zeal true coffee demands, and I considered the delivery of my Indonesian coffee, meaning how far it had come, meaning how close had it gotten before the roads were closed, the foothills impassable, before the driver was forced to turn around and would Linda even alert me to its eventual arrival and, additionally, I also wondered, how long does a blizzard typically last? Seconds later, Kleist reappeared, the belt of her bathrobe replaced by a leather belt cinched around her waist. I returned to the chair while observing Kleist flit haphazardly around the cabin, gazed at the blue-green veins of her legs, the gnarled knees jutting beneath the bathrobe's hem, and with a pair of fingerless gloves Kleist began caressing an enormous sculpture of marble, the obvious centerpiece of her collection, while exhaling clouds of fragrant smoke. This is *Medusa's Apprentice,* she said, *Uczeń Meduzy* in Polish, made by Nadia Poltorzycka, a young artist who died of typhoid in Bergen-Belsen, a beautiful woman whose parents recognized her talent and saved what money they could to send her to the prestigious *Akademia Sztuk Pięknych* in Kraków in 1937. Her work was heavily indebted to Rodin, just as every modern sculptor including myself is heavily indebted to Rodin, whether they admit it or not, in short, it refutes the hard outlines, focusing instead on volume and void, the synthesis of matter and absence and Kleist, circling the enormous creature, caressed the scales of marble and, though my understanding of sculpture was scant, I felt certain I was gazing at the work of a master because it made me *feel,* what I wasn't sure, but that was beside the point because naming or exploring the feeling was futile when all that mattered, I thought, was the feeling itself, and I recalled E. E. Cummings, who said: *since feeling is first / who pays any attention / to the syntax of things,* indeed, I thought, who pays any attention to the syntax, meaning the garnish, meaning the sugary patina, meaning the trappings of lesser minds predisposed to inspecting the feeling and cataloging the feeling instead of letting the feeling simply *be,* and I wholly agreed, because contemplating something beautiful and grotesque, ecstatic and bleak, turbulent and serene, allowing the work to consume one's spirit, was the intention after all, and how kindred were sculpture and literature, I thought, literature and music, I also thought, music and painting, all those modes of expression wondrously aligned to affirm life and touch the soul, and Kleist, with her two aged hands, had bequeathed a stagnant piece of marble the gift of movement because *Medusa's Apprentice* swayed even as it stayed in place, the scales of the monster, sharp and immaculate, thrilling in their graceful

exactness. After studying for two years in Kraków, Kleist continued, Poltorzycka began experimenting, sculpting small pieces
using soapstone and alabaster, less expensive materials and easier to acquire, but nothing was completed because she was sent
to Bergen-Belsen and didn't survive more than six months and
all that remained were the notes and sketches and, based on
those notes and sketches, said Kleist, I probed and expanded
and magnified the early work of Nadia Poltorzycka, I envisioned
the work she *would've* made had she not been murdered by stupidity. Kleist located a bottle of brandy, unscrewed the cap,
poured a glass, and nudged it into my hand. I studied the obsession Nadia had with Greek myth, her interest in classical sculpture, especially her fascination with *The Dying Gaul,* meshed
with *Fauvism* and later, of course, the work of Rodin, yes, she
said, I saw the work of Poltorzycka with blazing clarity and as
Kleist held forth I felt my limbs thaw, felt my blood begin to cir-
culate; I watched Kleist's shadow expand and swell across the
ceiling, her shadow and the shadow of *Medusa's Apprentice*
waltzing above, and perhaps it was the *looming lack of coffee* or
the disgust I felt toward my book-length essay but I was giddy
and overcome, tired and exhilarated, feelings typically opposed
suddenly dancing like the creatures overhead. Soon enough
though and my attention returned to the can of *instant coffee,*
snatching a glance each time Kleist disappeared behind *Medusa's
Apprentice,* and I considered the contempt a person must have to
put coffee inside of a can, no better than those bricks of freeze-
dried grounds my parents would buy and throw into the

refrigerator with as much regard as a stick of butter or can of soda, buying coffee with no more thought than a pair of socks and how much malice could be contained inside a human heart, I wondered, how much hatred of beauty? Had my parents never considered Selim II, I thought, the notorious Turkish sultan, better known as *Selim the Drunk,* celebrated for his generous disposition and love of pleasure, who sent a detachment of Janissaries across the Ottoman Empire, eventually to Tunis, each endowed with purses holding ten thousand ducats apiece, to find the legendary *Şehzade Roast,* a bean long rumored to be the best-tasting and most robust coffee bean in the world, a bean endowed with the properties of a mythical potion, the *Şehzade Roast* reputedly enjoyed by the great shahs and oracles of the Safavids, relished in Morocco, Mogadishu, and along the Horn of Africa, believed to be a powerful aphrodisiac, drunk amid the harems of Abu al-Mutawakkil, worshipped equally in Fez and Tangier, traded for slaves along the Gulf of Patras, and despite the grand vizier's arguments against the expedition Selim II wouldn't be swayed, thus the Janissaries departed and never returned, the last correspondence claimed they were in Tabriz, in northwestern Iran, said they'd discovered endless fields rich with *Şehzade trees,* squat, tawny, and vigorous, though by the time the message was delivered Selim II was long dead, and his son, Selim III, the current sultan, wary by nature, mistrusted the authenticity of the news, later confirming the Janissaries had been captured, imprisoned, castrated, and ultimately seized as part of Ramadan Pasha's harem and no one has ever proven the

Şehzade bean exists, most historians concluding it was a colorful fabrication, a fiction for one empire to gain advantage over another, and *this,* I told myself, was coffee, *this* was the drink whose history was as rich and expansive as the drink itself, awash with the richest cultures and most opulent stories, the dominion of art and the soul, the fortunes and calamities of history, subjects that interested my parents not one iota, yes, I escaped my hometown first chance I got, not due to my parents' antipathy toward coffee, although privately I'd always felt my parents' antipathy toward coffee symbolized their antipathy toward everything else, but I simply couldn't stay in the same city where my mother and father made their terrible coffee and drank their terrible coffee as if it were a chore, an act with no joy, simply one of the many duties they faithfully performed in the tedious routine of their lives, akin to the way they took umbrage at my interest in books, even though they claimed to *like* books, even though my parents were supposedly *educated,* they always held a strange apprehension toward books, literature in particular, as if a book required a practical purpose printed somewhere on the front or the back, preferably in bold, otherwise they became suspicious, and it was my obsession with reading that puzzled my parents, my affection for the poets of antiquity, followed by the Lake Poets, followed soon after by Tacitus and Cicero, then Bellow and Bowles, Cather and Crane, all of which preceded my Kafka phase and subsequent Proust phase, all of it troubled them, my love of books, literature especially, that baffled my parents, because the practical purpose of literature is ineffable, hidden too, requiring an effort from the reader with no explanation or guaranteed outcome, yes, literature is most remarkable in that it's unique to each person, meaning the things I felt or understood from reading Woolf, for instance, or Milton, for instance, or Musil, also for instance, among untold others, all which I'd consumed with an intoxication bordering on rapture, were particular to me, meaning anyone who'd read the same book would've read an entirely *different* book because literature, I always thought, was a wordless prayer, even though it's made up *entirely* of words, I thought, still, it's more akin to a wordless prayer, to transcendence and euphoria or, if not euphoria, then at least the *pursuit* of euphoria, yes, literature the earthly attempt of attaining these things and the beauty isn't in the attainment (which is impossible) but the *pursuit of the attainment,* the moment which dissolves as soon as you, meaning the reader, devour the words and are touched, yes, I always thought, and most people, including my parents, couldn't stomach the nebulous nature of literature and, by consequence, literature's eternal glory, because they wanted the practical purpose of the book printed either on the front or the back, preferably in bold, in order to be instructed on what the *book was about* as well as what they'd *get out of the book,* as if literature needed a utilitarian objective in order to exist and tell that to Melville, I thought, or Coleridge, I also thought, or poor murdered Bruno Schulz, I thought thirdly, because what I *loved* most about books is what my parents *despised* most about books, yes, the pursuit of a practical purpose, because literature is inscrutable, verging on mystical, and furthermore, I always thought, literature provides only a fleeting glimpse, never the entire view, literature a mere *suggestion,* I always thought, literature a *suggestion* and the reader supplies the materials, meaning the context and the imagination, to satisfy and complete the *suggestion,* most being unprepared or ill equipped or perfectly disinterested in bringing the context and the imagination to what they read because most people, my parents included, want a *coloring book* not literature, most people, my parents included, want a *smartphone* not literature, and literature demands you meet it halfway and you, meaning the reader, must bring the context and imagination; literature, such a lonely and noble endeavor, I always thought, lonely for the writer *and* the reader, and this doleful solitude was part of literature's allure which my parents eschewed and thought me strange for seeking, my parents always *wary* and *suspicious* of literature as they brewed their shitty coffee and drank their shitty coffee and as a consequence I'd minimized my enthusiasm for books whenever I was around my parents, always downplayed my passion in order to appear more engaged with the *real world,* as my parents called it, which, to me, was the furthest thing from reality, because I saw what they called the *real world* and thought, *no thanks,* saw what they called the *real world* and felt baffled and ill at ease, a whole childhood pondering if there were another world, a *substitute* world, either *more real* or *less real,* either-or, as long as it wasn't *this,* meaning the *real world,* because I was insatiable when it came to books, and each writer I discovered introduced me to another writer, another book, so that it became an endless obsession, more immense and elusive the more I read, a frustrating quandary, one which could only be solved, I realized, by reading more, reading incessantly until one died, yes, I think, and Montaigne solidified this obsession, gave his posthumous blessing on the unwavering belief that the most worthwhile life was the one dedicated to the pursuit of knowledge and so behind their backs I plummeted into literature, yes, *plummeted,* because literature, I'd felt, was the highest form of expression, literature like hiero-glyphics fossilized in stone, literature like sorcery and damna-tion and the sole reason for existence. And eventually I escaped, went to college, studied philosophy and ethics, read Diderot and Descartes; eventually discovered Montaigne which changed ev-erything, for better or for worse, oftentimes worse, nonetheless my love and ardor for Montaigne was the catalyst for writing *Montaigne and the Lugubrious Cherubs,* and Kleist, growing more cantankerous, eyes wizened by brandy, weaved between the pieces in her collection, dodging chunks of stone and discarded chisels, taking sips from the bottle, smacking her lips and mak-ing oaths, and I gazed at the can of instant coffee, thinking, *this'll do,* thinking a can of freeze-dried shit that at one time *resembled* coffee was better than nothing, better than the dark brandy Kleist had forced into my hand which I pretended to sip as she rhapsodized about the *paradox of stupidity,* the burden of tyr-anny and how Nadia Poltorzycka, unencumbered by her corpo-real body, perhaps an angel or a ghost, had spoken to Kleist, in-structing Kleist on the monsters and the serpents huddled inside the caverns of our souls, in short, the works she *would've* sculpted had she not been murdered, poor young Nadia filling her *Kraków notebooks* with sketches of golems and minotaurs, hyenas with the wings of vultures, yes, Kleist insisted, Nadia spoke to me and through my hands I carved *Medusa's Apprentice* and I tilted my head in an attempt to locate the head of the sculpture, part bird, part reptile, whose upturned beak grazed the ceiling of the cottage. Kleist continued taking swigs, making laps, weaving between her works; each time she vanished I'd locate the can of *instant coffee* and contemplate the slew of coffee-making procedures I'd enjoyed in my life, the dampening of the filter, the grinding of the beans, the percolation of my first coffeemaker like the softest but most persistent of rains, the gentle thrust of the plunger on a French press; I envisioned black coffee, creamy coffee, coffee with milk, coffee without, the *café de olla* drunk in Mexico and made in a clay pot or the Turks who used wooden pestles to grind their coffee in mortars; I envisioned the tiny espresso cups which contained the dark, aromatic liquid sending magnetic jolts into the blood, the custom of coffee-making an affirmation no doubt of one's passion for life. In college, following my Walser phase and Kafka phase, a year or so into my Proust phase, shortly before my Montaigne phase, I'd discovered Proust's deep relationship with coffee, his profound devotion to the *Corcellet* brand of coffee which, according to his housekeeper, had to be purchased daily from the *Rue de Lévis*, in the seventeenth arrondissement, the *Corcellet* coffee not only Proust's favorite brand but, from what I'd read, the only brand he would accept. Freshly purchased. Freshly roasted. Poured in a

Corcellet brand cup in fact, no other cup would do because Proust insisted drinking his *Corcellet* coffee in a *Corcellet* cup, Proust performing this ceremony of coffee-drinking in seclusion, a bib fanned across his chest, feet swaddled in silk slippers as he read *Le Figaro,* the very newspaper he once paid to publish his own anonymous and glowing review of *In Search of Lost Time,* where he wrote, in regards to *Swann's Way,* the book *almost suggests the fourth dimension of the Cubists.* Something so sad and tragic about Proust eager for his genius to be discovered, just as all geniuses wish to be discovered and almost always regret it. Reading about Proust confirmed my love for both coffee and books and invariably I envisioned Proust drinking cup after cup of *Corcellet* coffee, admiring the cork-lined walls of his room, his mind suspended between the conscious and the unconscious, and meanwhile Kleist was haranguing me about virtue, grace, and the unassailable *wall of stupidity,* an oil-spilt sea, she said, a dark so dense it was bereft of shadows, a gathering storm that would infect the masses, creating a phalanx, an *army of stupidity,* fixed on the *complete destruction of civilization,* annihilating every continent, eventually the entire earth, and despite her intoxication Kleist was unflinching, taking ravenous gulps, tossing wood on the fire, the gusts outside howling threats like an approaching invader, Kleist suddenly bringing up the subject of Ernst and his *nudism,* how her husband had been one of the founders of the *Nudists* at the Horner Institute in the '70s, years before they'd met, nudism being a popular movement that pervaded much of the Horner Institute in the middle years of the 1970s, and these

Nudists of the '70s were serious thinkers, Kleist insisted, nudity wasn't just a youthful impulse or empty gesture, serious work and serious research were still expected, but the *powers that be* were frightened of the institute's name getting sullied, afraid the Horner Institute would unwittingly become a *nudist colony* or, at the very least, be seen as one because they'd felt, rather absurdly, that it was a slippery slope. Ernst was ardent about his nudism, said Kleist, Ernst felt nudism was a moral imperative and the summers before we met and fell in love Ernst spent climbing *Karwendel* and *Ruchenköpfe,* enjoying a picnic upon their peaks, sunning himself in the nude while contemplating whether the Bavarian Alps were growing or shrinking. The *Nudists of the '70s* had taken over large swathes of the Zybècksz Archives for three consecutive seasons, said Kleist, but serious work was still expected and serious work was indeed completed because the *Nudists of the '70s* were first and foremost intellectuals and scholars, serious thinkers before anything else, artists and writers before nudists, inventors and painters before their practice of *nudism,* all of this, meaning the work itself, took precedence over the nudity because the *Nudists of the '70s* and the *Nudist movement* meant nothing without the ideas and work that compelled them, merely an empty vessel, an anemic trope, because the *Nudists of the '70s*, said Kleist, understood how quickly the flesh fails, how swiftly the human form frays and what remained was the work, the *Nudists of the '70s* fully understanding the blights of the body and it was the work and only the work that possessed the power to attain perfection, and the *Nudists of the '70s,* which included

Temporada and Rambuski, who'd written extensively on William Blake's angels as well as celebrated assessments of Blake's relief etchings, they too had dappled in *nudism* and furthermore, claimed Kleist, Tijn Auersberg, the theoretical physicist, yes, she gushed, him too, Auersberg's nudism practiced during the winter terms in the harshest periods of winter. In fact, Kleist continued, the *Rare Manuscript Room* and the Annex adjacent to the *Tsypkin House of Holocaust Research* were both built in the nude by the *Nudists* during the *Nudism of the '70s,* chiefly the summers of '74 and '75, and the Zybècksz Archives were considered as a World Heritage site during those years, both in 1974 *and* 1975, years, I might point out, when the *Nudists of the '70s* were running rampant, not in *spite* of the *Nudists,* but *because* of the *Nudists,* and I misspoke, said Kleist, because the *Nudists* weren't running anywhere, certainly not rampant, they were simply creating art and conducting research, in short, getting in touch with their souls while in the nude which, of course, made the *non-nudists* of the '70s resentful because what could be more boorish than a brilliant group of thinkers painting and sculpting, researching and creating art, as well as erecting the *Rare Manuscript Room* and the *Annex* while their cocks and tits were exposed, cocks and tits gazing at the breadth of blue sky, and a short distance away sat the fully clothed, evidently more conservative fellows begrudging the *nudists* and their sense of freedom and don't misunderstand, said Kleist, many of the fully clothed fellows of the '70s, meaning the *non-nudists* of the '70s, completed important work, but nothing compared to the accomplishments of the *Nudists themselves.* Furthermore, Kleist said, the bust of Marx, at one time the centerpiece of the *Pleasure Gardens,* before the *Pleasure Gardens* erupted into what they are now, a jungle, a maze, an erratic, unwieldy sprawl of disunity clawing their way into the knotty foothills which, though possessing pockets of beauty, mostly by accident, are nothing like the *Pleasure Gardens* of yesteryear, the understated and synchronized *Pleasure Gardens* of the '70s where a cohesive, underlying concept was apparent to anyone, even the dim-witted or blind, yes, *that* great bust of Marx, engulfed now in ivy, was indeed sculpted in the nude by Hilde Schjetne, the celebrated Bergen sculptor and polymath, yes, and Ezekiel Fernández, chess master and architect of *Bishop's Folly,* that peerless opening imitated ubiquitously the world over, he too, said Kleist, was a nudist who counted himself among the *Nudists of the '70s* and I'd heard mention of the *Nudists of the '70s* before I'd met Kleist, I thought, before I arrived as a fellow and, later, after my arrival, departing both Tanner Rooms following a day of research, I'd pass the *Rare Manuscript Room* and the *Annex,* long, two-story complexes, complete with Russian cupolas forever in disrepair, leaning toward the earth like grieving widows, their onion domes like limpid pillows and even in my wildest imagination I couldn't perceive building such structures in the nude and Kleist began tapping her pipe against one of the smaller sculptures, *Slaying of Faith,* she called it, sculpted by Wladyslaw Nowak, the *Prince from Danzig,* as he was dubbed by his fellow Jews, at least the Jews who cared about art, Nowak's work a study in compression and restraint, Nowak's work buried beneath the dust of history when Europe was overtaken by stupidity and Nowak was murdered by that very same stupidity while attempting to escape Treblinka and my reverie is broken by the chirp of the *smartphone*, tossed on the floor over an hour ago, and I curse my failure at silencing that infernal object, something which should be the easiest of tasks, I think, sipping my coffee, but it seems the further we slide or stumble or flounder into the future, the more humanity retreats and regresses, the more we become infants, idle and illiterate about the objects we've created, and I gaze at the *smartphone* chirping on the floor of the third bedroom and I recall my students stabbing the screens of their *smartphones* as if they relied upon these devices to generate the very oxygen necessary for their survival, stabbing the screens of their *smartphones* as if it were an act of life-giving sustenance, without which they would surely die, endlessly scrolling the surface of their *smartphones,* refusing to capitulate for even the briefest moment. And I approach the phone, see that it's Marcel and waver between picking up and not picking up, between talking to my son who, after all, just lost his mother, meaning my wife, or allowing the voicemail he'll most certainly leave to be collected with all the voicemails numbering, who knows, thirteen or fourteen by now, and I decide to answer the *smartphone* because I love Marcel, truly, the problem being the parts of myself I like the least, the traits which've made my life the most difficult, the stubbornness and boundless enthusiasm, the undiluted fervor, are the traits Marcel nurtures and amplifies, and I never cautioned him, I think, staring at the *smartphone,* I never warned him about the dangers of passion and ardor because day by day the world chips away at passion and ardor, the world, meaning society and other people, diminishes passion and ardor, devotion, zeal, call it what you want, the world annihilates these things if you don't keep them hidden away, I think, because the world, meaning society and other people, are the *enemies* of ardor and zeal, and I never told him this, never instructed him to hide what was most precious, a huge disservice, I think, because my own parents knew enough to instruct me on the world's cynicism and indifference purely by their own cynicism and indifference, yes, I think, my parents unknowingly prepared me for the world's indifference because the world's hostility toward passion is simply staggering, and no one wants to hear someone rant about *house music* or *downtempo dance music* for hours on end, I think, not my son's friends, not even his father, no, I think, keep what you most love secreted away, and I pray he doesn't want to rhapsodize to me about *deep house* or *downtempo dance music,* because I haven't the stamina, I haven't the fortitude, and if he begins a sermon on *deep house* or *downtempo dance music* there's a good chance I'll throw the *smartphone* against the wall because Marcel, I realize, is simply a younger version of me, and I picture him ordering a *turntable* or a *mixer* costing thousands of dollars because, he'd think, *fuck it,* just as I'd thought, *fuck it,* when I'd ordered the *Nuova Simonelli* espresso machine because my students were slothful and aloof and my wife was dying and my bovine-faced students were struggling for oxygen, the teachers too, everyone, I felt, trying desperately to breathe and I'd begun suspecting the *smartphones* were the culprit, the *smartphones* stealing oxygen and causing inertia on a cosmic scale, and now she's dead, I think, holding the *smartphone,* and I can't walk past her closet without a nervous breakdown or some sort of conniption, because for decades I defined myself through my wife's eyes and now that she's dead I can't see myself, can't see who I am, and for *fuck's sake,* I think, seeing Marcel's name quivering on the *smartphone,* why is the despair so arduous, the existential misery so intractable, why does the pain go away only to return sharper and more unyielding? And I think of the times I didn't have room for Marcel or worse, didn't *make* room for Marcel, how I was consumed with my book-length essay and later, following my return from the Berkshires, consumed, not with the essays of Montaigne or the life of Montaigne or anything remotely involving Montaigne, but countless titles, consumed with wigs, with dueling, with the misadventures of a scandalous Russian and not long after, well, actually, years later, my wife lost her mind, not all at once though, but gradually, over time, which is worse than losing someone suddenly, I think, because watching a person you love, a person who *defines* you, slowly dissolve is a fate worse than death, seeing them wither from inside a protracted agony, a disaster in slow motion, and toward the end came the fucking *spaceships,* terrifying her, which terrified us, meaning me and Marcel, *spaceships* recording us, she insisted, decoding our thoughts, she also insisted, rafts to ferry the dead, she said, *spaceships* filling the sky like raptors or birds of prey, and why did I push him away, I think, why didn't I make room for my own son who, I suddenly think, is exactly like me? Marcel and his endless sermons about dance music being a *refuge* and *celebration* of life, particularly queer culture, something he contemplated as recently as a month ago, I think, holding the still-unanswered *smartphone,* his mother still alive but barely, and Marcel meandering from God-knows-what subject into the celebration of queer culture within dance music, pontificating for thirty-odd minutes about the *celebration of queer culture within dance music* knowing full well I had no interest in the *celebration of queer culture within dance music,* nothing against either queer culture or dance music, I thought, but the human mind can only contain so many interests, the brain inflexibly finite in its concerns, and it was later in the evening, after I'd sedated his mother following one of her outbursts, something that occurred more and more often, usually when I'd tried feeding her, an operation that required untold amounts of stamina and me, straddling the chair beside her, stirring the soup, reassuring her with the sorts of things one says to an infant, *mmm,* I said, *looks delicious,* I said, *smells good,* I added, blowing on the spoon, taking a slurp myself, but she wasn't convinced, distracted as she was by the *spaceships* although by then, meaning that late stage, I'd covered all of the windows with curtains then towels and finally thick blankets which had the opposite intention as she, meaning my now-dead wife, only became more suspicious about what was behind all the towels and thick blankets, as in what are you trying to hide, she'd think, trying to unfasten the towels and thick blankets with lunatic curiosity, as in what is being kept from me and why had this strange man, meaning me, her husband of twenty-plus years, gone to the trouble of covering all of the windows in the house with layers of different materials, namely towels and thick blankets, and the answer to this, in her mind, was *spaceships,* and she'd gotten a grip on the bowl and thrown it across the kitchen, sending soup everywhere and it was a plastic bowl because I'd learned my lesson by then, but still, it was simply too much and I'd sedated her with the tranquilizers she'd been prescribed for her *fits of unreason* as one of the doctors had called it, *fits of unreason,* I thought at the time, what a great title for a book-length essay, *fits of unreason,* the term the doctor used to describe my wife's tantrums or meltdowns, when my wife, in his words, became *besieged by madness,* when she sensed the walls of existence encroaching or crumbling, and imagine for a moment, the doctor said, the world we perceive with utter lucidity but she, meaning my wife, sees with a diabolical terror, where you and I see a lake or a shopping mall or field of sunflowers, she sees the maw of an enormous, black-souled monster, and hence, he explained, her *fits of unreason,* and ignoring the soup on the floor, the walls, my clothes, I sedated my wife, as much for my own sake as hers because everyday tasks were becoming more difficult; she refused to eat or take baths; I'd surrendered most of the duties to the nurse, and that night, after I'd sedated her (my wife, not the nurse) and cleaned up the soup Marcel stopped by, peeked in her room as he always did, then plopped on the sofa across from me and I released a long sigh which, by then, Marcel was adept at reading, sighs weighed down by exhaustion and guilt and certainly grief. Then, seeing his chance, Marcel spoke about his *new opportunity,* the remix he'd been asked by a friend to make which led to a discourse on the long, storied history of *queer culture celebrated in underground dance music* which, I thought with relief, was something he'd talk about at length, allowing me to drift and nod and feign interest while thinking about things like my wife dying in the next room or my love of coffee from Ethiopia and Indonesia and did I have a preference because both, I reasoned, were easily the best coffee-growing regions on earth but did I prefer one over the other, I wondered, a question I'd posed to myself for years, because coffee from Ethiopia was the most fragrant in my opinion, the smallest beans too, smaller than anywhere else in the world, I thought, and if one placed a coffee bean from Ethiopia beside a coffee bean from anywhere else, say, Colombia or Vietnam or Papua New Guinea, it would make the size of an Ethiopian coffee bean, meaning its diminutiveness, meaning its dainty suppleness, abundantly clear and *motherfucker,* I thought to myself, I'd completely ignored the Rwandan coffee bean and the wonderful coffee grown in Rwanda, utterly fucking disregarded my unequivocal adoration for the Rwandan coffee bean which also ranked among my favorite coffee-growing regions on earth; all of this I considered while Marcel described the remix he'd been asked by a friend to make, his friend known for his ecstatic, maximalist, boundary-hopping songs, dazzling and vibrant, he said, dance music bursting with ideas and if he were forced to describe his friend's music in one word it'd be *Day-Glo,* no, wait, he said, *Queer,* no, wait, he'd said, *two words* were absolutely required to describe his friend's music, and those two words were *Day-Glo* and *Queer* because summarizing his friend's music in one word was simply impossible, even two words were an injustice because he was tempted to use the word *buoyant* too, buoyant as the third word to describe his friend's music, and this friend, DJ *something-or-other,* had entrusted Marcel with remixing his new EP of, in Marcel's words, *Day-Glo, deep house bangers,* songs awash with silky melodies and floating chords as well as dizzy polyrhythms steeped in the history of *queer underground dance music,* laced throughout with gospel samples, disco samples, snatches of older dance music to invoke the history and the *culture of house,* the DNA of his friend's music infused not only with the *queer underground* but the *African American underground* too, protest music born in New York and Chicago and Detroit because the culture of clubbing, said Marcel, was a culture of protest as well as escapism, music born from injustice, because of AIDS, he said, because of *poverty,* he also said, because of *systematic racism,* he added, yes, because *house music is Black music,* and the most sublime means of escaping yourself and the rest of the world along with *hundreds of strangers,* others too who needed to escape both themselves and the rest of the world, thus finding communion on the dance floor, consequently the invention of *house music* which is, in itself, he said, protest music, and Marcel was ecstatic, simply beside himself discussing the remixes he planned to make of DJ *something-or-other's* songs with a fidelity and exactitude that would honor his friend's music. I want to strip away the colors, he continued, I want to expose the bones of the song; Marcel insistent on bringing a minimalism to his friend's maximalist songs which normally, he reiterated, were blissful and euphoric, even a little *kitschy* as well as obviously *Day-Glo* and *Queer, buoyant* too, and through his remix, he'd bring a sense of urban gloom and hypnotic repetition, with hints of smoky jazz, *hints* though, not *out and out* jazz, just enough jazz, Marcel said, that the listener senses the jazz but doesn't realize it's jazz and for the listener, familiar with the original song which, as I've said, he said, is booming and celebratory, to hear the remnants and wisps of that original song but, in my hands, he said, songs made anew, cloaked seamlessly in the atmosphere of a traditional *downtempo house track,* keeping the gospel samples and the layered keyboards but removing the colors, the original song altered and transformed but still affirming its roots in *underground queer culture* and Marcel talked about the *culture of remixes,* talked about craftsmanship and taste, cosmic disco and retro-futurism; he spoke of organs and cymbals and pianos as well as the complex drum patterns requisite to any good dance song, and Marcel, I realize, holding the still-ringing *smartphone,* never remixed his friend's songs because *you-know-who* died, which wasn't a long period but it wasn't short either because there were the days preceding her death leading to the day of her death which led to the days that followed, including the preparation for the funeral as well as the funeral itself, and then, later, sitting shiva for a week, perhaps twelve days in total, too much for a person in the midst of this, meaning the death of one's mother, to remix an album of *celebratory dance music,* even I knew that, and I'm finding it hard to have conversations, I think, even listening to Marcel is a slow, uphill plod, because it's been years since I was fired or retired, depending on the version, and I rarely leave the house, my interactions with the outside world relegated to, well, I think, to nothing, I have *no* interactions with the outside world, only interactions with Marcel and I have no sense of time because the house is in a constant state of darkness or semidarkness, in essence a tomb, due to the towels and sheets I've not neglected, but actually *refused* to remove from the windows, towels and sheets hung to hide the *spaceships* from a person no longer alive, and this *counterfeit night,* as I've begun calling my existence, only aggravates my isolation from the world, the last five years one long *counterfeit night,* I think, one long *counterfeit night* since I've retired or was fired, depending on who's telling you, and part of me thinks my dead wife's dementia infected *me* because I have trouble talking to people, in fact I avoid it, no desire to remove the blankets or towels from the windows either, no desire to face other people, no desire to abandon this *counterfeit night* either, even my coffee is delivered, left at the door with no interaction, no conversation required, I think, holding the still-chirping *smartphone,* so no, I think, I have no reason to leave, no reason to interact with the outside world when I can walk aimlessly through the house in my pale-yellow slippers, careful to avoid my dead wife's closet, or sit at the roll-top desk and think up titles for a book I've yet to write and finally I answer the *smartphone* and ask Marcel how he is and he replies that he's fine, that it comes and goes and he doesn't say what it is that comes and goes because we both know that it's grief, a hole inside that won't heal and which, I'm beginning to suspect, only gets worse with time, grief a buzzard, I think, and our hearts the carrion, and yes, I say, I agree, it comes and goes but I don't tell Marcel about his mother's closet and how I avoid walking past it in order to spare myself from a fit or a breakdown or whatever the fuck is breaking inside and Marcel asks where I've been, saying he's left a ton of messages, and I tell him I was working on my book. Ah, yes, he says, your *French book,* which is what he's always called my book-length essay and suddenly I'm glad I picked up, happy to hear another voice in the endless procession of days; it's company, I think, an excuse to step away from the rolltop desk and the mountains of titles, *Trench of Sophocles* and *Gold Gray Ghosts of Babylon* and hundreds of others for a book that hasn't been written, I think, sipping my coffee, the bulk of the book mere detours into meaninglessness, no, I think, not *meaninglessness,* but certainly nothing involving Montaigne; pages infused with ashen, half-lit mornings, a flight of starlings, the somber skies over Bordeaux, Austrian coffeehouses, Russian duelists, subject after subject except the subject I was meant to write about, meaning Montaigne, as if I've been *avoiding* writing about Montaigne, consciously or unconsciously, who knows, and I have a dozen pages about Montaigne's manservant, Jean Brismontier, whose existence I discovered in the facsimile of a copy of Montaigne's diary, whose love of

decadent fashion, wigs especially, brought both fame and igno-
miny and after leaving the service of Montaigne, Brismontier
fled to Paris, becoming a celebrated, though controversial, wig
designer, tastemaker, and underground darling. My fascination
with this minor character required visits to the *Bellinger Wing*
and *Bustamante Embassy* as well as the *Porter's Lodge*, a squat
structure adjoined to the Chapel which, sitting upon Barker
Hill, commanded an abundant view of the defunct greenhouse
and topiary. Weeks before the blizzard and *looming lack of coffee*
as well as other subsequent dilemmas, tragedies really, and already the skies were charged with menace, already I discerned
the ponderous footsteps of disaster inching ever closer. Inside
the *Tanner Reading Room,* I transcribed from the facsimile of a
copy of Montaigne's diary, my hero's rigorously recorded entries
of his ancestral vineyard, his weekly rabbit hunts, as well as complaints about the kidney stones that plagued his days and on one
of these pages Montaigne referenced *Rudiments & Formules de
Donception de Perruque* (*Basic Wig Design & Formulas*),
Brismontier's strange and epicurean book of reflections and anecdotes on wigs and wig design. Montaigne called it a *slight, frivolous but happy diversion, eccentric like the young man I remember*
and I returned to the *Tanner Room* from the *Tanner Reading
Room,* swiftly signed the release forms, endured the pat down,
and raced to the *Bustamante Embassy* where I found an English
translation of *Rudiments & Formules de Donception de Perruque*
by Jean Brismontier, whose title page asked the fundamental
question: *does the man wear the wig or does the wig wear the man?*

Published shortly before Montaigne's death, *Rudiments &* *Formules de Donception de Perruque,* despite its title, wasn't stiff or pedantic but warmhearted and effusive; Brismontier spent little time on the rudiments or materials of wig-making, but waxed poetic on his favorite styles, from the *Le Coq* (a wig so long its tresses reached the rump of its occupant) to the *Danseur Méchant,* which mimicked the plumage of a tropical bird, to the ostentatious *Archipelago* where the silver hair, streaked with bands of crimson and tied in the back with ribbons, was curled in thick rolls not unlike cannoli floating above the ears of its wearer, and though future centuries would see the wig as an at- tempt at ambiguity, a way of fitting in to avoid standing out, no- tably the aristocracy, Brismontier didn't share this attitude. The wig was significant for its twofold intent: its *sheer superfluousness coupled with its fundamental imperative,* wrote Brismontier, a *tri- umphal adornment* and a *celebration of the spurious,* he also wrote, a decoration both *subversive* but also *outright necessary,* coincid- ing fortuitously with *fashionable grooming.* The hair bestowed upon our species, Brismontier laments in his introduction, is *weak and unfinished, disparate and coarse,* often thinning in man's adulthood and likewise turning brittle in the advancing years of women. Just as one shines the leather of one's shoes, Brismontier wrote, shoes made to protect the feet as well invite trends, why would one likewise not adorn their pate with coiffures that beckon the stars? Brismontier loved the wig for its *immaculate superficiality* and *beautiful pretense,* he wrote, for the sense of completing one's outfit because a soul lacking the wig, he resolved, was *culturally impaired* as well as displaying *outright disdain* for one's own upkeep. Once he turned up in Paris Brismontier surrounded himself with child prostitutes, cross-dressers, and dissolute highwaymen, all lurking in the subterranean catacombs, specifically beneath the twelfth and fourteenth arrondissements, making bootleg burgundy and conducting orgies, the hedonism which took place something of which Brismontier had only dreamed; men dressed as geishas and squires, emulating nobility, fucking endlessly in skirts and heels, with powdered faces, adorned in extravagant corsets, and it wasn't long before Brismontier's personality cast a spell on these wayward souls, leading them through the squalid streets of Paris, coaching them on the artful craft of plundering: fabrics, mink coats, mother-of-pearl buttons and especially hair, much of it collected from the floors of local barbers, larceny something Jean instinctively understood, as if he'd grown up in the densely packed streets of the French capital, not the rolling hills of Bordeaux, thievery an impulse swimming through his veins, he felt, a divine talent, not unlike a sense of direction or ear for music. The pillaged materials were used for Jean's first attempts at wig-making, including the breathtaking *Laquais de Pute* and the notorious *Archer's Cock,* a blood-red wig standing several feet off the head of its occupant which, the moment he modeled it in those cursed, noxious, and seemingly endless tunnels, catacombs suffused with venereal disease, an inexplicable miasma emerged which surrounded Jean and his invention, everyone felt it and, taking long strides, the clicks of his heels resounding through the tunnels, Jean felt the worship of his fugitive disciples, an unmistakable radiance surrounding the colossal blood-red wig, because the height of the *Archer's Cock* as well as the audacity and brilliance of the *Archer's Cock* was indisputable and his followers, pallid and pox ridden, gripping candles to illuminate the towering invention, shuddered in exaltation. Knowingly or not, they were looking at the future, though most of them wouldn't have one, meaning a future, because in less than a year their necks would meet the blade of the guillotine, largely for acts committed at the behest of Jean Brismontier who, not yet twenty-five, was envisioning blue wigs, lilac wigs, wigs with partridge nests, wigs containing hidden compartments for pouches of snuff or the secret correspondence of lovers. All the same, I wondered, why was I studying *this*, meaning Brismontier, and not *that*, meaning Montaigne, the most glorious essayist in history? Was my life merely procrastination and delay, a false endeavor never to bear fruit? It was quiet in the Porter's Lodge as I reflected on my inability to stay the course, my innate capacity for dodging the things that mattered most, my book-length essay, for example, my middling career as a humanist professor and Montaigne scholar as another example, neglecting to tell Marcel his love of *dance music* was a dead end as a third example, that loving what you love most means keeping it secreted away in order to protect it from the hordes, loving something means not acting on it for here I am, I think now, holding the smartphone, staring at the rolltop desk; decades of torpor and waste, hundreds of false starts gazing in accusation and yes, Marcel repeats through the *smartphone,* it comes and goes, and I know he's talking about grief, a cataclysm, a sinking ship on a frozen ocean, and without warning Marcel begins talking about Bogotá and Berlin, about how he plans to move to either city, meaning Bogotá or Berlin, and *begin anew,* and it's either Bogotá or Berlin, he says, he's not yet sure which because both cities have a vigorous *underground dance culture,* especially *electronic music,* he tells me, Bogotá and Berlin, though seemingly different on the surface, are actually cities *in accord,* he says, *sister cities* in a sense, cities eager to celebrate a love of *dance culture,* because both cities embrace the desire to record, produce, and perform *electronic dance music* and Marcel begins naming his favorite artists from Bogotá: Felipe Gordon, Adriano Lopez, Gerardo Pechón, as well as Colombia's fervent culture of *drum and bass,* though admittedly not his favorite, he says, is indicative of Bogotá, music drenched in *breakbeats,* beats like epileptic seizures, beats that force the listener to fear for their own sanity, beats which escalate, becoming harder and faster until the club reaches a *collective euphoria,* especially in *Chapinero,* an upscale neighborhood in Bogotá dotted with warehouses that double as clubs, flyers littered across the walls of *Chapinero* promoting the newest club or an upcoming rave, yes, Marcel says, because one of his roommates, Zach, just returned from Bogotá and can't stop raving about Bogotá, *Chapinero* in particular, a neighborhood abounding with international DJs as well as *underground clubs,* and though I was adamant about moving to Berlin, says Marcel, *dead set* in fact, even though I had my heart set on recording my first proper album there, meaning Berlin, Zach, my roommate, got me thinking about Bogotá, *Chapinero* in particular, where the clubs, which are almost always in warehouses, promote the newest in *drum and bass, tribal house, breakbeat,* guaracha, reggaeton, and *electric Cumbia* and afterward, according to Zach, says Marcel, the DJs and clubgoers fan across the streets of Bogotá, *Chapinero* in particular, drinking and dancing, bombarding the food trucks, eating *empanadas* and *arepas* and sure, he says, Spanish is the dominant language spoken in Bogotá, *Chapinero* in particular, but the language that stands above the rest, the language that requires no translation is the *language of music,* and once they're finished dancing in the clubs which double as warehouses, he says, once the clubs have closed and the sun begins to rise, according to Zach, says Marcel, they take to the streets, dancing endlessly into the night or heading to one another's apartments, because in Bogotá, *Chapinero* in particular, night never ends. Finishing my coffee, avoiding my wife's closet, I return to the kitchen, turn on the electric kettle, grab the grinder and select a roast from Veracruz, single origin and shade grown, because Marcel's sudden mention of leaving, of exchanging one country for another, can only be tolerated, I think, with another cup of coffee, and while Marcel explains how much he loves both Bogotá and Berlin, though he's never set foot in either, says he's quite certain he'll love it, tells me in frustration that he's simply repeating what he's told me in the five or six voicemails he's already left and *fuck me,* he says, you still don't know how to check your voicemail, do you? And on he goes about his desire to *begin anew,* his ambition to leave and make a *fresh start* because of *all of this* and he trails off because both of us understand what *all of this* means, the death of his mother, anguish like a plunged knife, and so on, yes, I get it, he and I both eminently proficient at comprehending the definition of *all of this,* and he doesn't need to say another thing, and he doesn't, because after saying *all of this,* something we both know only too well, what's left to say, so he trails off and I consider how much heartbreak a single person can endure because, in the scheme of things, I've been very lucky, in the scheme of things, I think, I've had very little heartbreak but for *fuck's sake,* I think, losing my wife feels like losing a *platoon of loved ones,* losing an arm or a leg, losing a language, perhaps the essence of my personality, because my wife was how I related to the world and now that she's gone I can't relate to the world, have no desire to relate to the world; instead I find myself hiding from the world with sheets and blankets and towels, sheets and blankets and towels I have no interest in taking down and I consider the heartbreak Kleist endured from the death of Ernst, the heartbreak no doubt inherited from her parents too because the destruction her parents witnessed doesn't evaporate, I think, it's bequeathed to the child, perhaps in the womb, something of which I'm utterly convinced because that night, weaving between her sculptures, she said as much. As night endured the blizzard gained strength and Kleist, cackling like a wounded bird, yanked away the glass of brandy she'd given me, and which I had pretended to nurse, and gulped it in a single motion. *Jesus Christ,* she muttered in disappointment, tightening her belt, preparing to seek another bottle of *whatever I come across first,* the only challenge, she confessed, remembering where she'd hidden the brandy, vodka, and endless other spirits she kept hidden from herself when trying to complete *The Boots of Stupidity* because I don't drink when I work, she explained, I drink as a *reward* for completing the work, and finding the booze took no time because Kleist kept bottles stashed everywhere. Kneeling beneath the cot, between the buckets of sculpting materials, the chisels and the polishers, hidden high in the cabinets of the cottage, her wizened face like the snout of a hunting dog, she eventually came upon a bottle and, without even the most cursory glimpse at its label, opened it and took an enormous gulp, a gulp like she'd crossed the Sahara, not a *mental Sahara* but a physical one and I glanced once more at the can of *instant coffee,* considered asking if I could make a cup, perhaps two, because my head was throbbing as a result of the *looming lack of coffee* which was no longer looming or approaching, no, it had *arrived* because, doing the math, I hadn't had coffee since nine or ten that morning, meaning I hadn't had coffee in over twelve hours and my chest was tight and raw, my head throbbed; an all-consuming dread had nestled in my soul. The depravity of man will not go unpunished, Kleist declared, her face suddenly in mine, the waft of schnapps hitting me in the face, her long nose and blue lips boring into me for a crime I hadn't known I'd committed but which her expression assured me I had, her bloodshot eyes boring into me, searching for something I didn't possess, and I sensed the disappointment she had in her

LESSER RUINS [177]

audience, meaning me, because Kleist savored someone with whom she could argue *and* drink, Kleist relished the push and pull of a sparring partner, a person equal in intelligence and tenacity, in short, *not* me, and the more she drank the more pugnacious she became, and there was no stopping her, I thought, not that I wanted to, what I wanted was a cup of coffee, perhaps two, even better, three, coffee stronger than the schnapps I'd been given and *fuck everything,* I thought, if given the opportunity I'd use half the can of *instant coffee* for a single cup, if that's what it took, coffee like mud, like black earth, the electric buzz, the transcendent sense of solace and well-being, what had become for me an *existential requirement,* and before I could say anything Kleist disappeared behind *Lap of Eurydice,* a sculpture which had radiated bad omens since the moment I'd entered, a beast more tail than torso, and instinctively I knew looking at *Lap of Eurydice* head-on would only invite agitated dreams. Stupidity, cried Kleist, stupidity, she repeated, hunched behind *Lap of Eurydice,* people talk about sloth and greed, she declared, envy and wrath, but I assure you it's stupidity, stupidity the deadliest sin, for it's the most common sin and the sin which borrows from all the others, stupidity a curse and a sin which I became intimately acquainted with through my mother, said Kleist, my mother instructing me on the stupidity of mankind, a plague and a blight to which no one is immune, her own death, said Kleist, which my mother blamed on stupidity, and rightfully so, because toward the end she had become an artifact of herself. Visiting from college I perceived my mother's rapid decline, the leaden weight of trauma from across the room; she wouldn't leave the bed and for the first time in my life she began to recite the names of the guards at *Gusen II* as if she'd seen them only yesterday, Richter and Krüger, Braun and Scholz, oh yes, she said, I can't forget Scholz, my mother bellowed, said Kleist. Scholz was evidently a long-held obsession which my mother never permitted herself to talk about until suddenly, at the end, she wouldn't stop, *Helmut Scholz,* my mother proclaimed, said Kleist, a man born to kill, who as a child must've contained a thousand murders inside his heart, the prisoners Scholz worked to death or shot from boredom, prompted by the sheer tedious-ness of camp life in *Gusen II,* who circled the barracks where we slept on slats, three apiece, joints poking into another, knees and elbows and chins, while Scholz crossed the courtyard looking for someone to shoot, to rid himself of the tedium of life in *Gusen II,* the goddamn tediousness of all that death, confessed my mother, said Kleist, Scholz tramping through the camp like a gluttonous wolf, seeking an answer to all that death, wondering perhaps if the vacuum of stupidity could be sealed off or con-tained with *more stupidity,* who took particular delight in shoot-ing the newly arrived at *Gusen II,* the handicapped and the el-derly, shooting people less trouble than flipping a lighter, and I remember seeing Scholz awaiting the new arrivals on the plat-form, my mother confessed, said Kleist, my mother's eyes vacant and glassy, like uninhabited galaxies, oh yes, my mother had seen Scholz marching back and forth upon the platform, the Jews herded off the trains and Scholz ticking the verdicts with his index finger, *this one labor, this one death,* my mother observing Scholz mouthing the words, *labor or death,* only two paths, only two fates, *labor or death,* his index finger casting judgments like God, and Scholz, like much of his Nazi brethren, was a drug addict, addicted to *Pervitin,* said my mother, Kleist explained, meaning *crystal meth* or *methamphetamines,* whatever you want to call it, I'm sure of it, my mother insisted, Kleist said, and due to Scholz's elevated position he was able to procure as much of the drug as he wanted and watching him emerge from the depot or the guardhouse or his château, that's what it was called, a *fucking château,* my mother spat, as if *châteaus* existed in death camps in the middle of Austria, anyone could see the man was completely removed, altogether absent from the surroundings he himself had fashioned, and Kleist reappeared from behind the sculpture, her eyes either gateways or dead ends, I couldn't tell. As a child I saw my mother laid to waste, she said, saw the scorched panorama of man's most haunting visions, said Kleist, saw what happened when man was exempt from the trappings of morality, all bestowed to me by my mother. Scholz and his blood-red eyes and wet snout, my mother ranted, Kleist said, his face like a hungry wolf, a wolf exhausted of searching for an end to the stupidity he helped author, a stupidity unleashed and proliferating, not an aberration, but a direct consequence of our own natures, all of this confessed on my last visit home before she died, my mother frozen in bed, not angry, just resigned. Yes, my mother confessed, what matter if the *Pervitin* was meant for the German soldiers as a *performance-enhancing drug,* my mother asked, said Kleist, wasn't the coordinated murder of millions of souls a performance as well? What did Scholz envision in that divine stupor, asked my mother, said Kleist, did he not realize he was not only living in hell but propagating it? Did he not realize he himself was an instrument of outrageous suffering? Each night he circled the barracks, waiting for the first cough, a cough as inevitable as the passing of time because the sickness and disease in *Gusen II* was everywhere. As soon as Scholz heard a cough he'd burst into the first bunker he passed, no matter where the cough originated, whichever was closest, he'd kick the door open and begin shooting at random, simply fire into that darkness crammed with cowering Jewish flesh, shoot until the gun was empty and then turn, skulk away, and vanish. Every night for three years, said my mother, Kleist said, more dependable than the rising sun. Those nightly strolls where the meth-addicted Scholz, with the eyes of a *dybbuk* and the countenance of a possessed wolf, kicked open doors at random and nothing could protect you, my mother explained, Kleist said, lying still, holding your breath, all of it useless, and after the war Scholz fled to Mexico, oh yes, my mother explained on my last visit home from school, my mother desperate and determined to speak the names of those guards before departing. I did the research, she said, it wasn't hard, and the others, Richter and Krüger, Braun and Winkler, they escaped too, although not for long; they ran west toward Mannheim until they saw their fates in the blood-red horizon which to them must've resembled the end of the world, and maybe they believed it *was* the end of the world because each bit down on the capsules of cyanide they'd been issued, committed suicide in a trench outside Wendenkopf, I'd later read, said my mother, Kleist explained, but not Scholz, Scholz changed his name, removed a letter here, added a letter there and *poof,* he was an exile living in Mexico, although, my mother explained, said Kleist, the monster added a *Berg,* added a *Berg* to Scholz, becoming *Scholzberg,* an exiled Jew living in Mexico, the *fucking audacity,* and with some false documentation he was suddenly a Hungarian immigrant in Mexico, Cuernavaca I think, changed his name and fled the deadly stupidity of Europe, disguised as a member of the tribe he'd tried to eradicate, and I wanted to find him, my mother admitted, ranted Kleist, but what would I do, she pleaded, prone in bed, eyes devoid of light, eyes that at one time were a rich cornflower blue but now glacial and barren, eyes beseeching the end, refusing to let me open the shutters, listing the names of those guards with a vindictiveness unique to the doomed, and Kleist excused herself for *another piss,* returning with another full bottle and eyes like meteorites, only too happy to discuss the subject of her childhood in Liezen and the Austrian anti-Semitism in which she'd grown up, because, trust me, she said, the Germans didn't invent hating Jews, not even the Nazis. They may have *mechanized it,* they may have put *into production* what the Polish and Austrian and Russian Jews had suffered for centuries, but it was always there, this anti-Semitism that drifts through the atmosphere of Europe like a vapor because Austria's hatred of Jews is well documented, she said, people hear the word *Nazis* and think Germany, but the stupidity which emanated from my neighbors, Kleist said, provincial Austrians who didn't sympathize with my parents nor feel any guilt for their roles in the attempt at their wholesale murders, no, my neighbors in fact regretted nothing but the *failure* of the wholesale murders of my parents, resenting my parents and me simply for being alive because in Austria there was never any sense of culpability, Kleist said, never any collective shame or regret, she added, only regret at having failed, yes, a sense of regret at having failed at the wholesale murder of my parents meaning, in essence, me, because obviously if they, meaning my parents, had successfully been murdered in *Gusen II* my existence would've never been a subject, my *non-being* an obvious *non-subject,* something which was blatant to me but not the provincial Austrians I'd grown up around, busy as they were wishing nonexistence upon me and my family and Kleist smacked her lips and released a cackle; the hatred of Jews after the war, she continued, was window dressing, or should I say their *anti-Semitism* which is just an academic word for stupidity, *anti-Semitism* a clever-sounding word, a *cunning* word to cloak the tedious and utterly uninteresting hatred of Jews because there's nothing less interesting, nothing more tedious, than hatreds without nuance, passive and indolent hatreds, said Kleist, hatreds without logic or reason, hatreds of entire cultures and peoples and thus hatreds of whole histories, and instead of simply saying *Jew-hater* which is what it is, they call it *anti-Semitism* as if there's some academic rationale, some written doctrine that supports their stupidity when the only conviction behind hating a group of people, any group, is the *dogma of stupidity,* just as bigotry itself is merely an excuse stupid people feel justifies their own stupidity. Anyway, said Kleist, *that* hatred of Jews adorned the actions of every non-Jew in Liezen while I was growing up, it drifted through the air like pollen, never seen in acts or spoken in words because it permeated the silence between words and imagine coming face to face each day with the very people who attempted but failed at your murder, walking along Siedlungsstraße or Rathausplatz and *there goes another kike,* they'd think, *another fucking Yid,* they'd also think, *another goddamn subhuman,* they'd think too because there is no bottom to the *stupidity of bigotry,* every Jew a reminder of their own failure at our wholesale destruction, she said, drinking from the bottle of schnapps, already half empty, every Jew a reminder of the people they never lifted a finger to defend, all the Yids and faggots and filthy Roma, they'd think, the people that disgusted them for reasons they never understood because it was indoctrinated the moment they were born, infused in their bottles of milk, drifting like spores, whispered in the halls at school, the bile your very presence provoked, well that was me, a child seeking some form of psychic survival, surrounded by the people of Liezen, a small village of Jew-hating Austrians disappointed at the failure of my parents' wholesale murder. Kleist cleared her throat, began looking for her pipe, misplaced somehow amid her aimless wanderings, still ranting about *chaos, decay,* and the *indisputable clutter* of human souls, a viscous soup, she said, a blood-red sea that swallowed everyone, the *giant maw of the blood-red sea,* she fumed, the blood-red sea intent on drowning us, sometimes quickly but often over years or epochs, the blood-red sea married to our destiny, that of a dead species, a species already extinct but *terrifically oblivious* of its own extinction, a species copulating in ceaseless ambivalence in order to perpetuate and avoid their own instinctive knowledge of the blood-red sea, the blood-red sea never sated, never appeased, no matter how many bones and teeth and claws it ingests because we're already dead, she said, already extinct, she added, Kleist finally finding her pipe, packing it, and meantime me dividing my attention between Kleist and the can of freeze-dried shit which an earlier version of me would've never considered drinking, coffee I would've scoffed at, and rightly so, but now wanted with ravenous longing and still Kleist raved about the *giant maw of the blood-red sea,* the venomous stupidity of human nature, a stupidity we boasted of without the smallest hint of shame, a species *bereft of shame,* a species on the brink of decline and utterly *bankrupt of shame.* And without pause night endured, the brutal winds pulverizing Kleist's cabin, the floor trembling, walls buckling, and luckily the fellowship cabins had been constructed a century earlier, built to withstand the terrific force of the harshest winter blasts, the unyielding winds and fierce gusts, forcing the walls of the cottage to contract and Kleist, suddenly rigid, suddenly cognizant, mistook a branch scraping the window as a sort of divine presence because she bolted upright, told me to *shut the fuck up* even though I hadn't said a word, I'd merely looked over her shoulder to make certain the can of *instant coffee* hadn't vanished while she held forth about the blood-red sea as well as anguish, stupidity, and the Austrian anti-Semitism in which she'd been raised, and in her eyes I saw the ink-black cliffs, sharp and nameless, recognized the conflict between her arthritic joints and the tenacity infused by alcohol, saw Kleist inching toward self-destruction, pleading with me once more to *shut the fuck up. Shhhh,* she whispered, quiet, she added, *shut the fuck up.* Putting a hand to her ear she bolted upright: Nadia is here, she screamed. Tears streamed down Kleist's cheeks; the bottle of schnapps was empty and whatever was outside, doom, treachery, strife, had invaded. Suddenly invigorated, Kleist's shadow inflated across the walls like the portents of another world. Nadia Poltorzycka has come to see our work, Kleist declared rapturously, her face grotesque and demented, like a mask of itself, Kleist leaning an ear toward the window and sniffing the air. She tightened her belt, began looking for her boots, circling the sculptures, kicking the tools, her words a concoction of some new language with a thousand words for horror. She disappeared behind *Medusa's Apprentice*, appearing a moment later gripping her boots, squatting on the floor to put them on. She glared in my direction, sit up straight, she barked, Nadia Poltorzycka is here! She's come to see our work! I straightened up, frightened for Kleist, but also thinking of coffee, of finally making a cup, the dark liquid instantly returning me to myself, making me human and whole, bestowing perhaps the courage necessary to write my book-length essay, and Kleist, suddenly ecstatic, suddenly weeping, tightened the laces of her boots, and

I wasn't sure if it was joy or horror or both at once but she wept, cackled, stood, grabbed another bottle, scotch this time, and threw open the door. Torrents of snow burst inside, pummeling Kleist, who bent forward, shouldered the wind, laughed with intoxication and told me she was fetching Nadia who was obviously lost because, she hollered, it doesn't snow like this in Poland, Nadia is lost, she yelled, and I must retrieve her and Kleist leapt into the darkness, into the merciless winds of a blizzard that continued for another two days and which ultimately swallowed her whole, the bottle of scotch discovered first, the pipe second, and her corpse three days later.

III

Bogotá or Berlin, says Marcel, Bogotá or Berlin, he repeats, he can't decide which, says he can't choose between the two cities and where he wants to live, says something else about *house music,* I think, or *warehouses that double as dance clubs,* I think, but grinding the coffee, a Mexican roast, it's difficult hearing Marcel, difficult understanding what he's saying about his decision to move to either South America or Europe, meaning Bogotá or Berlin, places, he explains, which embrace the young artist, places where a young person like himself is encouraged to create: music, writing, painting, dancing, whatever they love, and *get by,* not like here, he says, not like here at all, because attempting to make art in America is an uphill battle, he says, *a fool's errand,* he adds, not only is everything against you like the *structure* and the *culture,* but also the *structure of that culture,* dead set against you, and people too, because people in general want you to fail so they can feel superior in their decision not to pursue what they love and then tell you later how you were being young or selfish, or both, and it's time to wake up they'll say, time to face the music, they'll also say, meaning it's time to anesthetize your soul, time to spend your life ignoring or neglecting your soul in order to work, because nothing makes people feel better than the realization they've made the right decision, nothing better than feeling superior, that they're intelligent and pragmatic while you're reckless and foolish, in short, unserious, because most people are convinced that caring about art, thus the soul, is the pinnacle of folly, and for them nothing is better than knowing you're slowly dying right alongside them because nobody wants to die alone and *Jesus*, I think, I agree, but I'm not going to say so because I've already learned that lesson and it's a lesson taught through pain and experience and acknowledging these truths will only spur Marcel into making the same decisions as his father, and the water is beginning to boil and the coffee is ground and for a moment everything is okay, for this fleeting moment, I think, my nerves are calm and I steep the coffee, smell the coffee, a Mexican roast, and eventually I walk into the third bedroom with the coffee while avoiding my dead wife's closet because leaving the kitchen it's impossible to fully circumvent my dead wife's closet, in fact each time I enter or exit the kitchen I'm faced with the door to my dead wife's closet (still ajar) followed by the rolltop desk containing my work-in-progress, meaning my book yet-to-be-written, just a thousand false starts and suddenly I laugh, click my tongue, sit before the rolltop desk, and jot down *A Thousand False Starts* on a slip of paper, *A Thousand False Starts* as a potential title for my book-length essay because it's easily the most emblematic title I've come up with yet, symbolic of everything having to do with my book-length essay, notably its composition, and though *The Intrusion of Distraction* is a fortuitous title, an enviable title, the title, I think, gives too much away, and perhaps *The Intrusion of Distraction* works as a subtitle or an alternate to *A Thousand False Starts,* I think, but only as a subtitle or an alternate because *The Intrusion of Distraction* is simply too obvious whereas *A Thousand False Starts* is wonderfully vague and wonderfully nebulous, *A Thousand False Starts* can easily be applied to me as well as Montaigne, why not, and I underline *A Thousand False Starts* then highlight *A Thousand False Starts* so I don't lose *A Thousand False Starts* amid the mounds of paper and legal pads stained by rings of coffee and offhand sketches, not to mention receipts, pencil nubs, and napkins faded with the phone numbers of doctors who couldn't save my wife, as well as dozens of pages about Jean Brismontier; meaningless pages too about Alexei Voznesensky, the Russian fugitive, all this and more stuffed inside the receptacles of the rolltop desk, my efforts spent researching and writing about these obscure men leading nowhere, I think, dozens of pages written about Brismontier and Voznesensky and never visited again, every page a reminder of the time squandered doing *meaningless* work instead of *meaningful* work, this not that, chaos not certainty, dashing between both Tanner rooms believing I'd found some foothold into the work, and yet one can't know until the work is complete, I realized only later, one can't be certain until the time has been spent, and I remember how exhilarated I was reading about Montaigne's earliest conversation with Voznesensky while visiting the public gardens near his château on an afternoon excursion, how he had engaged in conversation with the duelist and found he enjoyed his company, enough to invite him to his châ-teau for the evening, sending him off the following day with food and clothing. And nothing more. That was it. A pointless anecdote taking up no more than two pages of Montaigne's diary and for what? What insight had it brought to my masterwork on Montaigne and the French Renaissance, the birth of the essay as well as the burgeoning potential of the human soul? And yes, I'd learned later that Voznesensky died from mysterious circumstances from injuries sustained in a horse-riding accident or a horse race or perhaps it had nothing to do with horses at all, but most of the stories involving his death seemed to mention a horse, I think, or at least a barn, colorful stories, sure, but to what end? Meanwhile Marcel on the phone, abandoning the subject of his imminent move abroad, instructing me instead on how to check voicemails on the *smartphone,* angry I've missed the voicemails he's left announcing his decision to move to either Bogotá or Berlin, angry too, I suspect, I haven't listened to any of the mixes he's *sent* or *emailed* since purchasing the smartphone, meaning the *links* to these mixes he's sent or emailed. The *settings* feature, he says emphatically, you need to go to the *settings* feature and forget the side of the phone for a second, you're obsessed with the side of the phone but the buttons on the side of the phone won't do shit if you don't go to the *settings* feature, the *settings* feature on the front, he says, where you can move the *voicemail* option wherever you want, his voice escalating, his exasperation growing, simply touch the *settings* button on the *home* screen, he says, the icon that looks like an old-fashioned telephone, and I know the icon he's talking about, the icon meant to represent an old-fashioned telephone that glimmers from the front of the *smartphone,* intended to invoke a nostalgia that doesn't exist because no one has the time to remember old-fashioned telephones, all of us moving too fast, more dogged and myopic than any time in human history, incapable of looking back, I think, incapable of being circumspect or discerning, all of us unequipped and unprepared to pause for even the briefest moment, paralyzed and incapable of reminiscing or remembering, in short, unable to take a moment and *simply reflect,* especially about things like old-fashioned telephones because there's simply *too much everything,* so when the icons of these old-fashioned telephones are gleaming from the faces of our *smartphones* it merely evokes a nostalgia that's unremembered and false because we've entered a new period, I suddenly realize, dire and dim, a moment when there's *too much history,* too many events behind us to remember or even consider, *too much history* to learn or begin thinking about, and once you touch it, says Marcel, meaning the *settings icon,* you can move the *voicemail* wherever you want and I don't have the heart to argue, don't have the energy to illustrate my disdain for *voicemails* which are merely an opportunity for human interaction, another intrusion separating me from the *mental Saharas* necessary to finally complete my project and *motherfucker,* I think, I'm nowhere near finishing my project, but I lack the heart to tell Marcel I'm not missing his calls, in fact I hear the chirps of his calls with deafening clarity; I simply want the *smartphone* to shut the fuck up, I think, because the *smartphone* is an intrusion on the mental lucidity and concentration required to create anything serious, anything novel and new, meaning my book-length essay, the *smartphone* symbolic of the world's vulgarities, nimbly annihilating the prospect of having an unfettered thought in this depraved world, all of it utterly impossible, and I understand, I tell Marcel, knowing I don't really understand, unsure in fact if he's instructing me on *voicemails* or *downloading mixes,* or both, neither of which I'm able to feign even the slightest interest in because what I want more than anything is to forever silence the chirp of the *smartphone,* but I humor Marcel, tell him that once we're off the phone I'll fix it, meaning the *settings* feature and the *voicemail,* I'll fix it, I say, so I can listen to your mixes and as well as your messages, but tell me about Bogotá and Berlin, and as Marcel explains with obvious frustration what he's already explained in several *voicemails,* he quickly detours into the names of dance clubs his roommate Zach visited while in Bogotá, *Fabrik* and *Amnesia* and *Los Capachos,* clubs celebrated for their *experimental house, acid,* and *underground techno,* music bursting with jagged beats and turbulent grooves, songs like shards of glass, beats like scattered mica, his roommate Zach had said, everyone seeking the divine in repetition, looking for enlightenment in repetition, in the incessant beats, the litany of chords, the sacred and the holy buried amid the *reiteration of rhythms* played over and over, and moving to Bogotá, says Marcel, makes more sense because of the *dance scene* in Bogotá, *Chapinero* in particular, where the music and the clubs, littered with *experimental dance music* but also with *Tropicanibalismo,* a genre inspired by traditional *Cumbia,* are literally everywhere, according to Zach, says Marcel, and instead of describing the *dance scene* in *Chapinero,* Marcel swerves into ruminations on *space-age disco, nu-jungle,* and *neo cassette underground,* popularized in the early 2000s, he says, *neo cassette underground,* his newest interest which he hopes will inform the album he plans to record either in Bogotá or Berlin, more than likely Bogotá, once he decides, an album that will incorporate *dub,* obviously, but also highlight *neo cassette underground,* and as Marcel explains the patterns or signifiers of *neo cassette underground* I can't help but drift, recall my now-dead wife's expression upon my return from the Zybècksz Archives at the Horner Institute, how baffled and distraught she was by my state of mind, neither of us knowing she would be losing hers, meaning her mind, in a few short years. The failure to complete my booklength essay, to make even the slightest *progress* on my booklength essay, in fact returning with hardly a thing about Montaigne, combined with the death of Kleist, all of it had impaired and enfeebled me. I was untethered, bitter, feeling demolished; the image of Kleist's lifeless body echoed in my mind, resembling one of her sculptures, stoic and resigned, the appendages on her shoulders like glacial wings, her ancient face entombed beneath crystals of ice lending her corpse a strange, pensive nobility and, admittedly, I didn't search for Kleist as hard as I probably should've, meaning not at all, because that night, following her lunatic flight, I'd scrambled to my cottage to make the shit-black *instant coffee* filched from her counter, coffee that was barely tolerable, coffee which tasted like surrender and defeat, coffee like a hundred nameless inflictions but, at the very least, brought me back to myself, and later, once the storm passed, I was hardly troubled, confident Kleist would return, agitated and hungover but alive and well, eager to talk about sculpture and nudism and the Bavarian Alps and whether they were growing or shrinking, convinced she'd emerge unscathed, the very thing I told the Horner officials angry I'd watched her flee into the night, however, following her exodus, I'd had more pressing issues, namely the *looming lack of coffee,* hence I'd scrambled to my cottage with Kleist's can of *instant coffee* like a stolen artifact, demons screeching, ravens circling, obscure pangs piercing my soul, and I made a cup, then a second, then a third, and after the fourth tiny epiphanies danced inside my skull and the world transformed from a desert of banality to a field of possibility; the stacks of notes, the half-hearted research, all my copious battles against mediocrity altered, turned ripe with promise, and ignoring common sense I made a *fifth* cup of coffee, adding four heaping spoonfuls instead of the recommended two because, I thought, *fuck it,* and I paced my cottage, gazed upon the desk inundated with false starts and bad ideas, anemic work sullied by insignificance which now, suddenly and miraculously, was bursting with life, and the winds clawed the cottage like the hands of God and the night grew darker and colder, and none of it meant a thing, the stacks of uninspired pages perched atop the desk like an adversary, a totem of my impotence, all of it promptly transposed, thanks to coffee, into a paradigm of order; I saw my salvation glowing before me, never had my objective appeared so lucid, my purpose unveiled with such purity. I laughed to myself, removed my frozen Horner-issued bathrobe and replaced it with another I'd purchased days earlier at the Zybècksz gift shop, and began whistling Bruckner's *Requiem in D Minor* while making circles in my pale-yellow slippers. I considered Montaigne's glorious works, thought to myself the world was good, my son was good, above all, my lovely wife who I had no inkling would be dead in little more than a decade was the embodiment of good, so much goodness I could hardly stand it, and though the coffee tasted like warm death, it spun webs of magic. Unhindered, I returned to my work and two days later the storm swiftly receded. The air was crisp, the light dappled, the sky endless. One morning, bouncing between both Tanner rooms, I passed Arnette Foster-Jones, the Afro-feminist scholar and urban planner, who halted me on the stairwell to give her condolences and naturally I became defensive, thought the condolences were meant for my work-in-progress, meant to mock my attempts at a book-length essay and I released a chortle, said it really wasn't any of her business, told her the seamless mix of literature and art, philosophy and biography, couldn't be forced, that subtlety was required, delicacy too, acumen and a flair for the subject didn't hurt either, and when an artist envisions something new, wholly original to a field of study and discipline, there exist no roadmaps or keys, no compass either, it's like walking in the woods at night, I told her, blindfolded and injured, not a *fatal* injury but certainly a debilitating one, a broken foot or bunions, and it's true, I admitted, I hadn't had much luck thus far, but all one needed was a good foundation, I said, a good foundation and the rest would follow and I happen to have a good foundation, I continued, meaning my thesis, *Montaigne and the Lugubrious Cherubs,* and this good foundation will ultimately see me through and Arnette Foster-Jones was miffed, insisted I misunderstood, claimed she had no notion of the genre or substance or subject of my work, not the faintest hunch of the area of interest my work entailed, insisting her sympathies were in regards to the sculptor, Kleist, whose body had been discovered that morning outside the *Tsypkin House of Holocaust Research* by a pack of search dogs and I promptly spat out the mint I'd been sucking, a habit necessitated by the revolting taste Kleist's coffee left in my mouth because each cup of *instant coffee* required a mint immediately after, because it wasn't simply a case of Kleist's *instant coffee* being terrible, which it undoubtedly was, but no amount of sugar or cream could mask its foul repugnance because, bizarrely, it was insipid *and* bland, an impossible combination curiously mastered by the can of *instant coffee* I'd seized from Kleist's cabin, and already I'd begun concocting nicknames for the terrible swill: *Hades's Blend, Excrement Roast, Fecal Latte,* charming monikers that lifted my spirits while I forced down another cup of that heinous swill that wouldn't make the grade at a gas station or truck stop or low-end kiosk, coffee so rank and repugnant it made a person question the decisions in one's life, the large and the small, the seemingly innocuous decisions made decades earlier, those so-called forks in the road culminating in the moment one found themselves holding the cup, gagging at the noxious flavor, outright marveling, as in how did I end up drinking *this*, worse, drinking this *willingly*, because it was truly terrible coffee, revolting not only upon consumption but even before taking the first sip, the moment one brought the cup to their lips and took the briefest, most passing whiff, before the first dregs even entered one's mouth, that fractious instant when the *cheapness* and *mediocrity* and *stench* of the coffee smacked the victim with a blatant and powerful blow, a warning impossible to ignore, and on a personal level I found the scent so uncivilized, so nauseating and outrageously odious, that following through, that is taking the actual sip, seemed not only foolish but against every natural instinct I had, yet I knew of no other means of masking the taste, of somehow making it less atrocious than it was, all to say that a strong mint taken promptly after each cup was not only necessary but imperative, not merely to erase the flavor it left on one's tongue like a bed of moss but to allow one the space to contemplate loftier subjects, the wondrous stories of de Maupassant for example or the sensuous splendor of love or the glorious assortment of Hindu gods, *thirty million* I'd think to myself, *thirty million Hindu gods*, or the waning shafts of sunlight along a meadow at dusk, really anything that inspired a sense of solace and well-being, and I thanked Arnette Foster-Jones for relaying the bad news, apologized for my outburst, and sprinted down the stairs toward the corridor separating the various ramps dividing the manifold wings housing both Tanner Rooms. Kleist dead, I thought, frozen to death, I thought too, holding back tears, wanting nothing more than to vomit, an urge precipitated by both the grief and Kleist's can of *instant coffee,* namely the grief because I'd never been good at grief, never been taught how to mourn, never been instructed on the ways a person finds purchase to the chambers of the human heart *in order* to mourn, how to handle the emotions dealing with anguish, despair, lamenting another's eternal absence, Kleist especially, the brevity of our friendship balanced by its intensity, all of it baffled me. I raced past the quadrangle and the *Steinhoff Collections,* through the frozen *Pleasure Gardens* whose accursed history was impossible to ignore; the pale sun, the receding snow, the ancient pines with shards of ice suspended from their branches, one the very tree from which Alessandro Costa had once hanged himself; I descended the low, solitary field (a verdant meadow in the summer, I'd been told), passed the fellowship cottages, nodded at Elena Troncoso (a formalist composing a discourse on the Linguistic Constraints of Critical Relativism), and, three cottages later, saw Liam Rankell, an abstract painter from the Labrador Peninsula. I ran until the *instant coffee* began crawling up my throat, forcing me to stop and have another mint because the taste of Kleist's *instant coffee* was reminiscent of death or dying or sickness at least, and I cursed the can of *instant coffee* with the faded green label, the can so large it seemed endless because no matter how many cups I drank, no matter how many scoops I used, it was impossible to diminish its contents and even Napoleon, I'd thought, exiled on Elba, certainly had better-tasting coffee, and Diderot, imprisoned in de Vincennes, enjoyed swill more palatable than what I coaxed from Kleist's can and standing in the patch of snow, sucking the mint, catching my breath, I considered both my *pathological need* for the *instant coffee* as well as my *pathological aversion* to the *instant coffee*, because I needed the coffee as much as I detested the coffee and after drinking a cup I'd gag, punch the air, vow it was the last cup I'd endure, swear to myself I'd renounce the *instant coffee* once and for all, make a pact with myself to wait for the roads to reopen and for the arrival of my Indonesian beans, beans so delicate and rich, so aromatic, they were almost holy, and I forbade myself from making another cup only to give in and acquiesce, roused by the *memory* of coffee which was only a memory of course and nothing proximate to the *instant coffee* I was currently drinking, yes, it seemed altogether implausible that what I was drinking shared a name with the coffee of my memory and, as if testing myself, I made *more instant coffee* under the dumb belief it would turn out differently, would somehow be an improvement when I knew this was impossible, impossible to extract gold from a pile of shit or, in this case, a can of shit. Still, the routine advanced unabated: *denouncing* the coffee then *drinking* the coffee, cursing it then brewing it, recognizing it for the lousiest dregs I'd ever ingested only to make another cup using an array of tactics: assorted temperatures, alternate steeping times, swapping between the pour-over and the Moka and back again, anything that might disguise the stench of ruin, each time yielding the same dense aroma, a scent so thick it was palpable, the smell itself an abomination, an assault on one's senses, a cup of black liquid reflecting back my own horror, the same horror I felt when I reached the *Tsypkin House of Holocaust Research* and saw the police gathered outside, heavy with paunch and authority, their unwieldy belts packing guns and cartridges and all manner of weapons and it was then I accepted Kleist's death as certain. The horror of the scene was countered by the sense of calm; a troupe of search dogs in repose, languid tongues and dark eyes regarding the world with indifference; a pair of Horner administrators in parkas sharing a thermos; and, a little further off, a clump of *scholarship poets* gathered beneath an enormous tree laughing at Christ knows what, the *scholarship poets* and their pea-green cardigans and gleaming boots, grinning and gloating at their preposterous *scholarship poets'* humor, jokes only *scholarship poets* would understand, gladdened perhaps by the turn of events and the drama certain to ensue and was there nothing sacred about the death of another, I wondered, nothing venerable about the demise of a great artist? I wanted to cry out, scream at creation. Kleist's body had already been taken to the coroner, a police officer explained, instantly advancing, asking my name, and upon hearing my name checking his notepad, confirming I was the one who'd spent several hours with Kleist on her *final night,* the exact words he used, *final night,* as if I'd foreseen the death of Kleist embodied in her sermons, that onslaught of words and denunciations that felt hopelessly eternal, the officer asking me a barrage of questions he claimed were *routine* but seemed deeply suggestive of, perhaps not *murder* or *homicide* or even *manslaughter,* but problematic, as in *how long had I spent* with Kleist that final night, as in how much had we had to drink, as in had she made any threats of self-harm, verbal or otherwise, as in, lastly, why hadn't I attempted to stop her? And me raising my hand, gasping for air, asking if anyone by chance had a mint because my pockets were depleted, the last mint sucked and savored on my way to the *Tsypkin House of Holocaust Research*, and the taste in my mouth was atrocious, my tongue an extra appendage, heavy and listless, the *instant coffee* churning inside my stomach like poison, and from the glut of officers a detective emerged, brandished a *smartphone*, thrust it toward my face, and asked me to identify the person on the screen, a sort of disfigured effigy, a sculpture of ice that had recently been a human, Kleist obviously, but was now a corpse, and I shuddered because Kleist was whiter than I'd thought possible, whiter than marble, because even marble contained the veins of other colors, blue and gray, even green, whereas Kleist appeared as a single color, no, a *noncolor*, a color drained of any color at all, including white, even worse, her eyes were open, gazing at the world or the afterlife or the quivering abyss wearing an expression of unabashed cynicism, aggrieved no doubt by the sweeping array of stupidity she'd faithfully endured. Once more I appealed for a mint, anything that would expunge the taste of shit inside my mouth because I'd completely run out, used up my last mint en route to the *Tsypkin House of Holocaust Research* and I felt the *scholarship poets* snickering nearby, whether or not they were I wasn't sure but I was faint and frightened, felt my knees buckle, same as last week when I'd collapsed outside my dead wife's closet, the smell of her clothes, the scent of her body, and I wept like I hadn't wept in years, decades perhaps, the sort of weeping that to an outsider seems overly dramatic and unnecessary, the sort of grieving I'd always found *uncouth,* uncouth until it's you, overly dramatic until it's your wife of decades that's died and me lying on the floor outside her closet, kicking the walls, wailing like a monster, a sense of existential terror amid the sudden realization that everything I'd ever known was less than a grain of sand, every book I'd read, every poem that nourished my soul, the whole catalogue of human philosophy mere exercises in futility, realizing as I wept how it all meant nothing, all those *thinkers* who knew so much until they didn't, their life's work merely a way of sustaining their own pride, of prolonging the inevitable, *and agony falls again,* I recited, *past comprehending,* Rilke writing about the death of Keats, yes, I thought, an agony past all comprehension, an agony that defies books and words, because all those books about death and words about death couldn't *defeat* death, couldn't even combat the grief *roused* by death because what's more triumphant and unequivocal than death, I thought, sobbing outside my wife's closet, the answer being nothing, nothing more triumphant and unequivocal than death, and Emily Dickinson, who'd measured every grief she met *with narrow, probing eyes,* more meaningless words, I thought, more declarations and gestures about grief and none of it granting a sliver of solace or respite nor the thinnest glimmer of hope, and Kierkegaard too, who'd avowed working out one's salvation *with fear and trembling,* books and poems and philosophy racing through my mind, infernal nonsense, while I kicked and wailed outside my dead wife's closet, all of it vanity and sentimental contemplation; *a stifled, drowsy, unimpassioned grief, which finds no natural outlet, no relief,* wrote Coleridge, who at least admitted helplessness in his pursuit to encapsulate or constrain grief which ended with no respite from this dark night of the soul, I thought, kicking the walls like a child having a tantrum, sensing the onset of an anguish uncharted, an aguish hanging over me this very moment, a week later, as Marcel gushes through the *smartphone* about *acid-licked basslines* and *blissed-out house tempos* and the way the beginning of the song dictates how much he'll love the song, the first beat or opening chord and already he knows, he says, already he's convinced how much he'll either love or loathe a song, the way the synths open, he says, the way they slowly build until the listener is acquainted with the song, recognizing the tropes but also taken aback by something new, a kick drum, a shifting pulse, because a perfect song requires both, he says, the familiar *and* the unfamiliar, both are essential; the soft pads, the persistent piano reminiscent of soul and disco, the sensory pleasure that reaches a place beyond language, but also something *other,* he says, the beginning of the song infinitely important as the song builds and accrues details, snaps and handclaps, hi-hats and lasers, all of it, meaning the song itself, must do what all good music does and that's *obliterate the bullshit of being alive,* and again he explains over the *smartphone* the difference between a *mix* and an *album,* a *remix* and a *club mix,* an *extended mix* and a *dub mix,* the difference between a *bridge* and a *chorus,* as if I haven't heard this lecture a trillion times, Marcel *reciting* and *preaching* through the *smartphone* his vigorous feelings about *electronic music,* why making a dance album will be easier in either Bogotá or Berlin because of the cultures in both cities and the *lack of culture* here, meaning America, and as Marcel proclaims his love of places he's never been I leave the study and wander into the front room, no notion of the time, no inkling if it's day or night due to the blankets and towels covering the windows and I lift the blankets and towels to peer outside and discover that it's dusk, notice the neighbors' trash cans positioned at the end of their driveways as if my wife hasn't died, trash cans dutifully arranged while I'm gasping for air and pacing in circles in my pale-yellow slippers, no different than last week and the week before and backward into infinity, the neighbors comfortably oblivious in their nests of stupidity, I think, neighbors dutifully going to work and returning home, making their meals while I'm circling this holding cell asphyxiated by sorrow or, in my more frivolous moments, searching for Montaigne and the trembling light, and why have I insisted on keeping the blankets and the towels hung across the windows, I wonder. Depression? Inertia? An unspoken ambivalence? Am I pacing in circles to avoid thinking of my dead wife, both the fact that she's dead and how she was once unbelievably alive? Yes, I think, recalling my wife, as beautiful as she was sophisticated, as accomplished as she was kindhearted, and even before we were engaged she insisted on reading *Montaigne and the Lugubrious Cherubs,* my master's thesis, to *understand my passion,* she explained, even though she later admitted having trouble getting through it, actually taken aback, she said, by the tone which felt both *condescending* and *misanthropic* and the spate of digressions littering the work which suggested a *deep longing for solitude,* in short, my rather strong feelings about the human race because it was obvious, she said, I had a deep love for humanity which was at odds with the deep loathing I also had for humanity. One can be both, I explained, myself and Montaigne for example, I told her, cursed by the need to reconcile a love of humanity with a dread of humanity, both of us embracing our species as much as holding them in contempt because, I said, *look around,* and my wonderful wife, now dead, found it curious that I'd acquired my master's degree on the strength of *Montaigne and the Lugubrious Cherubs,* which, though respecting the effort involved, felt more than a little antagonistic, as well as uneven, poorly researched, and a trifle *deranged,* she actually used the word *deranged,* laughing gently to help soften the severity of her review and perhaps my now-dead wife simply relished the challenge of marrying a man who contained a deep love of humanity while also possessing a deep hostility toward humanity, always trying desperately to rid himself of their company because it's true, I think, returning to the third bedroom, I want the company of my fellow creatures yet feel instantly nauseated by the company of my fellow creatures, and I love my fellow creatures *in theory,* I think, sitting before the rolltop desk, but not *in practice,* because my fellow creatures, to quote Kleist, are *pinnacles of stupidity,* each person *a perfect instrument of stupidity,* she declared, each person, she raved, *a perfect archetype of stupidity,* while the blizzard churned and the stars collapsed, mere hours from meeting her fate, a fate she invited and encouraged and perhaps always wanted and my wife with her wholesome heart mistakenly believed *Montaigne and the Lugubrious Cherubs* was an exercise in scholarship, not realizing *Montaigne and the Lugubrious Cherubs* was the essence of who I was, *Montaigne and the Lugubrious Cherubs,* though not without its flaws, contained the foundation of every belief inside of me, meaning the *substance of my soul* or, at the very least, what I'd yearned to become the *substance of my soul,* because my temperament and my beliefs were the antithesis of my now-dead wife's whose love of her fellow creatures was forthright and true, something I'd always attributed to her upbringing in a well-rounded, functioning family, she becoming, almost inevitably, a well-rounded, functioning adult, the stories from her youth like scenes from old-fashioned novels, tender stories with predictable plots and good intentions: birthday parties, summer vacations, loving parents who had no trouble displaying their affection, her adolescence a book where the ending was always going to be a happy one and this, meaning her well-rounded, functioning upbringing, carried itself into every facet of her life, my now-dead wife infinitely approachable and selfless until she wasn't, Marcel suspecting first, noticing her becoming angry which she never was, becoming impatient too, which she also never was, my wife forgetting the names of things and people, Marcel and I unnerved, worried the foundation of our family was coming apart, and I becoming more and more distraught, taking her to endless doctors who couldn't find anything wrong, *everything checks out,* they'd say, one after the other, blood tests, genetic tests, CAT scans, MRIs, cognitive assessments, and back again, repeated ad infinitum because even though *everything checks out,* they said, nothing made sense, as in my wife couldn't place the names of friends she'd known for over half of her life, and not much later a shadow pressed itself upon our lives but by then it was too late, no drug could fix or reverse her condition, *frontotemporal dementia,* the diagnosis ushered from the lips of the doctor in a tone unmistakable and grim, the woman I loved already diminished, already receding, and I sip my Mexican roast, so different from the *instant coffee* requiring a mint after each cup, a mint no soul loitering outside the *Tsypkin House of Holocaust Research* claimed to be carrying or willing to part with and the detective removed the *smartphone* from my face and tapped the screen to exhibit another photo of Kleist *the way she'd been found,* face down, slumped in the snow, instantly recognizable by her boots and I began to tremble and whimper, assuring those present this was a textbook case of shock and grief, certainly not guilt, that I *cared* for Kleist and *admired* Kleist, surely one of the greatest European sculptors of the past century and the detective seemed skeptical, mumbled something about the autopsy and how it, meaning the autopsy, would reveal everything and it's incredible, I shouted, not a single one of you motherfuckers has a mint because by then I'd become transfixed, heartache and hysteria, anguish too, all manifesting into a single obsession which was the taste of *instant coffee* on my tongue and the desire to purge that abhorrent taste with anything available, preferably a mint, and I'd become antsy and unraveled, a touch delirious, all compounded by the shock at losing Kleist, so fervent and robust days prior, the anguish something I'd deal with later, I thought, secluded in my cabin, by myself, and in a spasm of fury I pointed accusingly at the *scholarship poets,* said something about retribution and the disgrace of false mysticism, gibberish really, but the death of Kleist, the image of her ashen face anchored to a region beyond death, as well as the face of the detective, suspicious and sharp, all of it had me rattled and thrown off, evidenced by my heavy breathing, panting really, the dearth of saliva and my unwieldy tongue; I cursed the world, the *instant coffee,* my own stupidity; I struggled to answer the most routine questions posed because not only was I the last person to have seen Kleist that *final night,* the detective reminded me, but I'd spent a *considerable* amount of time with Kleist that *final night,* the detective sweeping his hand across the scene, a tableau as dumb as it was tragic; the Horner administrators in their heavy coats, the *scholarship poets* sharing cigarettes, the boarded-up entrance to the *Tsypkin House of Holocaust Research,* all of it, I thought, a spectacle stunning in its idiocy. Exchanging his *smartphone* for a notepad, the detective asked me to describe Kleist's mindset that *final night* and I released a strange cackle, said her mindset was the same as it'd always been, meaning pessimistic and dire, miserable and foreboding, meaning utterly without hope, no different than every conversation I'd ever had with her, likely no different than the last seven decades of her life and *fucking Christ*, I wheezed, have you not seen *The Boots of Stupidity*? Everyone was miffed, indignant at my behavior or Kleist's death or, who knows, the abrupt thaw in the weather, no one ever really knows what's taking place inside the minds of others, murder or revolution, neglected laundry, the sensual flesh of a dead lover, who can tell, every other human an eternal riddle, whether you've just met or shared a bed for decades, all of us a collection of mysteries both dumb and inscrutable. Especially cryptic were the Horner administrators who promptly approached, insisting I see Director Pleva in his office the following morning, nine o'clock sharp, and the detective, apparently finished, dismissed me with a wave. Quickly I stumbled back to my cottage in a stupor where, upon the steps, sat the package of Indonesian beans delivered in my absence. The next morning, reinvigorated by those sublime beans, I sat in the director's office: elaborate tapestries adorned the walls along with Persian rugs and a colossal painting depicting the scene of some ancient battle, all swords and armor and shimmering haunches. Behind Pleva's desk sat an array of death masks boasting past Horner luminaries like Algerian novelist Étienne Desjardins and Hungarian critic István Boros and, a little further up, Sergio Boschmann and Kumiko Fukagawa, the fabled mathematicians who'd rearranged the world's perception of the universe with their mind-expanding work in number theory and chaos mathematics, the expressions of those death masks conveying a mixture of triumph and religious euphoria and I recalled the outrageous stories of Boschmann and Fukagawa and the winter of

1967 at the Horner Institute, both nestled inside the now-demolished Citadel, consumed with their revolutionary work, refusing food and visitors, thronged by visions of transcending the void, of exposing the breadth of subatomic particles, from the dust upon the furthest planets to the veins inside a leaf, work requiring an enormous blackboard so large it was flown to the Berkshires, the vaulted ceiling of the Citadel the only building at Horner able to accommodate it, Boschmann and Fukagawa undertaking the completion of their proof, their masterwork, what later became known as the *Boschmann-Fukagawa Proof* which would illustrate, at long last, the *unbridled grandeur of the unadorned galaxy,* the particles of the galaxy *irrevocably undressed,* they asserted, exposed by means of their melodious proof, attainable at last to the *naked eye,* a proof, they claimed, that would leap beyond Schrödinger, beyond von Neumann and Meitner, the *Boschmann-Fukagawa Proof* merging the entire universe into a single digit, one solitary number encapsulating every object in the history of existence which, thanks to their exquisite proof, would be seen all at once like an enormous scroll, although not *like* a scroll, they corrected themselves, but *precisely* a scroll, a proof aiming to tell the history of our galaxy as well as the trajectory of our future, unspooled with no regard for proportion or constraint, the micro and the macro, the infinitesimal and the colossal, a series of undulating lines which represented the thread inside every single object and non-object in existence, even the objects we no longer saw, the *ghosts of objects,* explained Fukagawa, the less reticent of the two, a former lover of

Boschmann's and a polio survivor, banished from the most prestigious universities in her native Japan after a series of mental breakdowns both in public and in private, though for the proof to be understood, she explained, it must be displayed as a series of endless schema, first presented on the enormous blackboard flown in and deposited in the Citadel and later in a series of six cloth octavos published in sumptuous dark plum, and, once circulated, both Boschmann and Fukagawa were lauded across the globe, given fellowships and chairs at countless universities because no one argued against or challenged the *Boschmann-Fukagawa Proof* since no one was certain they understood the *Boschmann-Fukagawa Proof,* it was too obscure, said some, too impenetrable, said others; thus no one could *disprove* their proof just as no one was able to *prove* their proof, still everyone admired the *Boschmann-Fukagawa Proof* for its inherent beauty, its so-called *poetic simplicity,* venerated the proof, at least in theory, a work exhibiting both the horror and the sublimity of our galaxy, an endeavor which borrowed from *Ostrogradsky's Divergent Theorem* while remaining wholly independent of *Ostrogradsky's Divergent Theorem,* simultaneously drawing from and refuting contemporary vector calculus too, somehow simultaneously; the world of science and mathematics bewitched by the paradox of the work as well as its sublime arrangement, a conception of our collective past and our remote future contained in fewer than fifty typed pages, a proof representing the entire breadth and sublimity of the known universe, the ceaseless equations and supple seduction of quantum mechanics in order to arrive at their conclusion, a proof like a prophecy, glistening and austere, foretelling the collapse of our galaxy as well as its origins, and to the layman it appeared dormant and dull, but the work conducted to *achieve* their proof and what their proof represented had consequences both auspicious and disastrous because the few minds able to eventually corroborate and grasp the *Boschmann-Fukagawa Proof* suddenly saw the cosmos stripped down and ghastly, presented in a way that could never be unseen, like an unending massacre, said one, like a panic attack lasting for infinity, said another, the few minds able to ascertain the proof and what the proof represented were crucified by their own knowledge, attempting to sway anyone they could to abandon the pursuit of ever understanding the *Boschmann-Fukagawa Proof,* as it would forever wreak havoc on one's perception of existence and years later, in the middle of a lecture in Potsdam, Boschmann stopped mid-sentence, wrote something on a slip of paper, and took a vow of silence, still showing up at conferences and symposiums around the world where, sitting in the audience, nodding his patrician head, taking the occasional note, he refused to speak no matter how many acolytes and colleagues approached attempting to cajole a single syllable from Boschmann, who kept his vow of silence until he died at seventy-two from, of all things, a slip in the kitchen, and the death masks of both, meaning Boschmann and Fukagawa, surveyed the director's office with an aspect of phlegmatic gloom, Director Pleva settling in his chair, withholding even the most cursory of pleasantries to confess the misgivings he'd had about my book-length essay, doubts he'd harbored since accepting my application. I've wrestled with uncertainty my entire life, began Pleva, all jowls and pasty complexion, in fact when I interviewed for the job of director more than a decade ago after a stint at the *Basel Institute of Human Sciences,* my capacity for uncertainty was an enormous selling point, uncertainty as well as the anxiety that arises from uncertainty an enormous boon, so said my predecessor, confessed Pleva, and it's true, my uncertainty has paid off, uncertainty has helped me tap into the so-called *oddities* of untraditional talent, helped me detect the luminous when even the artist themselves doesn't see it, yes, in my decade here there have been countless examples, Camille Descoteaux for one, the Dadaist who, when she fashioned her dueling works outside the quadrangle, *Dans la Boue vs. Pariah,* which didn't seem like much at the time but went on to win the *Chevalier of the French Legion,* confirmed to me the significance of my uncertainty; it was then my uncertainty transformed to certainty, a chrysalis becoming a butterfly, though to be frank, he sighed, that's neither here nor there, the point being my uncertainty permits me to make one exception each season, that's right, I accept one applicant *outside the realm of conspicuous talent,* an applicant whose ideas are seemingly slight and second-rate, an applicant who is either mediocre or quietly brilliant, subpar or softly sagacious, in short, a genius or an idiot, one or the other since it's impossible to be both, someone I accept in the hopes the Horner grounds and the priceless works at their disposal will inspire, enflame, and speak to the deepest parts of their souls, for even one with the blandest heart must surely be swayed by the beauty of the *Pleasure Gardens* or the lithe and seductive architecture of the quadrangle, the quadrangle whose lines have always evoked a quiet sexuality, the composition of the quadrangle and the symmetry of the quadrangle and the murmurs the quadrangle produces on a warm night if one feels obliged or compelled to circle the quadrangle while extending a single hand along its envelope listening perhaps to the evocative purr the quadrangle produces, one feeling the quadrangle calling out to them in the tongue of ancient kin or the specter of a deity, in short, a *celestial presence,* and not the obvious aspects, said Pleva, no, not the stone nymphs carved into the facade or the angular doors that shocked the shareholders at its unveiling, I'm talking about the *skin* of the quadrangle, the outer walls that contain the quadrangle's character, I mean, am I mistaken? Am I wrong? This was our hope, said Pleva, this was our ambition, Pleva added, and this winter it was you, my exception, because I studied your application and the idea of your book-length essay about Montaigne seemed a touch *frivolous,* a touch *obvious,* but unusual enough to believe you might surprise us, interesting enough to make an exception, but let's be honest with ourselves, he said, we're all bombarded by noise and interruption and the frivolous clamor of the outside world, are we not? The point being to create one's work *despite the noise,* not to make art *about* the noise or *purported art* that chronicles the inability to make art because of the noise itself and then *call that the art.* Anyone can do that, doing that is simply a complaint, a mere grievance, I mean, am I wrong? In any case, said Pleva, it's all very charming, *your work,* it has the sheen of serious work but only the sheen because underneath there's nothing there, it's vague and naïve and without direction. What's it have to do with Montaigne, asked Pleva, as regards you and me and your fellow man? Tell me, am I mistaken? Am I wrong? Invoking Montaigne's name doesn't make you a *Montaignian* nor even a *Montaigne scholar,* frankly I'm not even sure it gains you entrance into the *orbit of Montaigne,* because you've had at your disposal a facsimile of a copy of Montaigne's diary which, according to my notes, you've checked out from the *Tanner Room* no less than eighteen times, eighteen times according to my notes, you've left the *Tanner Room* with a facsimile of a copy of Montaigne's diary to study inside the *Tanner Reading Room* and what's it produced? No, said Pleva with conviction, I've come to the conclusion your talent doesn't match your ambition, and what we've gained with your time here instead is the death of the great Kleist, a travesty, a tragedy, which I don't blame on you, of course not, no, even though you were with her that *final night,* and complaints now from the administrators as well as the current fellows, not to mention a few *scholarship poets* which, trust me, I couldn't care less about, the *scholarship poets* mere distractions, gnats at a picnic, a piece of food caught in one's teeth after a meal, still, they're a tradition, a part of the tapestry at Horner and so we let the *scholarship poets* flutter about in their meaningless circles reading their dumb poems and sharing their dumb poems and sending their dumb poems to even dumber journals, let them gossip and bemoan and fuck one another, let them exalt in their own ambition, you get it, what-ever it is the *scholarship poets* do, it's not hurting anyone, right? But there have been grievances about your behavior, *written grievances*. In the *Tanner Room* for one, as well as the *Tanner Reading Room;* erratic, they've written, antisocial, they've also written, mumbling to yourself *ad nauseum,* they've said, which is nothing too alarming at a place like this because we've had our share of misanthropes and eccentrics and an entire decade of nudism, but these *written grievances* were emphatic, using the word *charlatan* in regards to you and your work, yes, in fact, the word *charlatan* was bandied about six, maybe seven times in the *written grievances* I received, so much so I noticed a pattern in the use of the word *charlatan,* almost as if the grievances, their au-thors ardent and myriad, went out of their way to point out you and your outright *charlatanism,* the fact of you being a *charlatan* painfully obvious, they seemed to say, to even the most dull and dim witted, so you see, Pleva said, I'm in a bind, twiddling his thumbs as if concerned about a decision he'd have to make which I was certain he'd already made, the parade of death masks looming over his shoulders like a parody of all our earthly ambi-tions, each blithely mocking the chasm awaiting us, and I ex-pected to be dismissed or expelled, asked to go home, whatever the tradition was with pariahs, but Director Pleva wasn't upset, in fact he appeared blasé, merely suggesting I spend more time in my fellowship cottage for the month that remained, keep a low profile, and perhaps think twice about attending *bonfire night* and this scene was an augury, played out years later in not one but two emergency reviews, yes, I think, sipping my coffee, the act of explaining my work, the spectacle of defending and justifying myself before the tenured administrators of the community college, a pattern replicating itself in both the first and second emergency review, the second concluding with administrative probation and soon thereafter the *espresso incident,* the climax of months of complaints from students and faculty colliding when I decided to clean the *Nuova Simonelli* espresso machine during Humanities 102 or Philosophy 103, I can't remember, and years later, meaning now, the scene replays itself continuously in my mind, the shrieks of the students when the hose burst from behind the desk, discharging clouds of steam and jets of scalding water because I'd made the novice mistake of cleaning the machine while in *latte mode,* and a metallic screech rent the air into a thousand shards followed by an angry hiss that reverberated through the halls, the water scalding my arm, an unfathomable pain, and I wailed from the burns, and a startled student, mistaking the steam for smoke, pulled the fire alarm, which only added to the confusion, and I released a string of outlandish curses, *dickfucker, bitchtits, motherfucking savage Christ,* and on it went, a litany that prompted several students to brandish their *smartphones* and begin documenting the *espresso incident,* one getting up close like a guerilla filmmaker or aspiring auteur, attentive to each angle and frame, circling me while I beseeched God to strike me down and take the class with me, why not, I'd screamed, *fuck them all,* realizing only then the time serious burns take at announcing their severity is rather sluggish, notably the pain, the pain which doesn't decrease but multiplies with each second that passes, the pain like nothing I'd ever experienced, and I kicked the *Nuova Simonelli* espresso machine, cursed its very existence because my life was in shambles, notably a wife who didn't recognize me and a son endlessly pontificating about *underground techno* or *Chicago house* or the *aesthetics of trance-pop* and *Jesus Christ,* I thought, who cares? Meanwhile the fire alarm was signaling the neighboring instructors of a fire which didn't exist, the burns on my arm changing colors like mother-of-pearl and a student sitting in the front glimpsed the burns and fainted, the two students-turned-filmmakers instinctively separating; one opting for the fainted student and the other fixed sharply on me, holding the *smartphone* like a seasoned journalist, stepping forward and back at the optimal moments as I cursed all of creation, as I bristled with indignation, *goddamn jackals,* I raved, *fucking lunatics,* I bellowed, the curses long winded and scatological, directed at no one in particular but not without a certain vigor, and my slack-jawed students weren't so slack-jawed anymore, I thought, not so vacant and dim, invigorated by my outburst and the chaos at hand, yes, it was calamity and misfortune that roused their dull minds, I thought, bedlam that kindled their flaccid thoughts, and I beseeched Sarah, the least bovine of my students, to run to the infirmary for a first-aid kit and Alex, the second-least bovine of my students, to get towels and ice and I couldn't give a good goddamn where, I howled, just find them, towels, I shouted, and fucking ice, I added, a gauzy veil clouding my vision, edges becoming blurred, time itself turning muddled and formless, sped up or slowed down or both at once, I couldn't tell, and the fire alarm had given unnecessary urgency to the situation because the risk was altogether absent; I'd unplugged the espresso machine seconds after the explosion or blast or combustion, call it what you want, it's unplugged, I assured the class, holding back tears, attempting composure, arm blazing, temples throbbing, yes, I cried, the threat is minimal, likely nonexistent, and the four portraits of Montaigne looked down in consternation at what I had become. Was this how failure announced itself, I thought, with clamor and cacophony and the ridiculous bombast of farce? Was I the victim of some cosmic whim? Had I been singled out? Was my decline, grotesque and absurd, as farcical as it was trivial, altogether unavoidable? Days later I found myself in the dean's office, more solitary and solemn than the first and second emergency reviews, the dean alone, asking me to shut the door, offering a glass of water, explaining in a pinched expression the unavoidable consequences of the *espresso incident,* a moniker bestowed hours after the episode, the *espresso incident* the only thing being talked about, all of it captured on the *smartphones* and spread ubiquitously online, as popular in Beijing as in Auckland, sped up, edited, given different musical accompaniments, from bluegrass to hip-hop, slowed down to the sounds of barbershop quartet, someone in Belfast incorporating animation, adding fake applause, found sounds, animal noises, countless versions of the *espresso incident* sent soaring across the globe, the humiliation of my crack-up circulating for the enjoyment of

the dim-witted hordes; the blare of the fire alarm, the fainted girl
wholly neglected, the half-dozen students contorted with laugh-
ter, all of it projected seamlessly onto millions of tiny screens,
and in an analog world, I thought, the *espresso incident* would've
been just that, *an incident,* never making it past campus; fucking
smartphone, I fumed to myself, goddamn piece of shit *smart-*
phone, I fumed further, making it virtually impossible to suffer
an emotional collapse in private anymore, and swift action was
demanded, the dean said, the dean's tone caustic and grim, more
portentous than I'd ever heard, because it wasn't just the trauma
of the event, she said, or the fainting student, or the dangers of
having the espresso machine concealed beneath the desk, no,
she said, in addition to the *utter disregard for safety* it was also the
deception, meaning the installation of the *Nuova Simonelli*
espresso machine itself, ensconced beneath my desk, hidden under stacks of ungraded essays and an enormous biography of
Voltaire, the colossal appliance weighing well over three hundred pounds, meant for commercial use, discovered while I was
in the emergency room, rife with the stench of medicine and
mishap, the sudden talk of skin grafts which, thanks to the pain
meds, meant very little, yes, a cast of neighboring professors es-
corted by the janitorial staff had inspected the luminous machine in my absence, its countless valves and shimmering architecture illustrating a passion for coffee and its history, the
machine's complexity and artistry, the sheer force of its presence, an appliance which enticed me the moment I'd opened the
box, me thinking *what the fuck will I do with this,* me thinking

how is it even possible I've ordered something so gargantuan, like-wise knowing I would never return the *Nuova Simonelli* espresso machine because of its sensuous curves and stainless-steel frame which evoked passion and a contemplation approaching, dare I say, the celestial, as well as the lustrous reflection of my face, gratefully distorting the expression of a man whose wife was dy-ing, who went home, paid the nurse, and looked into the dishev-eled face of the only woman he'd ever loved, who on most days smelled of her own shit because the nurse hadn't changed her and *of course* I would keep the espresso machine, I thought, be-cause watching my wife dissolve extinguished the little faith I'd had in the world and the dean sighed, sorely disappointed, she said, dumbfounded, she added, confessing she'd seen no im-provement since the second emergency review, in fact, things had only worsened since the second emergency review, the sec-ond emergency review convened for a host of reasons including spontaneous outbursts of sobbing because I had begun crying in class, frequently too, sudden and abrupt pangs of despair, often without warning, startling the students ill equipped to observe the crude agony of an adult rapidly advancing toward late mid-dle age, manifesting in spasmodic outbursts of tears and sure, I thought, I'd no doubt become a bit *frenzied,* a tad *manic,* but my lectures were better and smoother and certainly *smarter* than they'd ever been; the four Montaignes peering down as I recited from Plato's dialogues or *The Tibetan Book of the Dead,* excerpts of Pizarnik's *Extracting the Stone of Madness,* whatever entered my mind, desperately trying to show those dolts the sheer multiplicity of the world while likewise avoiding thoughts of my soon-to-be-dead wife or my son's idiotic voicemails or the inevitable heartbreaking stupidity of being a living, breathing mammal, and it's not only the crying, said the dean, because there's the assignments too, she said, *ridiculous assignments,* she added, from the dioramas of Montaigne's château to the reenactments of Pushkin's fatal duel, none of this helped and, lest I forget, said the dean, the professors on both sides of my class and their *utter exasperation* over Stravinsky and *The Rite of Spring* or, more precisely, *the volume* at which I played Stravinsky and *The Rite of Spring,* and it's disturbing, they complained, a torment, they also complained, the professors and their students supposedly at their wits' end, a *plethora of outrageous infractions,* the document stated, read aloud during the second emergency review, *outrageous* and *infractions* underlined and in bold to lend gravity to the litany of improprieties. No, said the dean, following the *espresso incident,* she and I alone in her office, shades drawn, afternoon waning, golden light from the athletic fields faintly discernible, the community college simply *couldn't have it,* not explaining what *it* was, plainly confident we both well understood what *it* was without ever having to say *it,* though the dean never explained *it* or defined *it* and official-looking papers were shuffled across the desk pertaining to *immediate termination* but I didn't read the official-looking papers nor wait to find out because a sense of liberation had materialized, either from having a wife who was dying or the fact of never having been fired from a job before, never in my life, the determination to quit suddenly radiating from a place deep inside and I clapped my hands and stood, told the dean I was leaving and that was that, that I couldn't be terminated nor fired; I was taking early retirement, not knowing exactly what early retirement was or what it entailed and had I done the legwork necessary for retiring early, I wondered, was early retirement investing money or paying extra taxes or, conversely, withholding taxes, siphoning money into a shelter somewhere or perhaps signing a dozen dull forms labeled 10-A-50 or S-97? No matter, I thought, because my soon-to-be-dead wife's parents had left us some money, not a colossal amount, but enough to pay for a part-time nurse as well as assist me in caring for my wife, to hang blankets and towels on all the windows and recede from the world, for a few years at least, which is exactly what I did, and the dean smiled in sympathy, asked how she was, meaning my wife-who-hadn't-yet-died and I told the dean I appreciated her thoughts but my wife was suffering from *frontotemporal dementia* and there was no cure, that it was horrible and tragic and a litany of other things, all of them bad, but it was time at last for me to make a *heroic effort,* not only in the care of my ailing wife and her *catastrophic disease,* I said, but my masterwork, yes, by taking early retirement I'd finally have the time to dedicate myself to my *life's work,* the *foundation of an important and radiant work,* I said, *a critical work,* namely a book-length essay that would usher in a new genre, forcing astute readers to ask: is it an essay? is it a memoir? is it a work of incomprehensible genius and thus uncategorizable? Yes, I told the dean, she sitting, me standing, I would baptize the world with a wholly new genre of work dedicated to the *inner voice of the human soul,* a work based on the glorious essays of Montaigne, in dialogue with the glorious essays of Montaigne, an *appendage* to the glorious essays of Montaigne and speaking of him, meaning Montaigne, is it okay to retrieve my portraits? The dean shuffled some papers, cleared her throat, said my belongings had been packed in boxes outside of her office, currently attended by several security waiting to see me off campus and I smiled, told her the community college could keep the *Nuova Simonelli* as a gift, name it after me, place it in the teachers' lounge, hardly able to say the words *teachers' lounge* without laughing, yes, I said, enlighten the educators about what real coffee tastes like, I concluded, promptly leaving the dean's office to begin a new chapter, a chapter rife with doctor's appointments and medicines, with keeping my wife's deteriorating mind off the topic of *spaceships* and *dark beings,* one long *counterfeit night,* I think, swallowing the last drops of coffee while Marcel rhapsodizes through the *smartphone* about *samples* and how they, meaning samples, are like abstract art, samples the *musical equivalent of abstract art,* he says, and I want to get off the phone as I feel a cry coming on, not a hysterical cry, not like the cry last week outside my dead wife's closet, but a slow, simmering cry, the sort of cry that announces itself in a tremor, a mild upheaval that arrives in quiet waves, forcing one to retreat to the bed and cocoon oneself in the blanket, the bedroom desolate as a trench, colder than a coffin, but getting off the phone presents its own challenges because Marcel is implacable, more intent and fervent than the last time we spoke, Marcel explaining through the *smartphone* about how the best samples are exercises in *contortion,* the best samples a *perversion* of the source material, chopping it, slowing it down, playing it backward, yet managing to retain the *soul of the source material,* he says, beckoning to that *source material* throughout the song: a soul song, a church choir, an African American spiritual, the melody from an obscure reggae song, whatever the *source material* is, it doesn't matter, the point being, says Marcel, the song employs the sample to give a shade, a color, an ingredient that wouldn't exist without it, the sample expressing what the song itself cannot, the song in fact a skeleton without the sample, the sample creating a *sonic texture* for the song and hence the sample doubles as a *perversion* of the *source material* as well as a *deification* of the *source material,* a totem of admiration for the song itself and the genre to which the song belongs, and instead of crying I decide to make another cup of coffee, a light roast with overtones of fruit and a well-balanced acidity, the same drink Europeans realized after its introduction from the Turks helped assuage melancholy and gloom, opening ramshackle coffeehouses throughout London where the English quickly realized the effects of the beverage were similar to alcohol or opium and naturally the religious were suspicious of the dark liquid which, when served hot, changed the behavior of its drinkers and soon enough English apothecaries were endorsing the wondrous properties of the drink, meaning coffee, everything from digestion to temperament to the alleviation of pain and mental distress and it wasn't long before coffeehouses were sprouting up throughout London and its immediate outskirts, and while Marcel veers into his opinions on *techno,* which, he admits, are stubborn and complex, I walk into the kitchen with the idea of grinding some coffee, high elevation from Burundi, and I consider the ways a person enjoys their coffee and what it says about their personality and disposition; my now-dead wife enjoyed coffee with a hint of cream and sugar, sugar an absolute requirement for my now-dead wife, whereas I've always loved coffee black but also enjoy it with a hint of milk or cream, but never sugar, sugar a moral crime, I'd tell my now-dead wife, sugar in one's coffee a sign of *moral decrepitude* and *waning ethics,* both of us laughing, me sitting beside her with our coffee, both of us talking or not talking, often saying nothing at all, merely sitting beside one another in silence, drinking coffee, nothing as simple and profound, and in the beginning both of us watching Marcel sleep, in his crib and later his bed, the two of us slinking out of his room to enjoy our morning ritual of coffee, a custom as fixed and essential as getting dressed and me harassing my now-dead wife about adding sugar to her coffee, nothing more *lowbrow* and *insipid,* I'd tell her, nothing so revealing of *inferior taste* and *social deviance,* and adding sugar to your coffee gives me an actual *physical pain,* I'd tell her, a *violent tic,* I'd say, *a sense of repulsion* for which no words have yet been concocted, and both of us laughing, knowing it didn't matter, what mattered was being companions in this curious life, so strange and beautiful and undeniably tragic, me expounding to my wife about the beans, beans easily the most crucial ingredient in coffee next to water, that goes without saying, I said, the origin of the bean and the roasting technique of the bean, both of unequivocal importance, and when one drinks coffee one often forgets or is perhaps altogether ignorant about the beans, notably the origin of the beans, beans passed through ten or twelve different pairs of hands, maybe more, grown, cultivated, hulled, dried, roasted, and distributed by a litany of strangers across an array of continents, the history of coffee, in fact, as rich as the drink itself, a history as awash with humanity's stories as anything, Balzac's *Treatise on Modern Stimulants,* I told my wife, an exceptional work, minor though it is, Balzac emphasizing coffee's miraculous ability at not only alleviating sleep but also helping one concentrate for longer periods, meaning a drink not meant solely for the morning when one yearns to remove the delicate webs of the unconscious, but later in the day, when one is in the throes of their life's labor, for Balzac this meant works like *Cousin Bette* and *Père Goriot,* in short, Balzac's entire *La Comédie Humaine,* novels bursting with tyrants and outlaws, financiers and street urchins, all the myriad types that traipse this great, heartbreaking world, the beautiful and the villainous, the sturdy and the frail, the victims and the predators alike, and for me, I'd say, coffee is crucial for my book-length essay, my wife resting her head on my shoulder, stroking my knee, her sympathetic eyes, her chestnut hair, her quick mind and kind heart, yes, I see her now, smiling at my enthusiasm, at my ridiculous digressions, and standing in the kitchen I'm plagued by nostalgia, cursed with looking back at what's gone forever, even though I know it wasn't always perfect, of course not, she and I fought too, of course we fought, she distressed and disappointed, not just by my staying at the community college, but by my always teaching Philosophy 101 and Humanities 102, year after year, the same courses which ushered the same complaints, when I should've, in her words, been *evolving,* and what does it matter, I'd say, it affords me the time to work on my book, and sometimes she'd simply nod, her way of feigning agreement, but other times she'd roll her eyes because my now-dead wife had been listening to me talk about my book-length essay for years, had heard enough about my book-length essay to last three or four lifetimes combined or stretched lengthwise, yes, she knew the story backward and forward, and without saying it out loud, she wanted the ambition I had for my Montaigne book to be devoted toward everything else, the topic we most often fought about, although, as I said, we had a deep affection for one another and as fierce as the quarrels were, we always made up, always knew enough to forgive one another and it's outrageous that she's gone, I think, preposterous I have a closet bursting with her scent but not her. Dead, I think, gone forever, I also think, while Marcel's voice meanders through the *smartphone,* the two of us all that remains of a family, the *remnants* of a family, what a sick joke, what a fucking sham, so much agony and grief it's inexpressible, no words yet invented to capture how merciless undiluted grief is, how impossible to navigate a world awash with undiluted grief, just the two of us left and my wife not around to comfort us in her absence, I think, grinding the coffee, boiling the water, smelling the first fragrance of the coffee, trying not to cry, even though I want to cry, the primitive desire to cry overwhelming, forcing myself instead to think of Balzac and coffee, anything in the world besides the paralyzing inclination to cry, the tightening in my chest, the pang in my heart, smelling the coffee in an attempt not to cry, and it was Balzac, I recall, who said, *coffee connoisseurs begin as with any passion: by degrees.* Yes, it was by degrees that my wife lost her mind, a tragedy in slow motion, forgetting small things at first, but quickly larger things; instead of the house keys it became the house, instead of the car keys it became the car, calling me in hysterics, unsure of where her car was, not only where it was parked but what kind of car she drove, me attempting to calm her down but assailed by the fear in her voice, a voice that sounded nothing at all like my wife's regular voice, stiff and petrified, and the fact that she had no recollection of her car's whereabouts was terrifying, for me surely, but for her it must've felt as if the universe had collapsed; suddenly we'd crossed some intractable marker; her forgetfulness was no longer charming, some cute foible, but the first tepid drops of an approaching storm and I was frightened of asking her on the phone where she was for fear of my wife not knowing and what would I say if she, in essence, told me she was lost? And it wasn't long after, six months or a year, that she was forced to stop working, unable to drive or remember *where* she was driving and eventually the diagnosis of *frontotemporal dementia,* those terrible words, followed by a string of cliches; *no known cure, quick decline, hopeless case,* a dire diagnosis, astonishing how quickly her mental disintegration occurred, how rapidly she transformed from my companion to a helpless stranger: her disheveled hair and chapped lips, her eyes either dim or filled with mania, the deadly conviction there were *spaceships* hovering over our street, a dull, typical American street, a street endowed with loneliness and mediocrity and lawns manicured to reflect a sense of order that never existed, the disintegration of her mind something from a nightmare and standing in the kitchen attempting not to cry while the coffee steeps, while Marcel preaches about synth chords sticky as taffy and ectoplasm, wanting desperately to weep or, at the very least, soothe my nerves by listening to Stravinsky and *The Rite of Spring* but attempting this on the *smartphone* has already proven impossible when I can't even silence the goddamn chirp, the *smartphone's* chirps which will continue once I hang up and deep into the long remote future, Armageddon could come and the world would be left with only rubble and the chirps of *smartphones,* those chirps rising from the detritus of civilization, chirps inexorably tied to our fates, chirps alerting us of sales on cereals or collapsing democracies, car accidents or abducted children, and *fucking Christ,* the updates, I think, the number of updates for these contraptions is beyond comprehension, the updates of updates that suddenly need updates to correct the last update before the next update, and I pour a cup of coffee from Burundi, return to the third bedroom, and sit at the rolltop desk, finally prepared to work on my book-length essay, not only the titles but the work itself, yes, I think, finding the passages with promise, ignoring the endless bibliographical tangents citing wholly unrelated works, but focus instead on the excerpts taken from the facsimile of a copy of Montaigne's diary gathered at the Horner Institute. It's time to merge them together, I think, time to assimilate the best elements of *Montaigne and the Lugubrious Cherubs,* the poetic parts, the profound parts, time to sift through my notes and commence at long last with my life's work, enough dawdling, I think, enough procrastination, I also think, time to merge the best pieces to create a *sustained piece of original thinking,* a book-length essay unlike anything anyone has ever read, vested in the works of Montaigne but radiating outward like an enormous flower or the birth of a galaxy, yes, I think, *the birth of a galaxy,* meant to encompass the fractured modern world but seen anew, although before this I must endure Marcel's pontifications about *dance culture,* about his sudden decision to move either to Bogotá or Berlin, one or the other, and what will I do when he's gone, I think, the news of his move so unexpected it hasn't even registered, and I imagine Marcel adrift in some other country, *crate-digging* and *spinning records,* and Marcel won't mention the drugs of course, but I'm no idiot, I know about the drugs, or at least *suspect* the drugs, Marcel probably using the drugs while *turning* or *spinning* records; coke, ecstasy, pills, designer drugs, you name it, I can see him now, bathed beneath the flickering lights, sweating from the cocaine and the pills, everything more vibrant, he thinks, more urgent too, in short, *better,* and I've met his friends and his roommates, other DJs mumbling in slothful somnolence, resembling sleepwalkers, worse even than my slack-jawed students poking their tiny screens while waiting for their thoughts to be interrupted, and for the last five years it's only been Marcel, the nurse, and my now-dead wife inside the house, no one else, except of course last week, following the funeral, after sitting shiva, when I'd removed the sheets and blankets from all of the windows for the sake of the mourners and the rabbi and my dead wife's friends, everyone dressed in black because of ritual, because of etiquette, and me replacing the sheets and blankets the moment they left, watching the last mourners getting in their cars, and me wasting no time, dashing around the house and once more darkening the interior of the house by covering all of the windows, Marcel following me as I returned the sheets and blankets to their rightful place, meaning the windows, Marcel asking what I was doing because she's gone, he said, she's dead, he added, insisting there were no *spaceships* and of course there aren't, I replied, but there's *everything else,* Marcel baffled as I explained I'd grown accustomed to the darkened house for countless reasons, the primary reason being the world *out there,* the world *out there,* I said, chafed and harassed, did it not? Yes, I went on, attaching a sheet across the front windows with electrical tape, not allowing Marcel a chance to respond or even disagree, the world *out there,* I continued, didn't *feel right,* the world *out there* demanded the grotesque and the preposterous, cared more in fact for the grotesque and the preposterous than the profound and I'd even say, I said, the world out there *recognized* and *subscribed* to the grotesque and the preposterous, celebrated the grotesque and the preposterous at the *expense of the profound* and besides, I said, fastening another blanket, I've become accustomed to this *counterfeit night,* Marcel following me through the house, suddenly worried for the sanity of his father days after burying his mother, the interior of the house once again enveloped in darkness, like a crypt, I bragged, like a wasteland or the holding cell to an abyss and *Jesus Christ,* Marcel screamed, what the fuck does that even mean? But now, sitting at my desk, sipping coffee, Marcel ranting about different brands of synthesizers, proclaiming his love for *Afrobeat* and *dubstep,* my mind meanders, one moment Dylan Thomas then John Keats, next the coffeehouses of Aleppo and following this, the cafés along the Golden Horn, those pungent coffeehouses of Istanbul made famous by Zafar Ul Hakim, legendary barista who refused to ever turn anyone away, offering tiny cups of strong black coffee, often on credit, my mind veering suddenly to Erik Satie's *Vexations,* Satie's simple and yet oft-misinterpreted instruction to perform the piece, meaning *Vexations,* 840 times in succession and the performer, meaning the pianist, better have a comfortable stool, I think, he or she better be hydrated and committed to performing the single sheet of music that makes up *Vexations* 840 times in succession and once more I'm struck by grief, by nostalgia, by the sting of anguish, thinking of my dead wife and the tragic farce of existence, how the moment you have a grip, a foothold, the slightest sliver of understanding, something slips, a breakdown, a car accident, a heart attack, ceaseless cataclysms pervading our lives, meanwhile Marcel is explaining his feelings about UK *bass*, a trend heavily influenced by *dubstep* and *grime,* and I like it okay, he says, but I don't love it, I mean I could take it or leave it, he says, but I can't imagine listening to an *entire album* of UK *bass;* it's too frantic and frenzied, it's meant for the club, for dancing or driving around with friends and nothing else, so the quality and the musicianship isn't as high and perhaps it relies too much on gimmicks, uses gimmicks in the place of melody because, in my opinion, UK bass is completely *devoid of melody* and although bass is *imperative* in good dance music, bass in fact *essential* in regards to dance music, when it's only used as a propulsive device of the song, the bass I'm talking about, it's nothing more than a gimmick, I mean it, and I admire the experimental and the *avant-garde* as much as the next DJ, sure, but never at the expense of melody, because I'm a real sucker for melody, and lots of people swear by UK bass, but the dream, *my dream,* is to make an album like Lindstrøm or Prins Thomas or Aksel Schaufler, aka Superpitcher, those German and Norwegian artists whose songs are inundated with swirling textures of color and unmitigated joy, and likewise have no qualms experimenting with *shoegaze* and *modern pop,* music as connected to *Krautrock* as *dance music,* says Marcel, especially *Norwegian Space Disco, Norwegian Space Disco* the epitome of my dream because by focusing on joy they reach the pinnacle of solemnity, by invoking wonder they exhibit the aspiration for serious thought because historically it's the clowns who are the truth-seekers and, speaking of clowns, I almost forgot Todd Terje, says Marcel, Terje, whose exuberant songs wink at the listener, telling the listener there's nothing more important and profound than this moment, dancing with a thousand strangers, laughing and crying, collectively experiencing the joy of existence; ground shaking, walls trembling, eyesight pulverized by the strobes, by the music and the joy, yes, my dream is to make an album akin to Lindstrøm's *Where You Go I Go Too,* a masterpiece of electronic music, of dance music and headphone music, of *undiluted euphoria,* and Lindstrøm smiling mischievously on the cover of *Where You Go I Go Too,* in black and white no less, the humility and knowledge that he, meaning Lindstrøm, has produced a masterpiece, he knows it, the discerning listener knows it, *Where You Go I Go Too,* a record as timely and timeless as anything ever recorded, a journey as well as a fable because the title track, *Where You Go I Go Too,* a twenty-eight-minute song, swells and unfurls, collecting details the way an avalanche or landslide collects pebbles and soil as it charges down a mountain and in this fashion Lindstrøm collects drums, lasers, strange bells and remote crackles and the sheer exhilaration and rhythmical persistence of *Where You Go I Go Too,* says Marcel, exhibit new details with each listen and I sit at my desk, sipping coffee, half listening to Marcel, while contemplating the grueling effort needed to complete my book-length essay, Marcel ranting about the radiance of *electronic dance music* and the *ecstasy of electronic dance music,* especially *Where You Go I Go Too,* a masterpiece by Lindstrøm, he says, an unequivocal masterpiece, he insists, and I recall Kleist and her masterpieces, not only *The Boots of Stupidity,* created in the neighboring cottage, but the entire arc of her sculpting career, her first exhibition in fact, *Death of Beauty,* at the *Museo de Arte Moderno* in Mexico City, back in the '80s, how Kleist abandoned her first show, she confessed, leaving the sprawling, seemingly endless metropolis of Mexico City, her first international exhibition, she explained that night, what turned out to be her *final night,* powerful gusts shrieking outside as Kleist weaved between her works and I'd barely sat down and Kleist busy navigating between her newest collection explaining how she'd left the *Museo de Arte Moderno* situated in the center of Chapultepec Park, not far from Chapultepec Castle, fled the incredibly influential show, she said, a *pivotal exhibit,* she added, but I left, she said, and not because of *artistic anxieties* or concerns over the quality and consonance of my work, something, she admitted, she never had any qualms with, no, she said, swigging from the bottle, the liquid clear and potent, because I've always been confident and honest with myself, she said, when the work was brilliant I said so, when the work was uninspired, when it simply wasn't good but paltry and slight, I said so too because above all an artist must be honest with themselves, honesty in fact the only virtue an artist must possess, everything else only hinders, everything else only baggage, but honesty with oneself is vital, and at some point you have to step away from the work, step away and shrug, washing your hands of the piece: a painting, a poem, a play, whatever it is, and say with utter finality: *this was the best I could do* because creating a work of art is no different than walking a tightrope or skating across the blade of a knife and if you *dawdle* or *second-guess* or *rearrange* too much, the original idea, the seed and inspiration of that idea is molested, you've already failed for any number of reasons: perfectionism, endless revisions, perhaps not knowing what you wanted in the first place and you've fallen from the tightrope or knife blade that is artistic creation, though this wasn't the case with my first exhibition, *Death of Beauty,* because *Death of Beauty* was a powerful collection, sculptures I was proud to exhibit, but, as I said, she said, hours before the opening I got it in my mind to leave and this is what I did. I left.

I took a bus to Cuernavaca to look for Scholz, the man who'd tortured my mother and father and countless other Jews so long ago in *Gusen II*, murdered countless Jews too, then stolen a Jewish name and escaped and fled to Mexico, according to my mother, said Kleist, supposedly living in Cuernavaca, at least from what my mother said, muttered Kleist, the cabin convulsing, winds speaking in tongues, yes, said Kleist, I'd already conducted the research, very basic research, but enough to know there existed the *possibility* that Scholz, now Scholzberg, was indeed alive, as my mother claimed, and I kept this with me the entire trip, the research I mean; on the flight, in the hotel, walking the radiant streets of Cuauhtémoc and Tacubaya and Juarez, and all the time the research was calling out, speaking to me in my mother's voice, insisting I abandon the show and go to Cuernavaca with no idea what I would do when I arrived, but I did it, I left the environs of Mexico City because I'd thought to myself: I couldn't be this close to Scholz (now Scholzberg) who may or may not still be alive, and not make the effort to set my eyes on him, possibly confront him, I simply couldn't, so I left the exhibition, left the *Museo de Arte Moderno,* walked away from my first international show, took a bus to Cuernavaca, leaving Mexico City, a city which never truly ends, Mexico City merely *tapers*; one might disengage themselves from the twelve lanes of traffic and the endless congestion, but the clamor extends beyond one's sight, the largest Spanish-speaking city on the planet you know, a city that expands the further you flee, a city that keeps its grip the harder and farther you try to abscond, spreading endlessly, a city that's famously horizontal, that's famously unending, because there's the slums and shantytowns, houses the colors of candy, endless neighborhoods winding into the hills, yes, said Kleist, swigging from a bottle, navigating effortlessly between her sculptures, me sitting in the single chair inside her cottage frightened she might detect my furtive and desperate glances at the can of *instant coffee,* because I was doing both concurrently, that is listening to Kleist's story of fleeing Mexico City for Cuernavaca while simultaneously stealing glances at the can of *instant coffee* while thirdly contemplating the dread and agitation in regards to my current coffee situation, meaning having none, and Kleist was drunk and myopic, acutely so, the amount of alcohol ingested coupled with her unwavering ardor, boisterously describing how she fled Mexico City for Cuernavaca, and I sat listening, thinking of coffee and meanwhile also enthralled by the story of Kleist absconding her first show, *Death of Beauty,* to find a Nazi. So I left, said Kleist, I took the *Pullman de Morelos* bus, watched Mexico City recede as we headed south; I had virtually nothing to go on, merely a sheet of paper containing some incidental facts and an old photograph of Scholz (now Scholzberg) who by then must've been close to seventy years old, I thought, said Kleist, an age much older than either of my parents had reached, and it wasn't only his last name he'd changed but his first too, from Helmut to Max. He was born *Helmut Scholz,* which sounds almost laughable it's so *ss-sounding, Helmut Scholz,* like an angry command, like the bark of a German shepherd, like a name fabricated for a Nazi in some terrible novel, an aggressive name even for a German speaker like me. Anyway, I sat on the bus heading to

Cuernavaca with no idea what I was doing. I was young, twenty-five or twenty-six, and I gazed at the photo of Helmut Scholz, who was roughly the same age as I was when the photo was taken and how had this man, hardly into adulthood, taken it into his mind to murder those *already-dying Jews,* the *vestiges of Jews,* the transparent ghosts of *once-healthy Jews,* all of them well on their way to death from typhoid and dysentery, malnutrition and hard labor, but Scholz must've believed that that wasn't enough, must've resolved himself to exercising his legs, taking those solitary evening strolls and amid those solitary evening strolls he must've also thought: I'll wait to hear the first Jewish cough of an *already-dying Jew,* kick open the closest barrack door, and commence firing bullets into the dark, killing those *already-dying Jews.* Every single night for years, the sweltering summer months, the glacial winter nights, time itself ponderous and unending, unfurling like an insipid scroll, Scholz's ritual utterly inflexible, my mother had said, Kleist explained, no different than every aspect of his world, his routine rigid and scrupulous, and it may have been the methamphetamines or his own brutal nature, who knows, but his evening walks were as horrifying as they were reliable, although you and I know, Kleist said, winking in my direction, the real villain was stupidity, stupidity the true architect of those deaths, stupidity rearing its head in a place already *drenched* in stupidity, the death camps a place where stupidity *swelled with ambition,* the death camps the culmination of stupidity's most aspiring enterprise because where can stupidity go after a *death camp,* Kleist asked, nowhere, Kleist answered, stupidity can go nowhere after a death camp, because a death camp is stupidity's *logical conclusion,* a death camp, in fact, is the *culmination of stupidity,* the place where stupidity finds the most agency, a place stupidity can call home because stupidity knows no higher realm than a death camp and who even thought to place these two words beside one another, *death* and *camp?* Almost funny, don't you think? A *death camp,* slightly humorous, she said, if it wasn't so saturated in stupidity, if it didn't make one lose hope in one's own species, prompting the desire for a swift and expeditious extinction for all of us because a species clever enough to conceive of and create a *death camp* needn't exist, although at that young age my philosophy of stupidity's universal dominion was not yet refined; to me it seemed just another eccentric theory of my mother's. In any event, said Kleist, I sat on the *Pullman de Morelos* bus, heading south to Cuernavaca, and I wondered what had occurred in Scholz's short life to produce the urge to walk the grounds each night, pacing between the barracks, waiting for the first Jewish cough to start firing into the cowering Jewish darkness, one of those corners occupied by a young Jewish man, my father, another occupied by a young Jewish woman, my mother, both crouched in the corners of different barracks along with the other Jews, all of them trying to do the impossible, namely not cough, namely to disappear, Scholz's proximity announced by those menacing steps, as arbitrary and exacting as death itself, smoking a cigarette, I imagined, his neck irritated by his starched collar and razor burn, calmly preparing to empty his gun. And what was I doing leaving Mexico City? I thought. What was I doing abandoning my first show? Something powerful was pulling me, Kleist said, weaving between her works, stopping behind *Medusa's Apprentice* to clear her throat, but I was *compelled* to abandon my first show; something nameless and immense was dragging me toward both Cuernavaca and Scholz (now Scholzberg), an obligation to my parents perhaps, or those dead Jews, because even if my sculptures *discussed* or *attempted to tackle* the destruction of Europe's humanity it was only ever artifice, only decoration, because as much as I've always bowed at the altar of artistic creation, always *prostrated* before the steps of artistic creation which, in my opinion, is the *complete opposite of stupidity,* it pales in the shadow of the death camps and genocide, meaning stupidity's most indelible achievements, the same as slavery and apartheid, the hatred of an *unknown other* clearly stupidity's most remarkable exploit, the suspicion and contempt and degradation of an *unknown other,* the notion of *superiority* over an *unknown other* the mountain upon which stupidity fans its wings and exults, and thus I learned at a very young age the limits of art, because even art has limits, *especially* against stupidity which will always be victorious, Kleist emerging from behind *Medusa's Apprentice,* peevish and stubborn, her bony feet with their blue veins exposed for she hadn't yet heard the call from Nadia and fetched her boots, Kleist still pacing the cottage, sniffing out bottles, illustrating her trip to Cuernavaca where, she admitted, she was more than a little concerned about her absence at the *Museo de Arte Moderno,* considered the effect her absence would have on her career, especially her first show, *Death of Beauty,* and likely it would ruin everything, she said, my career abruptly ending the moment they noticed I was gone, the curators and critics assuming I was arrogant or ungrateful or difficult to work with and so on, though this of course wasn't the case and instead of my desertion offending anyone it made me appear strange and enigmatic, those bourgeoise *chilangos* and *chilangas* highly curious about this young Austrian sculptor so absorbed by the deconstruction of mankind, the broken limbs and dislocated joints that made *Death of Beauty* such a singular collection, sculptures portraying the collapse of Europe using the symbol of dislocated limbs, each representing a European capital; the cracked femur of Prague, the dislocated elbow of Rome, a rib protruding from the flesh illustrating Zagreb, all those limbs poking out from the primordial abscess of European civilization, sculptures like pulled teeth, *as beautiful as they are disturbing,* said Guillermo Mendoza when asked to describe my work, Mendoza notorious for his rigorous opposition to modern sculpture but somehow finding something *timeless and soul shattering* in my first international collection, *Death of Beauty,* famously celebrating *Death of Beauty,* shocking critics and connoisseurs who followed Mendoza's every move and likewise sought Mendoza's every opinion, particularly on sculpture, Mendoza who saw in me a successor to Anne Truitt, Truitt who also refused the use of industrial processes, who was unwavering in her insistence on using her own hands because one must *touch* and *palpate* the material, I'd always said, Kleist explained, always I insisted on using my own hands to sculpt because it must be tactile, if you aren't using your own hands to touch and roll the clay between your fingers, touching and feeling the surface of the material, how are you a sculptor? And when Truitt wrote that she was *on the track of square and rectangular shapes, articulated back into the depth of the ink,* Kleist said, yes, I understood that, when Truitt wrote that the shapes were *echoes of the structures she'd seen on archaeological sites in Mexico, Mayan temples* she'd written, Kleist said, I understood that too, and most importantly, when Truitt wrote that she *suddenly grasped the fact that art could spring from concept, and medium could be in its service,* it confirmed what my spirit had known all along, my works an absolute inevitability, fashioned already in my mind, fashioned perhaps before I was born, seeing them fully formed in my dreams and only needing my arms and hands to create what I'd seen in my mind's eye, a dream made manifest, and my work wasn't as minimal or sleek as Truitt's, it certainly wasn't as approachable either, but the method was the same, the tangible depth, the obsession with memory and nostalgia, and what she, meaning Truitt, saw as the boundary between gravity and verticality was for me the boundary between heaven and hell, meaning earth and sky, because the earth is undoubtedly hell, we've proven that time and again and, without exception, every single piece from *Death of Beauty* sold, purchased by a wealthy *chilango* or *chilanga* or some moneyed connoisseur visiting the Mexican capital, what at the time was known as the *Distrito Federal* or DF meaning of course Mexico City, and while I was on a bus heading toward Cuernavaca each of my sculptures was purchased for an exorbitant price, my name suddenly being whispered throughout the galleries of Latin America as a *vital new name in European sculpture,* a person to *be aware of,* and hence the custom of never attending my own shows, a habit or ritual inadvertently begun when I decided to leave Mexico City for Cuernavaca to find a retired Nazi who'd had a hand in torturing my own parents, to behold in person the face of Helmut Scholz (now Max Scholzberg), a phony Jew, a phony Mexican too, uncertain if he were even alive and if he were was he the same man my mother insisted had stalked the grounds of *Gusen II* committing atrocities with all the gravity of a child skipping stones? And sitting on the bus I held the photo of young Helmut Scholz whose face, like all monsters', was forgettable and mundane, whose visage looked no crueler or more benevolent than the next, an expression that in no way exhibited the depth and scope of his savagery. And I imagined the man I was approaching, the elderly Max Scholzberg, who may or may not have still been alive, the bus half full, Mexico City finally behind us, the bus drifting through veils of fog, and I considered the ease with which the erasure of a human being was accomplished: the addition of some letters on a forged passport and one could go from a murderous Nazi to an exiled Jew, the most audacious and cruel feats of history accomplished with ease, whereas the everyday chores, renewing one's driving permit, applying for a position at some university, are riddled with impediments, infested with bureaucracy, everyday chores awash with hurdles, but escaping one's murderous past, exchanging continents, doctoring one's identity, outrunning an obscene body count, that simply requires a smattering of hubris and gall because that's how the modern world is arranged, the villains forever the most accommodated, and I recalled my mother's depiction of Scholz walking amid the barracks of *Gusen II* waiting for the first cough, kicking down the door of the closest barrack and committing mass murder as the shots burst and the prisoners wailed in terror, wails in Hebrew and Polish and German, all of which sounded exactly alike because what's the difference between the wails of a Pole or a Croat or Romanian? Nothing. No difference at all between the wails of a Pole or a Croat or a Romanian, nor an Italian or a Swede for that matter, because terror has a single language which requires no interpreter, yes, wails of infinite terror that forever haunted my mother, that echoed in her head while I was growing up and instinctively I always knew something was amiss, something stolen from my mother which couldn't be replaced, my father too, though in a different way, how my parents described Europe after the war: Berlin and Pforzheim and Dresden the mere skeletons of cities, the *replicas* of cities, they explained, as if the destruction and the ruins were a reflection of the German soul, no, the *European* soul, because even when the world ends, my mother said, it still exists, it stubbornly continues, corpses heaped in stacks, carts littered amongst city blocks, suitcases ceaselessly strewn about, the contents of entire kitchens, kettles, pots, pans, utensils, all for the taking, not that there was much to eat, at least not at first, the maimed walking aimlessly in circles, my parents too, spending months sleeping outside, afraid of strangers, meaning everyone else, because anyone they'd known before the war was either dead or missing, although probably dead because, as I said, she said, being born a Jew in Europe during those years was the *pinnacle of misfortune,* and, long story short, said Kleist, I discovered that Helmut Scholz (now Max Scholzberg) was indeed still alive, something I discovered quite quickly because once the bus stopped I found myself in downtown Cuernavaca, opposite the Jardín Borda, all the lovely colonial buildings which, if I hadn't been hunting down a retired Nazi, I would've visited and enjoyed, and have you been to Mexico, Kleist asked and before I could tell her no, that I had never been to Mexico, she'd moved on, relighting her pipe, meandering once more between *The Boots of Stupidity,* emitting clouds of smoke like a wakened volcano. Well, she said, Mexico is the *opposite* of Austria, because when walking in Mexico a person wants to know what's taking place behind all of the Mexican windows whereas in Austria it's *revolting* to imagine what's taking place behind all of the windows, a person wants to shut out any notions of the Austrian lives taking place behind all of those Austrian windows because no sane person, no person with a functioning frontal lobe, has the desire to see the private lives being led behind the windows of Austrian homes, and where Mexico is warm Austria is cold, where Mexico is *possibility* Austria is *impossibility* and I swiftly fell in love with Mexico because in Mexico I felt closer to the earth, felt myself touched by the vault of sky, the teeming flora, everything the *inverse* to Austria, meaning vibrant and alive and sure, Mexico, like Europe, is drenched in death and melancholy too, because it's earth after all, but an *unspoken* melancholy, a melancholy *with imagination,* whereas Europe's melancholy is an *imagination-destroyer,* so yes, I felt an immediate affection for Mexico because of the aforementioned sky and flora, not to mention a government generous enough to receive thousands of European refugees, one in particular, a solitary Jew, having no idea he was in fact not a solitary Jew but a German mass murderer, a retired Nazi, and Kleist exhaled an enormous cloud of smoke which hung suspended like an omen. Anyway, I quickly found my way to the tax offices because I may be an artist but I'm also industrious and intelligent and quite cunning which I've had to be coming from where I've come from, meaning provincial Austria and, being more specific than that, a young Jew from provincial Austria with two impaired parents, parents ostensibly murdered or *half murdered* decades before I was born so, in a sense, I was raised by the *phantoms of parents,* the *husks of parents,* parents whose hearts beat and limbs moved but whose souls contained no light, and as a consequence I learned to be self-sufficient and pragmatic, hence I knew the tax offices are where one goes to find out virtually anything they need to know about the local residents, taxes, properties, and other practical details, and it turned out that Scholz (now Scholzberg) was indeed alive, not some phantom of my mother's demented imagination but a real living monster with a conventional Jewish name. My Spanish was lousy but the woman at the desk was kind enough to help; we each spoke enough English to understand each other. I handed her the single sheet of research I had, she in turn handed me copies of papers describing their illustrious citizen, name, address, properties, all perfectly public, papers describing the very man who'd murdered countless Jews while at the same time producing countless ghosts, including the children of those ghosts who were, in a sense, ghosts themselves, yes, because by taking a life you've altered destiny, a murder lives forever, a murder sets into motion a series of events that the murderer can't control and by murdering those suffering Jews Scholz had given birth to a population of ghosts of which I'd always counted myself and, following this logic, Scholz was as much my parent as my own mother and father. That's right, said Kleist, another bottle drained, tossing a log on the fire: Scholz arrived in Latin America shortly after the war, December of '46, disembarked in Chile, where he promptly disappeared. Two years passed and nothing, then in '49 Scholz (now Scholzberg) reemerged in Quito and the following year in Mexico, Puebla to be precise, eventually settling in Cuernavaca, where he started a small factory, paper and pulp, became successful too, opening another three mills in the outskirts of the city, mills employing roughly four hundred people, four hundred Mexicans, added Kleist, unearthing a bottle of white wine amongst the chisels and the dust, unfastening the cap, taking a generous swig and I was amazed by the array of alcohol she was ingesting, both in quantity and variety, because I'd never witnessed anyone consume so much in such a small span of time and instead of crippling or undermining her movements, each swallow inched her closer to some epiphany, each gulp conveyed a lucidity of purpose known only to her, projected in the way she marched between *The Boots of Stupidity* recounting her departure from Mexico City to Cuernavaca. I also discovered, she continued, that Scholz (now Scholzberg) was never married, was enjoying the twilight of his life living outside Cuernavaca, in Privada Villaflores, a small distance away, what turned out to be a lavish estate with walls surrounding the perimeter complete with pieces of glass poking from the top to discourage intruders, a quiet area with winding streets and jacaranda bursting from both sides which provided shade even in the middle of the day. I called a taxi and had it drop me near the address, I stood across the street holding the photograph of Scholz (now Scholzberg), observed the wall topped with broken glass like sharpened teeth and didn't know how long it would take to catch a glimpse of the man, to compare the young Scholz with the elderly Scholzberg, but I was resolved to stay until I'd seen him, really set eyes on him, and I would've waited outside for an hour or a week, it didn't matter, and cars passed, though not very many since it was a quiet part of Cuernavaca, in other words a wealthier area and, judging from my vantage, Scholzberg's estate was expansive, the heavy branches of abundant trees rising over the wall, a distant roof confirming its capaciousness, and I stood in place for over two hours, surveying a gate in the wall where I assumed the cars came and went; meanwhile I studied the black-and-white photo of Scholz, the firm and exacting uniform of the Third Reich, the sharp collar angled against his neck like a piece of architecture; I wanted his visage imprinted upon my mind so that when I finally saw him, coming or going, gazing in my direction or looking askew, I'd have no trouble seeing the resemblance between the young Nazi and the old phony Jew and sure enough it happened; hours had passed, I don't know how many, three or four, when the gate opened and I stood frozen. My chest constricted. The anticipation at glimpsing this man suddenly induced a physical reaction. I wanted nothing more than to run away. To escape. It wasn't fear but something far deeper and more ancient, a relic of hatred chiseled in my bones, because here was the moment I'd long sought and I wasn't scared, but *petrified,* incapable of moving, fastened to terra firma as if my shoes were nailed to the mantle of the earth. Moments later a small car, a Renault, backed out through the gate and the driver got out, a young man in a dark suit and driver's cap, after a minute I saw a small Mexican woman in a uniform, a servant or a housekeeper, escorting an elderly man from the interior of the property toward the car, not that he was *that old,* but old enough, and I began to tremble, not because I was unsure if the elderly man was Helmut Scholz but because I was *absolutely certain* he was Helmut Scholz. I gazed at the man and had no doubt it was the man who'd walked the barracks of *Gusen II* decades before, weaving between the huts of his victims and me, his ghost-child, his foul progeny, struggling to stand, unable to control the anxiety that washed over me in waves of vertigo, and the deepest part of me wanted to cough, wanted to see if the old man still had it in him to recognize the cough of a Jew, but I was stricken by panic, paralyzed, even though, curiously, I was able to note small details, the sleek silver hair and powder-blue cardigan which implied decades of easy living, and it was immediately clear he'd *never* been Max Scholzberg, was only ever Max Scholzberg *on paper*, because anyone with two eyes could see he was born Helmut Scholz and would forever remain Helmut Scholz, a man whose name, *Helmut Scholz,* belonged to him and no one else, his nose like a bird of prey, his angular skull, his glacial eyes, it left no question because people's inner natures manifest in their outward physical appearance (if you know where to look) and Helmut Scholz was of this type, a man born to pursue those weaker than himself, a man who'd murdered Gypsies and Jews simply because he could. When an allotment of earth was relinquished to horror, filled with stupidity, here was a man who'd *flourished,* a man who'd found his calling on a tiny allotment of earth, meaning *Gusen II,* and I still hadn't moved, still hadn't remembered to breathe and I hated myself and cursed myself, my cowardice and incompetence, my youthful hubris, because when it was clay, when it was bronze or a block of stone I had the strength of a regiment, I could invent gods, but faced now with a true decision, one of flesh and blood, I was paralyzed. Tears ran down my cheeks and still I stood in place like an idiot, a dullard. I watched Scholz getting into the Renault, watched the young driver in the suit and cap shut the door, saw the housekeeper wave goodbye. I was engulfed by despair. What was I doing in Cuernavaca? In Privada Villaflores? What was I planning to even do? Exact revenge? Torture him? Murder him? Nonsense. Of course not. It was absurd, the whole thing. I'd flown across the world to Mexico City only to *leave* Mexico City, hopped on a bus and gone to Cuernavaca to see for myself the man who'd helped shape my identity, an odious relative, my only remaining lineage to the twentieth century when you think of it, which I did, at that very moment I thought of it and understood Scholz was my only living link to the senseless past. With the car gone, the gate closed, and I didn't do a thing, didn't try to sneak onto the property, didn't try chasing down the Renault, because I understood I was a fool and a coward, a host of loathsome attributes which I couldn't stop calling myself and if a stranger had seen me, crouched beneath the verdant trees, they would've called the police or notified the closest asylum because I was literally falling apart; hours I stood across the street, weeping for myself, my parents, the tumult of history, this planet which makes exiles of all of us. I wasn't waiting for anything, certainly not Scholz who solicited nothing but a sense of overwhelming doom; suddenly I had no desire to ever see him again, especially up close, his face spawning a hatred so deep it was prehistoric; I was simply trying to put myself back together or keep myself from falling apart, which amounts to the same thing. And I gazed at the wall, the shards of glass sticking out like indignant teeth, teeth desperate for a mouth to fill, hungry for sinews to sink themselves into, the patches of bougainvillea erupting in beautiful explosions, and Kleist paused, her posture suddenly rigid, belched, and sighed. Anyway, she said, I stayed past dusk, certain I would never forgive myself, wanting more than anything to vanish, to disappear forever. But life is relentless, it stops for no one, the trauma, the hardship, they're immaterial, life continues, with or without you. It doesn't judge because it doesn't care. And time too, time doesn't ask permission. It was dark when I left, when I felt I could control my legs and began heading back to Cuernavaca, taking my time and only decades later, this winter in fact, while creating *The Boots of Stupidity,* did it dawn on me that rapture was never the theme of my work and never had been, it was *stupidity,* stupidity my theme and obligation, my lifelong obsession, even after I met Ernst, amid those young happy years of marriage, it was stupidity, had *always been* stupidity. My life's work, every single sculpture and every collection, was simply outrage at the burden of history which devours each one of us, the stupidity we as a species allow to proliferate, the stupidity we foster and encourage and as a species have always chosen over the competent and the kind, by which I mean the *thoughtful,* because as I said, Kleist said, stupidity is the strongest element in the universe and anytime stupidity senses kindness or thoughtfulness its only duty is to stamp it out, to obliterate it, and tonight I drink to celebrate my impotence, I drink in honor of stupidity's prowess which took both my parents and is doing a hell of a number on me, stupidity encroaching upon entire generations and those generations' progeny, all waiting to be annihilated by the jaws of stupidity and walking back to Cuernavaca I began to sense my good fortune, the quiet luxury of being an artist, my shame tempered by the anticipation of future works, works fraught with human limbs forever frozen and forever attempting to break free, because even then my hands were anticipating the touch and feel of *future totems* symbolizing the base stupidity of our species and Kleist was well on her way to total inebriation, minutes from hearing Nadia's voice, minutes from ranting about the *giant maw of the blood-red sea* and suddenly there's silence on the *smartphone* and I sense Marcel has posed a question I didn't quite catch, something about *Afro-house,* a genre of dance music from South Africa that, in his humble opinion, is incredibly innovative, and I ask him to repeat the last question, hoping it was, in fact, a question, because staring at the mound of papers, the countless receptacles of the rolltop desk, the scent of my now-dead wife permeating everything, I haven't heard a single word Marcel has said, I've merely peppered the conversation with *uh-huhs* to mollify Marcel because I love him, painfully so, but I'm desperate and sad, *desperately sad,* trying to collect myself, to focus on anything but my wife who's only been dead a week, seven short days, but attempting to *avoid* thinking of my now-dead wife I'm unable to contemplate *anything* except my now-dead wife, and I try to think of coffee instead, of cortados and espressos, I try to visualize endless beds of beans spread beneath the majestic sun, and for no reason at all I consider the French campaigns in Egypt and Syria, I recall Thomas-Alexandre Dumas Davey de la Pailleterie who'd led the charge and whose son, Alexandre Dumas, a son of mixed birth, was legally freed when his father brought him to France and who, over the course of his life, wrote more than *one hundred thousand pages* including *The Count of Monte Cristo,* had dozens of affairs as well as numerous illegitimate children and though I know nothing of Dumas's attitude toward coffee I'm incapable of imagining his life's work, meaning the writing and the fucking, without fervently believing Alexandre Dumas was a devout disciple of coffee, yes, I think, a safe bet, and why am I thinking of this, why am I contemplating Alexandre Dumas and his *one hundred thousand written pages* as well as his sexual escapades and whether or not he drank coffee when I have my own pages to consider, my life's work, including hundreds of discarded titles like *Vacant Voices* and *Days of Dark Drudgery,* a catalogue of terrible titles, many of them flirting with alliteration, *Momentary Montaigne* and *Fathomless Fortunes of Fury,* titles all equally tedious and trite, all further perpetuating my own failure, each scrapped and abandoned, shelved inside the countless receptacles of the rolltop desk, each tossed title a token of my own impotence, and inevitably my thoughts return to my now-dead wife, can't think of anything except my now-dead wife because whenever I think of coffee I somehow think of my now-dead wife who, even in the darkest days, I loved, maybe more than ever, because seeing her suffer, watching her forget herself, accessed a pain that was novel and new, touched a part of my soul I'd never known, even when she raved about the *dark beings* and the *spaceships,* ships I always imagined as silver and sleek, which, she insisted, hovered soundlessly over the neighborhood recording her thoughts, how the *dark beings* had invaded her mind, implanted recording devices inside her body and toward the end, in the darkest days, she didn't even recognize me, convinced her own husband was an extraterrestrial, a *shapeshifter,* she'd said, and on those days, the darkest ones, if Marcel wasn't around, if the nurse had gone, I'd sit beside her and weep, overcome by sorrow, a throbbing in my chest like a cataclysm, our conversations reduced to arguments about what was real and what wasn't, those fruitless attempts at convincing her there weren't any *spaceships* hovering above our heads, no *dark beings* either, that I wasn't an extraterrestrial but the very man she'd met at the *3rd International Conference for Social Sciences, Aesthetics, and Disaster Management,* the very man she married soon after, who'd loved her for decades, even when we fought, even when we'd stopped making love, hadn't made love, in fact, in years, how we'd gone through seemingly interminable periods of isolation, both of us removed and distant, how we sometimes considered separating but didn't, how we'd make up because we always reconciled, yes, I think, even when we fought, even when she called me selfish and myopic, which I undoubtedly was, we always found a way to return to one another, how she made me a better person, I think, how she improved me, I also think, even when I was distant and insensitive, a touch self-involved, how I chose the pursuit of *mental Saharas* over them, meaning my wife and son, and over time, years and decades, the way my wife saw me was ultimately how I came to see myself and now, her hardly gone a week, I don't know who I am, don't know how to see myself and I wonder if I should make more coffee or talk to Marcel, actually *pay attention* to Marcel, because he hasn't bothered to repeat the question I never answered, if it was a question, Marcel talking about his favorite electronic artist of all time which, inevitably, is Four Tet, because Marcel loves Four Tet more than life itself, always happy to declare his love for Four Tet to anyone willing to listen, an artist he loves *more than life itself*, his words, and he's never had any hesitation expressing his passion for Four Tet, because his love and admiration for Four Tet know no end, and the only reason I want to make an album like Lindstrøm's *Where You Go I Go Too,* he says, is because I'm *incapable* of making anything approaching the radiance and artistry and, shit, I might as well say it, *polyrhythmic complexity* of any of Four Tet's albums, not even Four Tet's singles, says Marcel, because to describe Four Tet as simply an *electronic musician* is to make an enormous miscalculation, not only a miscalculation but a huge *disservice,* an *enormous understatement,* because Four Tet's music pushes the boundary of what music is, has *always* pushed the boundary of what music is, the marriage of the electronic with the organic: jazz, folk, hip-hop, house, Afro, garage, psychedelic pop, even though it's all sequenced and preprogrammed, a fact Four Tet happily admits, it's all delicately constructed, not to mention the way he's able to fashion a collage of samples: of birdsong, of Tibetan bells, of human voices, disembodied and ghostlike, and also dub, *don't get me started on dub,* says Marcel, and you can just as easily dance to a Four Tet record as sit down and *deconstruct* a Four Tet record, because Four Tet's skills as a *beatmaker* are utterly unsurpassed, Four Tet the *pinnacle of electronic dance music* and Four Tet doesn't rely on the tropes of *Chicago house* or *Detroit techno, UK garage* or *breakbeat,* no, he completely ignores the tropes and cliches of those genres, yet still retains *wisps* of the tropes and cliches of those genres, as if by ignoring them he some-how *incorporates* them, genres which are ever present in his music, and my desire to make an album of *deep house* has more to do with my *limitations* than my *capabilities* because, for fuck's sake, I'd *love* to make an album like Four Tet, he says, believe me, but I simply don't have the ability, no, it would end up anemic and derivative, all the things I can't stand about *half-baked dance music,* even I know that, and Marcel has a lot more to say about Four Tet, which he does, and I'm lost once more in the contemplation of my now-dead wife and her decline, long at first then suddenly not, how I'd hired a physical therapist to help her exercise because without the therapist she would've spent all day in a stupor, sitting motionless, staring out of the window looking for *spaceships* and *dark beings* while I circled the house avoiding the rolltop desk and trying not to cry, and after the therapist came the nurse, and after the nurse came the assortment of pills laid out in chronological order of when she was supposed to take them, meaning when I was supposed to give them or at least *try* to give them, a plethora of tablets and capsules: painkillers, sedatives, antipsychotics, antinausea, a cornucopia of multicolored medicines which grew in number the longer she was alive because on top of losing her mind she'd developed a tremor in her right leg that appeared all at once and wouldn't go away, her right leg tapping the floor, making tiny, inadvertent kicks, thus there were a host of different drugs which had to be given in a specific order, at a specific time, and the nurse was practiced in doing this, meaning the dispensing of myriad medicines to a lunatic, in this case my wife, but at night it was up to me, utterly alone in dispensing these medicines which was no small feat, a fucking nightmare if I'm being honest, me coaxing her, humoring her, invoking the *spaceships* and the *dark beings* to distract her, lifting the sheets from the windows and attempting to make a game of it, *look* I'd say, *the spaceships,* and together we'd look into the claustrophobic night, the silent street, virtually treeless, absent of pedestrians, each house a perfect replica of the other with the arbitrary decoration, a flag in support of some team or a tiny stone fountain being the exception, but most nights, if she didn't suspect me of being a *dark being,* I'd coax her to the window where we'd gaze into a night that was never really a night because the sky, at best, was a dull soupy gray, the sky blending immediately with the light pollution, thus we'd been deprived of a night sky, *an authentic night sky,* a night sky replete with comets and stars and satellites for longer than either of us could remember, probably for decades, no doubt different than the night sky in Bordeaux, in Montaigne's time, the sort of sky Montaigne would've seen centuries before, affirming our own finite stature amid the infinite, something my wife would've mentioned before she'd lost her mind, her constant disappointment in our species for plundering everything, meaning the ocean, meaning the forests, meaning the natural world, everything in her case meaning exactly that: *everything,* another example of our inherent stupidity Kleist would think, and sometimes my wife's profile was frighteningly alive, evidently untouched by lunacy and amnesia, yes, and I remember those rare occasions when a small, wistful expression emerged which reminded me of better times but it quickly passed, transformed once again into a stranger, and later I'd attempt to give her the pills and sometimes it worked but more often it didn't, and when she was finally asleep I was relieved but terribly alone and I'd walk the house in my pale-yellow slippers, much like now, avoiding work on my essay because, *fucking Christ,* I'd think, how can I imagine approaching my masterwork when I have her, meaning my soon-to-be-dead wife, asleep in the bedroom we'd once so happily shared, where we made love and read books, where she patiently listened as I reeled off the names of promising titles, *Night's Symmetry, Metaphysics of Sorrow, Cloistered Acts* and hundreds more, and how terribly unfair and arbitrary are sickness and disease, I think, how merciless is death and its utter finality,

even though it arrives for all of us, even though it's the great equal-
izer, as they say, it doesn't mean we can't curse it, I think, doesn't
mean we can't abhor illness and death, and Marcel is meanwhile
elaborating on the most thrilling and dramatic aspects of Four Tet
and all I want to do is destroy something, attack and ravage illness
and disease, yes, I think, the ceaseless sorrow of life which is hate-
ful and cruel and ends far too soon, and toward the end it got so
bad she refused to eat, howling at the walls, at the *dark beings* and
she'd begun shitting herself too and I only ever minded *for her,* not
myself, because seeing my wife lose herself to *frontotemporal dementia* was no different than a world war, and the doctors who
specialized in dementia, who'd made their careers studying all
types of progressive brain diseases, held no hope. Her comfort,
they insisted, was the most important thing, her comfort, they
maintained, was tantamount, and the thing to do, they instructed,
your main priority, they added, was to make her comfortable, pac-
ify her, agree with her because, they reasoned, who does it hurt?
Even the *spaceships,* I asked. Of course the *spaceships,* they answered, as well as the extraterrestrials and the recording devices,
they instructed, the recording devices which grew in detail the
worse she became, as if she couldn't remember her husband or her
son, but with enormous mental dexterity, in perpetual waves of
byzantine logic, was able to describe the myriad details of the recording devices brought to earth by the *dark beings,* recording devices intended to study her thoughts, she raved, to study her *human heart,* she added, long cylinders made of a material not found
on earth, she claimed, which held manifold transmitters sending

signals of information to the *spaceships* with beeps and chirps and can't you hear them, she'd scream, can't you hear the recording devices implanted in my brain, she circling the living room, her hair in disarray, an expression both petrified and aghast, the nightgown smeared with soup and medicine, me utterly baffled about how to assuage my wife's madness, part of me wanting to see what she saw, wanting to share in her delusions, so that neither of us would be alone and the irrational tic I had of trying to talk sense to her, a dumb habit impossible to quell, as if dementia were something to be argued away and whatever she sees or thinks she sees, advised the doctors, if it doesn't get her worked up, simply agree, go along with it instead of arguing with her and I'd sit beside her and weep, unable to contain my sorrow, the house immersed in darkness, sunk in a silence so strong it felt punitive and eternal, the nurse gone for hours, and occasionally she'd sit beside me, ranting about the *galaxies of dark beings* or the *processors* forged on distant planets or the *phalanx of angels* soaring among nebulas, although, once or twice, a sliver of lucidity, a glimpse of her former self surfaced, asking why I was crying, what was the matter, and for the briefest moment I thought the disease a lie, the diagnosis a malicious trick, but this lasted no longer than a sneeze, and once more she'd disappear, engulfed in oblivion, and Marcel won't stop rambling, won't give himself a single respite from talking about *electronic dance music,* and I can't sit still any longer, I simply can't, and I interrupt Marcel's discourse on the saintlike stature of Four Tet's talent and invite him over, ask him to please stop by and show me once more how to *download* songs, how to turn off the ringer too, just stop by, I say, stop by and show me again how to use this cursed *smartphone,* and Marcel is silent, and I leave the third bedroom, begin pacing the house, making circles, careful to avoid the closet, passing through each room, circling back, heading toward the kitchen as Marcel ignores my question and explains instead how his album will incorporate both *jazz* and *house* and also inevitably reflect his new life as an *expatriate,* that's the word he uses, *expatriate,* either in Bogotá or Berlin, he hasn't decided yet, and the *sequence of songs* is of utmost importance, he says, because the *sequence of songs* can *make or break* an album, the *sequence of songs* the chief ingredient to a great album as well as the most *invisible* ingredient, and there are countless challenges with the *sequence of tracks:* starting too fast or too slow, having a string of songs whose rhythms resemble each other thus provoking a feeling of monotony, endless dangers and pitfalls in arranging the ideal *sequence of tracks,* and the opening track is *essential,* of course, he says, that's a given, but of greater importance is the *second track,* yes, he says, the *second track* on an album, because the *second track* does the heavy lifting, a lot more than the opening track, because the opening track, well, that's fucking obvious, he says, it *has* to be great because without a powerful opening track the album is already over, people don't have the time, if the opening track is shit the album is finished because there's millions of hours of recorded music in history, it's infinite, but the *second track,* Jesus Christ, I could go on all day about the *second track* including the understated importance of the *second track* because, more than setting the tone and mood on the first half of a record, the *second track* is also letting the listener know it's not a fluke, that the brilliance of the opening track wasn't some fortuitous act of God or chance, but a continuation of the grandeur that the first song introduced, because there's *literally thousands* of albums whose first songs are great but the second track, the track that by *sheer necessity* must be great, isn't, and I could name a *dozen* albums right now whose opening tracks are incredible and which purposefully or not mislead the listener into thinking the rest of the album is that way too, meaning incredible, but in reality the rest of the album is *fucking shit,* and I want to reach through the *smartphone* and strangle Marcel or embrace Marcel or kiss Marcel on his head because I love him terribly, so much so my chest aches but *fucking Christ,* I think, enough already with the *electronic dance music* and the *deep house* and fucking *Four Tet* and why can't we say the things we need to say, I think, why are we talking about everything in the world besides what we should be talking about, meaning the grief and despair, the misery and anguish, how his now-dead mother is gone forever, the *giant maw of the blood-red sea,* I suddenly think, what an apt expression, no weapon against *the giant maw of the blood-red sea,* I suddenly agree, and I continue circling the house, into the second bedroom and back out, wanting to interrupt Marcel and ask him once more about coming over, ask Marcel to stop by so, at the very least, we're less alone, and did Marcel hear my question, I wonder, did he simply ignore my invitation to come over? And I continue circling the house, into the third bedroom and back out, through the living room and into the kitchen, Marcel raving through the *smartphone* about the dance scene in

South America, Santiago in particular, which, though not as robust as Bogotá, he says, is rapidly growing, all of South America in fact, like Nicola Cruz from Ecuador, Nicola Cruz with his incorporation of Soca rhythms, and walking through the living room I feel irrevocably alone and I interrupt Marcel's discourse on the burgeoning *dance culture* in Santiago and ask him again to come over, repeat my desire to see him, just stop by for a bit, I say, and Marcel is silent, doesn't answer for what seems an eternity and during this eternal silence I consider my future like an open book with hundreds of pages remaining, yes, I think, with a surge of optimism both startling and swift and certainly out of character, I realize my life's not over, even if it feels that way, even if it feels like the end, which it undoubtedly does, it's not the end because a single life contains countless endings, just as a single life contains countless beginnings, and years remain, I think, boundless hours of reading books about Montaigne and working on my book about Montaigne, hundreds, perhaps thousands of cups of coffee too, *future cups of coffee,* I think, smiling, months, perhaps years, to complete my book-length essay, my life's work, which I'll dedicate to my wife, of course, clearly, because she suffered so much, even before her illness, suffered me and my moods and my endless anxieties about everything really, embracing me, encouraging me, enduring my hysteria for philosophy and French literature, especially Montaigne; her tenderness as I recited the titles as they came, *Splendor at Night* and *Lesser Ruins,* yes, I think, but she's gone, everything black and destitute, my thoughts viscous and cold, thickened by sorrow, but I'll finish my work even if it's only for her, to honor her suffering, and I continue pacing the house, walk into the bedroom, leave the bedroom, pass through the hall as I consider literature, and I recall Bellow who famously claimed *More Die of Heartbreak* or Sebald who said *behind all of us who are living there are the dead.* I think of the solace of literature and poetry, especially the radiance of poetry, and in my mind I begin to recite poetry which has always succored me in my darkest moments, poetry an endless comfort, I think, and Emily Dickinson who famously wrote, *each that we lose takes part of us,* and *fucking Christ,* I think, what a line! Also: how did she know? Also: how was she able to express such wisdom in a single line? Because it's true, I think, each person we lose takes something from us, just as they take something with them when they go and Dylan Thomas too, *the time-faced crook,* he wrote, *Death flashing from his sleeve,* he also wrote, meditating on time or grief or death, perhaps all three, words like shards of bitter truth; *undead eye-teeth* and *graveward gulf,* words I've recited hundreds of times, never entirely sure what they meant but also *absolutely certain* what they meant, because that's poetry, still pacing the house, faster in fact, considering D. H. Lawrence and his "Ship of Death," the poem where he, he being Lawrence, held death in his sights: *already our souls are oozing through the exit of the cruel bruise,* he wrote. *Already the dark and endless ocean of the end is washing in through the breaches of our wounds, already the flood is upon us.* Yes, I think, that's death, the flood, the cruel bruise. *Oh build your ship of death, oh build it!* I recite, walking into the kitchen, circling the kitchen, only to leave the kitchen. *She is gone! gone! and yet somewhere she is there.*

Nowhere! Me reciting D. H. Lawrence while envisioning the sinking ship of death, the cruel bruise, walking into the third bedroom to just as quickly leave the third bedroom, and I think of Neruda's "Song of Despair" where he writes, *oh flesh, my own flesh, woman whom I loved and lost,* and it's terribly true, and later: *like a jar you housed infinite tenderness,* how this perfectly embodies my now-dead wife who did indeed house infinite tenderness and how poetry reaches for the infinite which it can never reach because that's impossible and besides, I think, that's not the point, because poetry's purpose is to capture and illustrate the *struggle* for the infinite which is all that matters and then, a little further, Neruda writes: *it is the hour of departure, the hard cold hour,* and I'm especially stricken by the words *hard cold hour,* the words *hard cold hour* especially fierce, overwhelmed suddenly by recognition of *the hard cold hour* which I must face, barren and bereft, and this could mean a litany of things, I think, ditching the *smartphone* and settling into my work or perhaps *the hard cold hour* is walking into my dead wife's closet, taking a deep breath and finally letting the grief consume me once and for all so that if I don't die I'll be reborn, finally able to pay attention to Marcel, actually hear his words, his passion for music, his sadness too, and he still hasn't spoken, still hasn't answered my question about coming over, and I hope he agrees, hope he says yes to stopping by so I can cease pacing the inside of the house like a madman, windows blacked out, the inside a catacomb, the inside of the house darker than the *spaceships* my wife imagined, and I hope he stops by so I can embrace Marcel which will no doubt be difficult, even awkward, because we hardly ever embraced, I think, passing through the living room, in fact I can't remember the last time we hugged, and I'm tired and I'm scared and I'm tired of being scared and before I walk into the closet, before I face *the hard cold hour* I decide to return to the third bedroom and sit at the rolltop desk, the very desk my wife laughed about when she'd come home that night and noticed its sudden appearance, pressed against the same wall she used for her work, laughed and shrugged, asked instead about dinner because it had been a long day, she said, she was exhausted, and again she asked about dinner and what we should do because the refrigerator was empty, both of us had neglected getting groceries, Marcel sleeping at a friend's, Marcel still so young, and she didn't care about my purchase of the rolltop desk, whatever helps you finish your work, she said later, I just need something to eat, taking off her shoes, glancing at the newly installed rolltop desk but still not ready to bring it up, not ready to argue with me about appropriating the wall in the third bedroom that hours earlier had been her workspace, the elephant in the room in the shape of a rolltop desk, yes, I think, *the hard cold hour* is upon me and I'm not even sure what *the hard cold hour* is, only that it's upon me, and I have to face it, have to gather myself for *the hard cold hour,* to quote Neruda, and finally I stop pacing and sit at the desk, push away the stacks of notes and legal pads, the scraps of titles that never fit, which never felt right, pick up a new legal pad, clean and impartial, ready to start anew because the opening of my thesis never felt right and it's been decades since I wrote *Montaigne and the Lugubrious Cherubs* which seems so tedious now, so misguided and ambitious, me so young, and there's nothing so sad as life, I think, nothing as glorious either, but certainly sad, mostly sad when you think of it, terribly sad if you're paying attention, and on the other end sits Marcel and his silence and inside his silence I hear a bird take flight or a sound that resembles God or what I imagine God sounds like, and being superstitious I rip the first page from the legal pad and toss it on the floor, write my name at the top of the second page, stare at the second page and forget everything else, put everything else behind me, because shouldering everything else, the pain, the sorrow, Marcel's silence, I'll never complete my life's work, and for the first time since she died, either for luck or from superstition, I say her name out loud and it feels good against my lips, and I say her name out loud a second time and it sounds good too, and saying her name, I realize, nothing bad has happened, and a third time I say her name and it's not from superstition but for luck and Marcel still hasn't spoken, still hasn't said if he'll come by, nor asked why I've said his mother's name aloud, three times in fact, and I gaze at the blank page and the blank page welcomes me, the blank page spreads its arms like an immense field, a perennial night, and Marcel still hasn't spoken, still hasn't said a word, and for a fourth and final time I say her name out loud, prepared at last for the hard cold hour.

MARCEL'S MIX

Happiness (DNA 5) – Crooked Man (DFA Records, NYC)

LCL – Nonduality & Elayas (Apparel Music, Milan)

Momma, It's a Long Journey – Felipe Gordon (Shall Not Fade, Bristol)

True Romance – Bella Boo (Studio Barnhus, Stockholm)

Cecilia – Sofia Kourtesis (Ninja Tune, London)

Nowhere Good (feat. Bella Boo) – Axel Boman (Studio Barnhus, Stockholm)

Swelter – ATRIP (Shall Not Fade, Bristol)

Han Jan – Peggy Gou (Gudu Records, Berlin)

Hearts at Whole – Smallpeople (Smallville Records, Hamburg)

You Might Be Surprised – Jordan Brando & China (Shall Not Fade, Bristol)

Water Is – Tibi Dabo (Crosstown Rebels, London)

Love Salad – Four Tet (Text Records, London)

The Love Truck – DJ Koze (Pampa Records, Hamburg)

Final Credits – Midland (Classic Music Company, London)

Closing Shot – Lindstrøm (Smalltown Supersound, Oslo)

Be a Man You Ant – André Bratten (Full Pupp, Oslo)

So Weit Wie Noch Nie – Jürgen Paape (Kompakt, Cologne)

ACKNOWLEDGMENTS

For love and support,

Richard Haber and Janice Haber

Judy Haber

Erra Davis (The Pea)

The team at Coffee House Press

Jeremy Davies and Abbie Phelps, class acts, great humans, and indispensable editors who supported my vision

Kyle Hunter, for the design

Zenyse Miller, for the invaluable proofread

Danielle Bukowski, my incredible agent at Sterling Lord

For stalwart friendship,

Chloe Aridjis, Andrea Bajani, Matt Bell, Trevor Berrett, Axel Boman, Amina Cain, Laura Calaway, Chris Cander, Ryan Chapman, Mieke Chew, Buddha Chowdhury, Heather Cleary, Hernan Diaz, Thu Doan, Danielle Diamond, Rikki Ducornet, Danielle Dutton, Barbara Epler, Linda Ewing,

Archie Fairhurst, Boris Fishman, Carlos Fonseca, Rodrigo Fresán, Felipe Gordon, Peggy Gou, Laura Graveline (ThunderDome), Rodrigo Hasbún, Natalia Heredia, Troy and Carolyn Kavanagh, Kim Kiefer, Zoë Koenig, Tynan Kogane, Kompakt, Sofia Kourtesis, Hilary Leichter, Hans-Peter Lindstrøm, Aurelio Major, Alexander Maksik, Maureen McDole, John Mesjak, Valerie Miles, Idra Novey, Efrén Ordóñez, Daniel and Sophia Peña (Daniel, you're the best), Robert Rea, Resident Advisor, Ron and Candace Restrepo, Martin Riker, Barbara and Pablo Ruiz, Patrick Saunders, Damion Searls, Amy Shaughnessy, Erika Stevens, Studio Barnhus, Soichi Terada, Cristina Tortarolo, Carla Valadez, Elizaeth Whitefig, Paul Wilson, Mandy-Suzanne Wong, Shinichiro Yokota

The Can Cab Residency in Catalonia, Spain, for two uninter-rupted weeks to write.

The Department of Fine Arts & Letters at Berchtesgaden.

Coffee House Press began as a small letterpress operation in 1972 and has grown into an internationally renowned nonprofit publisher of literary fiction, essay, poetry, and other work that doesn't fit neatly into genre categories.

Coffee House is both a publisher and an arts organization. Through our *Books in Action* program and publications, we've become interdisciplinary collaborators and incubators for new work and audience experiences. Our vision for the future is one where a publisher is a catalyst and connector.

LITERATURE
is not the same thing as
PUBLISHING

Funder Acknowledgments

Coffee House Press is an internationally renowned independent book publisher and arts nonprofit based in Minneapolis, MN; through its literary publications and Books in Action program, Coffee House acts as a catalyst and connector—between authors and readers, ideas and resources, creativity and community, inspiration and action.

Coffee House Press books are made possible through the generous support of grants and donations from corporations, state and federal grant programs, family foundations, and the many individuals who believe in the transformational power of literature. This activity is made possible by the voters of Minnesota through a Minnesota State Arts Board Operating Support grant, thanks to the legislative appropriation from the Arts and Cultural Heritage Fund. Coffee House also receives major operating support from the Amazon Literary Partnership, Jerome Foundation, Literary Arts Emergency Fund, McKnight Foundation, and the National Endowment for the Arts (NEA). To find out more about how NEA grants impact individuals and communities, visit www.arts.gov.

Coffee House Press receives additional support from Bookmobile; the Buckley Charitable Fund; Dorsey & Whitney LLP; the Schwab Charitable Fund; and the U.S. Bank Foundation.

The Publisher's Circle of Coffee House Press

Publisher's Circle members make significant contributions to Coffee House Press's annual giving campaign. Understanding that a strong financial base is necessary for the press to meet the challenges and opportunities that arise each year, this group plays a crucial part in the success of Coffee House's mission.

Recent Publisher's Circle members include many anonymous donors, Patricia A. Beithon, Theodore Cornwell, Jane Dalrymple-Hollo, Mary Ebert & Paul Stembler, Randy Hartten & Ron Lotz, Amy L. Hubbard & Geoffrey J. Kehoe Fund of the St. Paul & Minnesota Foundation, Hyde Family Charitable Fund, Cinda Kornblum, Gillian McCain, Mary & Malcolm McDermid, Vance Opperman, Mr. Pancks' Fund in memory of Graham Kimpton, Robin Preble, Steve Smith, and Paul Thissen.

For more information about the Publisher's Circle and other ways to support Coffee House Press books, authors, and activities, please visit www.coffeehousepress.org/pages/support-coffee-house or contact us at info@coffeehousepress.org.

COFFEE HOUSE PRESS began as a small letterpress operation in 1972. In the years since, it has grown into an internationally renowned nonprofit publisher of literary fiction, nonfiction, poetry, and other writing that doesn't fit neatly into genre categories. Our mission is to expand definitions of what literature can be, what it can do, and to whom it belongs.

FURTHER FICTION TITLES FROM COFFEE HOUSE PRESS

For more information about Coffee House Press and how you can support our mission, please visit coffeehousepress.org/pages/support-coffee-house

Professors may request desk copies at coffeehousepress.org/pages/educators

Lesser Ruins was designed by Abbie Phelps.
Text is set in Arno Pro.